A Sucker for Love

By J.T. Smith

Acknowledgements

First and foremost, I would like to thank GOD for providing me with the patience to make this project happen. I would also like to thank my parents, Sarah and Joseph Smith for making me happen. I would further like to thank the rest of my family and friends for the constant encouragement they have provided me with throughout the years. And finally, I wish to thank Vern Attles, Teowonna Clifton and Norma Johnson for their input with this project.

CHAPTER ONE

The loud music was beginning to give me a splitting headache. The Electric Warehouse was rocking Brooklyn on another Friday night. The place was congested with all walks of life from New York City partying down. I honestly couldn't believe that at one point in my life, I actually enjoyed the ear-splitting music that was booming through the dozens of speakers that were dispersed throughout the club. Old age, I guess. Upon further reflection, it probably wasn't the music itself that gave me such a headache but the songs that were being played.

See, I dig hip-hop music just as much as the next brother does, but damn! How many variations of songs about living in the hood, getting paid, banging women, and driving expensive cars could there possibly be? I shook my head in amazement as I listened to the lyrics of an obviously new joint that some rap group had just dropped. After sucking every ounce of suds out of my bottle of Guinness, I checked my watch. It was already a quarter to one in the morning.

"Time to take my ass on home," I mumbled to no one in particular.

The only reason I didn't leave right then and there was because I didn't drive. I spun around on my stool to look for my roommate, who was somewhere on the packed dance floor. It was a wasted effort, as I saw that he was heading directly towards me holding the hand of some young woman that he'd obviously just met. That was evident to me by the way the two were smiling at each other. Not sincere, warm, or heartfelt, simply protocol.

"How come you're not out there on the dance floor, J.C.?"

The slight glaze in Tucker's eyes told me that my boy had downed one-too-many Coronas.

"Look, I'm about to break out of here. What are you going to do?" I asked, ignoring his question. Tucker gave me an annoyed look.

"Javier, I want you to meet uh..." He turned to the young woman beside him. "What's your name again, sweetness?"

A look of annoyance quickly flashed across her face. It subsided just as fast.

"Michelle."

"That's right, Michelle," Tucker echoed.

I quickly gave Michelle the once-over: standard ruffled sleeve blouse, standard polyester bell bottom slacks, standard black, thick-heeled clogs, and standard multi-colored weave attached to her head.

"Nice to meet you, Michelle," I uttered.

Michelle smiled at me, revealing one, highly polished, gold tooth that outshone all the real ones.

"You from the South, too?" she asked, obviously picking up on my slight Southern accent. I nodded my head in agreement.

"Yep, we's both be from South Carolina," I mocked.

The two of them laughed together. Tucker then put his arm around Michelle and pulled her closer to him.

"Michelle here is going to be in The Equalizer's next video!"

"Is that right?" I asked, unimpressed. (The Equalizer was the latest rapper on the East Coast to make it to the big time.)

"So how long have you been dancing?" I asked.

"Three years."

Her gold tooth blinded me once again.

"That's good," I replied before refocusing on Tucker. "I really need to get home. I still plan on going to the gym in the morning."

Tucker scowled at me once again. "We're about to leave right now. Okay?" he chimed before turning to Michelle.

"You wanna go find your cousin, baby?"

"Okay," Michelle replied before turning around and disappearing into the crowd. Tucker turned back to me and flashed his infamous, cheesy smile.

"Uh, my man..."

"Hell, no," I replied, cutting him off before he could get started.

"But, look here..."

"But my ass! I know what you're about to ask me, and the answer is no! If I need to get a cab, let me know now!" I had known Tucker for most of my life, so I could read him like a book. Every time we went out to a club and he pulled a sister to hopefully take home, she always had a friend or so-called 'cousin' that had to tag along as well, or the whole deal was off. Eleven times out of ten, it was some chick who was either solid enough to play starting nose-guard for the New York Jets, or she looked like something that the cat brought in.

Folks, don't get me wrong. I myself would not be labeled the most handsome chap that a young lady could run across in Brooklyn. I stand about six foot, two inches and weigh two hundred and ten pounds. I have a slightly muscular build. And since I'm talking straight from the heart, I'll let the truth be told. I have always been a little picky when it comes to whom I chose to shake the sheets with. I mean with AIDS going around and whatnot, who wouldn't be? My roommate, Tucker, was well aware of this fact, but he never ceased to try me.

"Come on, J.C. I don't know how this girl looks, but I swear this will be the last time!" he pleaded.

"You said that shit earlier this summer when you brought those two thieves over!" I quickly reminded him.

When Tucker and I first hooked up together in New York City, we got an excellent deal on a spacious two-bedroom rental on the second floor of a brownstone in tony, gentrifying Clinton Hill. Our landlord, Mrs. Rodgers, was an elderly woman, originally from Charleston, South Carolina. She took a shine to us right away. Since we weren't shelling out the high-ass rent typical of New York City life, we were able to furnish our place quite nicely. Ever since then, Tucker has been bringing over everybody and their 'cousin' to show the place off. On this particular night, he had showed up at one o'clock in the morning with a couple of new friends that he had met over in Bed-Stuy. If those two women had been any skinnier, they would have been invisible.

To cut to the chase, those sisters probably would have gotten away with robbing us blind that night had my cell phone not begun to ring just as they were about to leave. (No one else I knew had the theme from *Sanford and Son* as his ring tone.) Tucker and I turned up almost a thousand dollars worth of merchandise that those two skinny winches were escorting out of our place, including my lovely Miles Davis CD collection.

"It's not going to be like that this time!" Tucker pleaded.

"You don't even have to do anything. Just talk to the girl some?"

"Listen, Negro, let me say this to you one more time..."

I was about to really go off on my boy when Michelle returned with her so-called cousin. I had to do a double take when I saw her. This girl was the finest thing that I'd laid eyes on since I stopped wearing Pampers! Five-foot-five, one thirty something, a low-buzzed haircut. (I have always been a sucker for a bald-headed black woman. My former probation officer would gladly attest to that.)

Michelle's cousin, who had on a cute one shoulder cocktail dress, sported a devilish grin on her face. The sister was slamming too hard. An alarm immediately went off in the back of my mind. *Okay, J.C., what's the catch? You know this is too good to be true.*

"Guys, this is my cousin, Tamika. She's from Jersey," Michelle announced, blinding me once again with her dazzling grin.

"Hello," Tamika smiled as she spoke, revealing a perfect, non-metallic smile.

"Hi!" Tucker and I both replied in unison.

"Tamika," Michelle continued, "this is Tucker and Javier."

I took the sister's hand and gave her my most heartfelt smile. A sense of excitement overcame me as I scanned Tamika's hourglass figure. *This sister has definitely got it going on.* I thought to myself.

"Are you enjoying yourself tonight, Tamika?" I inquired.

She frowned slightly.

"No...not really."

"What's wrong?" Tucker and I asked in unison once again.

I turned to Tucker and gave him a subtle, yet firm 'take-a-damn-hike' look. Tamika flashed a little frown before she answered.

"Well, to be honest with you, it seems to me like you brothers up in here don't know how to dance too tough."

Tucker and I immediately looked at each other.

"Let me take a stab at it with you, Tamika," I offered. *Later for the gym!* I thought as I took Tamika's outstretched hand and led her towards the dance floor. Even though there was some garbage of a rap song playing at the moment, it didn't matter to me because if this sister wanted to dance, then that's what she was about to do.

After squeezing our way out onto the congested dance floor, I began to stretch my joints a little as I swayed back and forth to the beat, which really wasn't all that bad. Once again, it was those materialistic lyrics that ruined the song for me personally. Back in the day when I was a young pup, I could jump out on the floor and dance like there was no tomorrow. But at the ripe old age of twenty-six, I had to be more careful. (Once you're past twenty-five, folks, things on you begin to hurt if you use them too long.) After limbering up, I began to focus on my dance partner. It was time to see what type of girl Miss Tamika really was. It has always been a rule of mine that, when dancing, and especially when dancing with a woman for the first time, to let them lead. If a sister wanted to be reserved while getting her groove on, I could dig it. But, if a sister wanted to try to get her freak on while out on the floor, that was peachy with me, too.

Tamika was a little hard to gauge at first because she simply closed her eyes and held her head back as she swayed to the beat. After she did this for a while, I thought to myself, *This sister is clearly the reserved type.* I sighed with relief. Tamika briefly looked at me and flashed another radiant smile as we whirled around each other. I was a bit astonished when I felt a little, (and I mean just a little, fellas,) flutter erupt in my heart. Immediately, 'The Question' popped up in my mind. *Could this be the one?* Could Miss Tamika be the sister I was destined to meet, marry, and love for the rest of my life? Along with 'The Question' came some of the required secondary questions or questionettes as I like to call them. Did the sister have a man or husband? Hell, did she have a job? What about good credit? What type of education did this sister have? Oh yeah, let's not forget about the children factor. All of these thoughts wandered through my head as I beheld this mesmerizing chocolate goddess.

What the hell? I thought to myself. *There's no time like the present to find out.* I was just about to open my mouth and ask Tamika a few of these questions when the deejay put on another record with an even faster tempo.

"Oh shit! That's my song!" Tamika yelled out. She then began to gyrate wildly to this new beat. My jaw dropped. Tamika spun around, bent over, and shoved her ass at me in perfect time with the music.

"Hey!!! Ho!!!" she began yelling.

Oh well, it was a nice thought. I reflected to myself as I joined Tamika in her frenzy. *I can still make the gym in the morning if I hurry up and get my ass on home.*

I awoke to my alarm buzzing at exactly seven. For some strange reason, my skull was pounding. I shut my eyes even tighter and massaged my temples.

"Damn," I moaned out loud.

As I began to roll across my king-sized mattress to the opposite side of the bed so that I could turn my alarm off, I encountered an obstacle in the way.

"What the heck?"

I quickly sat up in my bed. There, snoozing next to me was Tamika. She stirred a little before opening her eyes.

"Morning, baby."

The smile that she provided me quickly faded when she saw the dumbstruck expression on my face.

"What's the matter, Boo?"

"What are you doing here?" I countered.

Tamika began to laugh softly.

"You so crazy."

"That might be true, but you still didn't answer my question."

Tamika sat up in the bed as well.

"You don't recall begging me to come home with you after we left Sammy's Place last night?"

"Sammy's Place?" I asked her in amazement.

(Sammy's Place was the official after-hours spot in Brooklyn over on Fulton Street. It would be considered just another hole in the wall if it weren't for their hot wings, which were the best in town.)

"When did we go to Sammy's Place?"

Tamika eyed me suspiciously. "You don't remember us leaving the Electric Warehouse and going over to Sammy's?" she asked with raised eyebrows. "Hell, I guess not after all that liquor you were drinking."

Suddenly, I knew why my bedroom was slowly spinning around. I am what some folks would call liquor intolerant. Just two glasses of the stuff and I'm as drunk as a skunk. Now beer's another story. I can sip on some brew 'til the cows come home, wake up the next morning, and get to work early, if need be.

"Liquor, huh?" I asked as I massaged my temples again.

"Yeah," Tamika replied. "Don't you remember any of last night?"

"I'm afraid not."

Tamika stared at me in amazement.

"Not even the bet you and your roommate had going about who could eat the most chicken wings?"

I shook my head "no." This new information suddenly explained to me why my stomach was boiling. I almost knocked Tamika out of the bed in my rush to get down the hall to the bathroom. If it wasn't for her being in the way, I would have probably made it, too. Vomit flew everywhere as I dropped down on my knees and held onto the toilet bowl for dear life. My worshipping the john was interrupted by a knock on the door.

"You alright in there?" It was Tucker.

"Does it sound like I'm alright?" I retorted before retching my guts out again. Tucker walked into the bathroom clad in boxers and a T-shirt. He bent over and stared at me with a wicked grin on his face.

"Aw, what's da matter? Baby tossing his cookies?" he taunted.

I glared up at him through blood-shot eyes.

"You think this shit is funny?" I snarled.

"Well, yeah, kinda…"

"I'll show you what funny is as soon as I..."

Once again I dropped my head down into the toilet bowl and began hurling more of my stomach's contents.

"If I was you, I'd concentrate on the job at hand," Tucker advised before turning around to walk out. "Oh yeah, make sure you put some bleach down in here when you clean this shit up."

After washing myself and cleaning the bathroom floor, I returned to my bedroom, where I found Tamika checking out my CD collection.

"I see you're into jazz, huh?" she beamed.

"A little bit, yeah."

I walked up behind her and scanned my Miles Davis section. All of his discs were still there. (Yeah, I know it was foul, but I was not taking any chances.)

"Uh, you about ready to go home now? Cause I usually do the, uh, gym thing on Saturday mornings."

Tamika turned around to me with a look of confusion on her face.

"I thought you told me last night that we were going to go get my kids this morning and head out to the IHOP for breakfast?"

"Kids? What kids?" I stammered.

Tamika stepped back from me and folded her arms across her chest.

"My kids!" She placed her arms akimbo on her curvaceous hips and continued. "Last night I told you that I had three little girls and you said you wanted to meet them. You was the one who offered to take us all out to breakfast this morning!"

Do not panic. I thought to myself. Also, I made a mental reminder to make sure that I kicked Tucker's ass twice when I got the chance.

"Look, Sister," I began...

"It's Tamika!" Her demeanor had definitely changed now.

"Look, Tamika, to be perfectly honest with you, there's no telling what I may have told you last night, because I was drunk. I normally do not drink liquor because it messes my head up really bad, and apparently that's what happened last night."

Tamika rolled her eyes as she glared at me. Still, I pressed on...

"So, I really don't remember anything that I may have told you last night. I'm very sorry."

I sat down on my bed as Tamika continued to scowl at me.

"So the part about you wanting to marry me was a lie, too?"

I shot back onto my feet.

"Say what?!"

Tamika's piercing glower continued.

"You told me last night that I was the type of sister that you were looking to marry!"

Now, it really *was* time for me to panic. I slowly counted to ten as I evaluated my options. They all boiled down to the same objective: get away from Tamika before things turned violent.

"Uh...Tamika, once again I do have to apologize to you because obviously I was talking out of my head last night," I said, trying to console her but knowing I was on thin ice. At that moment, Tucker knocked on my opened door. He had covered his boxer's shorts with a pair of jeans.

"Michelle and I are going out to breakfast in a little bit. You guys wanna tag along?"

Tamika and I slowly glanced at each other.

"Hell, no!" she yelled. "This motherfucker here is full of shit!"

Tamika jumped in Tucker's face and stayed in it as he began to back his way out of the doorway and into the hallway.

"You told me last night that your damn roommate was all of that! The perfect gentleman, a good man!"

Tamika continued to berate me as they moved further down the hall. Being no dummy, I seized the opportunity being presented to me, slipped into one of my warm-up suits, laced up a pair of matching cross-trainer sneakers, and grabbed my gym bag. I darted down the hall past Tucker and Tamika and out the front door to safety.

"Javier! Yo, Javier!" I heard my roommate call as I slammed the front door behind me.

CHAPTER TWO

Once outside, I smiled to myself as I clicked off the alarm on my jade-green Nissan Pathfinder and climbed in. I started her up, slipped my *Miles Live Around The World* CD into my disc player, dropped Jada, as I lovingly called my sports utility vehicle, into gear, and pulled off.

The streets of Clinton Hill were already busy. As I headed toward the gym, I reflected on the escapade that had just gone down. I'm sure that most sisters and quite a few of the brothers would think me weak for cutting out like I did, but to be honest with you, I didn't see it that way. Like I said earlier, liquor and I do not mix at all. It took a few noble attempts at hard drinking down at South Carolina State to make me realize that truth. Also, as I've stated previously, Tucker knew that I couldn't drink liquor, so the way I saw it, he was the one responsible for the mess that I'd gotten into in the first place. I was quite sure my roommate had slipped some booze into whatever beer I drank last night; I knew better than to order liquor for myself.

But there's another reason, actually the main one, I jetted from the crib like I did. If I hadn't hurried out there, I would have missed

The Truth down at Bronze's Gym. That was the predominately African-American gym where I worked out on Tuesday, Thursday, and Saturday mornings. To simply call Dionne Williams, or The Truth, as she is more commonly known to the male members of the gym, fine would be an insult to her. The reason she is called 'The Truth' is because, compared to her, every other sister who frequented that gym was a damn lie.

There have actually been several fights to break out in the facility over brothers wanting to jog on the treadmill next to her, or use the exercise bike nearest her. Personally, I've always been content just to gaze upon her beauty. She's actually part of my inspiration for getting up early in the mornings to go and work out in the first place.

I found a space in the already crowded parking lot and jumped out of Jada. I shook my head in wonderment as I walked through the gym doors. *Why does this damn crap always happen to me?* I pondered as a cute employee I'd never seen before swiped my membership card for me.

"Have a good workout," she instructed with a smile.

"Definitely," I replied.

We grinned at each other for a few seconds before I walked away from the counter and headed into the men's locker room.

"Did you see that fine-looking sister at the front desk?"

I turned around and saw that it was Tony Edwards, one of my frequent workout partners coming in after me.

"Yes, I did."

"Well, don't get your hopes up too high because I'm about to scoop that up," Tony announced.

"I don't recall saying I was interested in her."

"Well, just in case..."

Tony walked up to me and we gave each other a quick pound with our fists.

"So, how you doing, Javier?"

"I'm just chilling. And you?"

"Everything's lovely."

We selected lockers and began to put away our belongings.

"How's the old lady?" I asked.

Tony's wife, Brenda, was a touchy subject with him, as she was always threatening to leave him because of his infidelities. However, since I was still buzzing from the night before, I didn't think first before I asked him.

"She's alright, I guess."

"You guess?" I prodded further. "What's up with that?"

Tony finished putting up his things and then slammed his locker door closed.

"Brenda and the kids went over to her mother's last week. She talking about she's had it with me this time."

"Gee, I wonder why?" I smirked.

"Fuck you," he snarled.

I stepped over to Tony and nudged him on the arm with my elbow.

"You know I'm just kidding with you. Look, if you love her and still want to be with her and whatnot, then go get your ass on over to where she is and tell her! If not, then get ready to shell out some serious alimony."

"You know I love my wife, but..." he hesitated.

"But, what?"

A look of confusion appeared on Tony's face.

"But, what?" I repeated.

"I still gotta get my groove on," he finally explained. "You know, get me a little stray every now and then to keep it real."

I looked at him in utter disgust. "The only thing that's gonna be real is those lawyer fees if you keep it up, Homeboy."

Tony rolled his eyes at me.

"You doing your chest today?" he asked, ignoring my last remark.

"Naw, you go ahead. I had a little too much to drink last night, so I'm taking it light this morning."

I went over to the water fountain to douse my burning throat. (Isn't it funny how a person could drink all night long and be so thirsty the next day?)

"The twelve-step program really helps," Tony hissed as he walked out of the locker room.

As I programmed my treadmill for a thirty-five minute run, I reflected upon Tony's mentality and once again shook my head in wonderment. My father had a saying that summed up the marriage question for me nicely: "Why get married if you know you still wanna fool around? You either do one, or the other." Daddy had told me that once you did find that certain someone, that the urge to stray would go away. (As well as your freedom, but that's a different issue.) But to marry someone and still think that you could fool around on her without getting busted? Those days were long gone.

After making sure that my sneakers were tied up properly, I began running at a pretty nice clip. In no time at all, sweat, or should I say alcohol, began to drip from every pore in my body. I looked around to see if The Truth had gotten in yet, and she had. She was on one of the new step machines climbing away. Sure enough, there were four brothers around her trying their utmost to keep up with her pace. I couldn't help but laugh at the sight of them.

Personally, I wouldn't want to be involved with a sister like The Truth unless I was absolutely sure that she only had eyes for me. (Like there's actually a way to tell?) I mean, really, if a brother didn't mind fighting jokers off every time he took her out in public somewhere, then I'd say, "Go for it." She would simply be a source of too much drama, and Daddy always said for me to avoid conflict as much as possible.

I had actually thought about bringing Tucker to the gym and letting him meet her, but then reality set in. Since Tucker was nothing but a straight-up dog, in the end, The Truth would just be another sister hating my guts for introducing him to her.

The tragic irony about my roommate Tucker is that he started out as one of the most faithful, young, black men that a sister could ever want to meet. When we were in college, you couldn't get him to look at another woman if he was involved with someone. I tried to hook him up with several young ladies who were interested in him back in the day, but he wasn't game. A starting wide-receiver on our football team since his sophomore year, Tucker would not have had any problems finding female companionship on campus. In fact, he used to get quite annoyed by the endless advances he received from admiring female fans who dug his six-foot, one-hundred-seventy-five pound muscular frame.

Paris Greene changed Tucker, took him off the straight-and-narrow path he'd been on. She was a year behind us in school and one of the flute players in the Bulldog's 'Marching 101' band. (They kicked ass everywhere they played.) She and my man hit it off right from jumpstreet. One day after football practice, at the start of our sophomore year, Tucker and I were heading back to our dormitory when we happened upon the band practicing on the adjoining field. I have to admit that Paris Greene was the finest young thing out there on the field that day. She stood about five feet, seven inches, weighed about a buck twenty-five, and had a nice coffee-colored complexion. Her silky, jet-black hair draped her face as she and the rest of the band stood sweating underneath a hot mid-August sun. Paris looked as if she were about to pass out from heat exhaustion. She was waiting in line at the water fountain. Ever the smooth operator, Tucker stepped up to Paris. "Would you like a sip of some Gatorade," he asked, handing her his unopened bottle.

From that point on, there was no looking back. If she didn't spend her leisure hours on the sidelines watching him practice, then he spent his breaks on the sidelines watching her practice. Those two went steady for the next three years. No other sister could tickle my man's fancy. Tucker got engaged to Miss Greene right before he entered the Army as a second lieutenant through the school's R.O.T.C. program. They were married a year later after Paris graduated from the university, joining Tucker at his military station in Korea. My man was in marital bliss. Every time we talked on the phone, he sounded as happy as can be.

Then early one morning, hours before sunrise, he dialed me, hysterical. He had come home earlier than expected from training in the field that day and found his wife in the kitchen getting it on with a member of his unit. That soldier had faked illness so he could be excused from the unit's exercise. Tucker kicked homeboy's ass and gave him a very legit medical excuse. He quickly divorced Paris and then got him a full-fledged membership in the dog pound.

Tucker had tried to be an honorable black man but his cheating ex-wife put an end to that. Nobody would get the chance to make a fool out of him again. I personally cannot condone my roommate's behavior, but I do not say a word about the trail of women he brings home. As long as his half of the rent is paid on time, I am cool with whatever.

I slowed the pace on my treadmill because I didn't want to overdo it with my left knee. A vicious tackle by a Morgan State linebacker during my next-to-last home game as the Bulldog's quarterback had killed my dream of being a professional football player. I had two scars from two knee operations to prove that. The tragic fact is that I'd been getting good press in several sports publications, and had even had a few pro scouts come and check me out that last season. Believe me when I tell you I cried like a baby when the doctors told me that I couldn't play anymore.

I was depressed for a whole damn year. My so-called girlfriend at the time, Milagros, promptly informed me that she thought we needed some space. (Why do women shoot that crap to you when they're ready to kick you to the curb?) My not being able to play pro ball altered her financial future, so the gold-digger started scouting her next sugar daddy.

But enough of that old misery. The Truth just stepped onto the treadmill next to mine. Sure enough, three other brothers suddenly felt the urge to run as well. I chuckled softly to myself as I eyed the curvaceous rear end that fitted snugly into the dark purple and black jogging pants that girlfriend wore. Her gray midriff T-shirt revealed her perfectly toned abs and waist.

The Truth flashed a smile my way as she programmed her machine. Stunned by her beauty, I tripped and I busted my ass on the treadmill.

"Are you alright?" The Truth asked while speeding her jogging pace.

"I think I'll live," I replied, slowly picking myself up from the floor. My left knee felt like it was on fire.

"Damn," I grimaced.

"What's the matter?" It was The Truth again.

"I got a bum knee. Football injury in college."

"Where did you play at?"

"South Carolina State University, the Bulldogs."

"I've visited that campus before. Everybody was hanging out on that wall by the cafeteria."

"Yeah, sounds like you've been down there alright," I laughed in acknowledgment.

A small explosion went off in my knee. Again, I grimaced in pain. The Truth slowed the pace on her machine.

"You sure you're going to be alright?"

"I'm positive. I've done this before, unfortunately."

"Well, you should go home and ice that down for a few hours and stay off it awhile."

"Boy, you sound just like my doctor," I teased.

"Actually, I'm a nurse."

"I bet you're a freak, too," I muttered to myself absentmindedly.

"What was that?" she asked. "I couldn't hear you."

I quickly gave her my choirboy smile. "I said, that it was...nice to meet you."

"Nice to meet you, too." The Truth revved her machine's speed back up. Looking at her wiggling away on the treadmill, I felt a familiar bulge growing in my pants. I quickly limped off toward the locker room before I endured any further embarrassment.

CHAPTER THREE

Brooklyn's wide variety of black people is what drew me to that borough. Where else could you walk down a major street, say like Franklin Avenue, and easily pass brothers and sisters of so many different nationalities? More importantly, where else could you find so many beautiful black women concentrated in one locale? These were the questions I pondered as I stepped out of the G train stop at Smith Street and headed toward my job on Court Street. As I reached my building, I glanced up at its ominous, dull-gray façade and took a deep sigh before continuing inside.

There are few professions in New York City that are more dismal than working for the Human Resources Administration, otherwise known as the Department of Social Services. If somebody asked me how I ended up being a caseworker in Brooklyn, New York, I couldn't tell them. Everything happened in a big blur.

When I came up North five years ago, a neighbor encouraged me to take the civil service examination after watching me bounce from one meaningless part-time job to another. I scored pretty decently on the test and about a year later, I was canvassed for a position with the Department of Human Resources, which I foolishly accepted.

I reached my ever-cluttered desk and dropped into my chair. As soon as I began to psych myself up for the on-coming day's events, my phone began ringing. It was only a quarter 'til nine. I had another fifteen minutes to prepare myself mentally. *What the heck,* I thought, *might as well get this started.* I picked up the phone.

"Hello. Human Resources."

"Mr. Collins?"

"Speaking..."

"This is Maxine Washington."

"Yes, Miss Washington? How can I help you?"

"I went to pick up my damn food stamps yesterday and my card got denied! What the hell's going on?"

"Miss Washington, please don't use profanity," I stated politely.

"Fuck that! Me and my kids gotta eat!"

I took a deep sigh.

"Let me look at your case and see what's going on."

"Please do!"

I put my angry client on hold and typed her info into my computer. I then discovered that her case was being closed for failure to provide information about earned income she received during the last working quarter. Her name had come up as a wage match on our computer system. I inhaled and exhaled deeply three times before I picked the receiver back up.

"Miss Washington, are you employed?"

"I got a little part-time job, yeah!"

"Well, you had until last Tuesday to send us some information about this job, which you've failed to do. So now your case is being closed," I stated firmly.

"Closed?" she shrieked. "What the fuck you mean my case is being closed!"

"Miss Washington, please do not..."

"Fuck that! Nobody told me anything 'bout I had to send info about my new job to you!"

"A letter was sent to you in the mail, Ma'am."

"Well, I didn't damn get it!"

My head began to pound, signaling to me that it was time to end the conversation.

"Well, the bottom line is this, Miss Washington. You got a job that you've failed to let this agency know about. And if I'm not mistaken, this is not your first time doing this. You then failed to provide documentation of your income as was requested to you in writing. So now your case is being closed."

"Looka here, motherfucker! Don't think that you are all that just because..."

I interrupted her. "Miss Washington, I'm afraid I don't have the time to listen to your abusive language. I have to go now. Bye."

With that, I politely hung up the phone. I massaged my temples as I slid down in my chair and stared up at the ceiling, wondering, for the umpteenth time, *What in the hell am I doing in this God-forsaken place?*

"That's what you get for answering your phone before nine o'clock!"

My co-worker, Mandy Jackson, was grinning at me as she touched up her makeup with the help of her handheld mirror.

"Good morning to you, too, Miss Jackson," I growled.

She continued her reprimand.

"You're going to learn one day."

"That could have been another worker calling in sick, or late," I explained.

"Was it?"

She had me on that one.

When I first started at Social Services, Mandy was one of the few workers there who actually took the time from their own hectic workload to show me the ropes. That wasn't easy to do. Never before in my work life had I been in a place where you had to fill out so many forms in order to get shit done. I used to go bonkers trying to remember what form went along with what action. A lot of trees get cut down because of DSS; a lot of trees.

After we got to know each other well, Mandy introduced me to her cousin, Juanita.

Juanita Harris was the last black woman I was seriously involved with. I use the word *serious* to describe my dealings with her because girlfriend turned out to have some real serious issues. When we were first introduced, I had to keep pinching myself to make sure that I wasn't dreaming. She was so perfect. Weave-less hair, gold-less teeth, no six-inch fingernails, no kids, and a good job. She seemed too good to be true. *Okay, what's the catch?* That's the alarm that goes off in a brother's head when he thinks he's found a potential mate.

Juanita made it obvious to me from the word "go" that she was very interested in me. During our initial conversations, she was aggressive in her queries about my life. And I was so impressed that she didn't ask me all of those materialistic, bourgeoisie, surface questions. You know the ones: "Where did you go to school?" "What did you pledge?" "What type of work do you do?" "Who do you know?" and let's not forget, "What type of car do you drive?" Juanita kept the conversation neutral by discussing hobbies and interests. Neither of us thought the New York Knicks were all that. And that was a definite sign of compatibility.

Juanita gave me her phone number before I had even thought to ask her for it, and we began dating. We went to the movies, caught some slamming concerts, and did the whole 'dining out in New York City' thang. It was after one exceptionally succulent meal of shrimp scampi with oysters on the side at Jonah's Seafood, the trendy, eating place just below Harlem on Madison Avenue, that Juanita allowed me to accompany her home and spend the night.

I thought that I had found heaven on Earth. Miss Harris was the most affectionate, energetic, and skillfully agile woman in bed that I had ever been with. The very first payday after our initial sexual encounter, I ventured down into Lower Manhattan to look for an appropriate expression of love for my future wife.

Alas, after many glorious days, and many more scandalous nights, my dream world began to slowly unravel. It all began when Juanita decided to go back to school at New York University and pursue a second degree in psychology to go along with her first one in childhood education. She began taking these courses that required reading some really deep books. The majority of our limited conversations, when she *did* have time to get together with me, were spent discussing the various theories that she had read about. I had never seen a person so enthralled by her studies.

And then she had to go and sign up for that damned Black Male Behavior course! Eerie and irksome? Juanita became an entirely different human being. We'd be at the movies and I would turn my head to ask her a question, only to realize that she was watching me instead of the film. The same would happen when we were in bed together. I'd stir awake in the middle of the night to see Juanita gazing over at me.

At first, I thought nothing of it. I was sort of flattered. I actually thought that the sister was that much in awe of me. But then, she began questioning certain habits of mine. The order in which I dressed in the mornings, my eating manners, even my signature on a check. When she got around to interrogating me about my childhood and my relationship with my deceased mother, I knew I had to react. I sat Juanita down one Friday night and told her that it was going to be either me, or that damn book that she was reading for her class. I put my foot down.

Juanita helped me pack up the few belongings I had at her place the following day.

Needless to say, I was devastated. And the constant ragging from Tucker didn't help much, either. He stayed on my case for damn near a whole month, laughing about how I had let a book take my woman away from me. He said that he could see if it was another man, or even another woman, but a bunch of bound, printed paper? I consoled myself by sitting in my room, blasting my favorite songs on my stereo system. *'You Can't Hurry Love'* by The Supremes was good therapy. Still, it took me a while before I could even converse with Mandy again because I was so embarrassed.

As I was leaving the office later that day to go out to lunch, Mandy grabbed my hand when I passed her desk.

"Where you heading to?" she inquired.

"The House of Pork."

"You going back over to that swine place?"

"That's correct."

Mandy frowned at me for a moment before digging into her purse.

"Get me a large Pig in a Cup, and a side of fries."

I smiled to myself as I headed to the elevators.

The House of Pork was a small eatery and always crowded. No sooner than I found my place in the back of the line, my mouth started watering. The aroma coming from the kitchen made my stomach start to growl. Looking around, I couldn't help but laugh to myself. You see, once you walk through the front doors of The House of Pork, you'd know immediately how the establishment derived its name. Pictures of pigs in various poses are on the walls, in the windows and even hanging from the ceiling. All of the tablecloths are also decorated with little pigs and piggy salt and pepper shakers sit atop the tables.

After a five-minute wait, I finally made it to the front counter, where a cute little honey, sporting a pink cap complete with a pig's snout on the end, smiled at me.

"May I take your order please, Sir?"

"Yeah, let me have a..."

"Yo, J.C.!"

Damn! I spied Tucker coming from the restaurant's kitchen. During the time that Tucker was in the Army, everywhere he was stationed at, Fort Hood, Texas, Fort Bragg, North Carolina, and also various military installations in South Korea, people went absolutely crazy over the way my man could make barbecue. He would get invited to every cookout around, mainly because he would be the one they wanted to run the grill. And when he did attend, he would always bring some of his grandmother's special barbecue sauce. Tucker set it off just right on the grill. Tucker's food was so good that people paid for him to come over and cook for them.

As demand for his services rose, so did his fees. And when the word got out to the commanders on base about how good his cooking was Tucker began catering some military events as well. So after Tucker got out of the Army and hooked back up with me in New York, it was only natural that he stuck with his talent. But in Brooklyn?

When Tucker told people about his plans to open a restaurant in Brooklyn that would serve primarily pork, nobody, myself included, thought he would be able to pull it off. Everybody tried to talk some sense into the brother. We explained that there were too many 'conscious' brothers and sisters in Brooklyn who didn't eat pork. Tucker simply stated that a large majority of these so-called 'conscious' people originated from the South, and they were still the first ones in line at family reunions back home for some ribs and hash. They merely renewed their 'consciousness' once they got back on the New Jersey Turnpike, or touched back down at one of the city's airports.

When we told him that there were too many people from other foreign cultures in Brooklyn that outlawed swine, Tucker had a simple come-back. "They did not eat swine, because they have not tried mine."

Tucker ignored every bit of negative culinary and entrepreneurial advice he heard. Instead, he went to the bank, got a small business loan, found a good location for his endeavor on Livingston Street in downtown Brooklyn, and opened up shop.

Business started out a little slow, until Tucker began handing passersby free samples of his cooking. Since then, he has actually had to turn down requests for some catering jobs because he could not accommodate everyone.

Tucker even started home delivery to some customers, especially certain members of the dreadlocked community, who did not wish to be seen ordering pig in public.

"What's up, partner?" he greeted.

"I'm just ordering lunch."

Tucker turned to the cutie that had taken my order.

"Whatever he wants is on me."

"Okay, what's the catch?"

Tucker gave me his famous 'full-of-shit' grin as he strolled from behind the counter and pulled me aside.

"Why can't I give my roomie a free meal every now and then?"

"Because I know that you don't give stuff away without getting something for it in return." Tucker stared at me, pain shooting out of his eyes.

"Now that hurts. But you're absolutely right," he replied. "I need you to drop some money off at the bank for me on your way back to your office. I have to cover some checks I wrote for the business. The money needs to be there as soon as possible so I don't get hit with any insufficient funds fees."

"Why can't you do it?"

"Cause we're real busy right now. Plus, I gotta keep an eye on my workers. You do remember when we used to work together at the Burger Bungalow, don't you?"

I couldn't help but smile. The Burger Bungalow was the local high school hangout spot back in the day when we were coming up.

Both Tucker and I worked there, briefly. We both got fired for hooking up our amigos with free food. I admit that it was a stupid, dishonest thing to do. But hey, what can I tell you? We were just trying to be cool with our friends.

I walked inside of the Bank of Brooklyn holding two bags from The House of Pork in my hands. One contained my lunch, and the other bag contained over four thousand dollars in cash. Thankfully, the place wasn't too crowded, so I was able to get to a window quickly.

When I stepped up to the window, a cute, twenty-something sister with nice brown skin and no heavy makeup looked back at me through the bulletproof window. I read girlfriend's gold countertop nameplate.

"Good afternoon, Keisha."

She looked me in the eye and grinned. There was not a gold tooth anywhere to be found. Not bad at all.

"Good afternoon, Mr...?"

"Collins."

"And how may I help you today, Mr. Collins?"

I sat one of the bags I held on the counter and slid it under the window to her. I then turned around to survey my surroundings. I was giving Keisha the nonchalant treatment, as if dropping off big amounts of money at banks was nothing but something for me to do.

"I appreciate this, Mr. Collins, but I've already had my lunch."

I quickly turned back around.

"What?" I asked.

Keisha then shoved my lunch back under her window to me. I felt like such an ass.

"Sorry, wrong bag," I brayed.

"I thought as much."

Keisha laughed softly as she accepted the right bag from me. Needless to say, I was ready to get the heck out of there and back to my miserable job.

"Here's your deposit slip, Mr. Collins. And do enjoy your lunch."

"Thank you, I will." I grabbed the deposit slip and quickly made my way to the nearest exit.

Mandy was devouring a box of moon-pies when I got back to the office.

"What the hell took you so long? You know we only have an hour for lunch!"

"I had to make an unexpected stop," I explained, handing Mandy her lunch.

"You was probably out there whoring around."

"Naw, I didn't have enough time."

"Whatever," Mandy replied as she began attacking her Pig in a Cup lunch, a container of chopped barbecue soaked in Tucker's grandmother's special sauce and topped with coleslaw.

For being such a smart aleck, I started to keep Mandy's money but didn't. Daddy always said that right makes might.

"Here's your money back. The food was free."

Mandy's eyes lit up and she squealed with delight. I wondered if she did that because the food was that good or because it was free. It was probably both. While pulling out Mandy's money, I noticed that Tucker's bank deposit slip had a phone number neatly written on the bottom of it. It was Keisha's.

I sat down at my desk smiling, but quickly stopped and sighed when I saw all of the messages on it from clients who had called to complain to my supervisor while I was out. No rest for the weary.

CHAPTER FOUR

I called Keisha Dixon and we decided to get together for lunch the following Saturday in Harlem, where she lived. I gathered from the couple of phone conversations that we had prior to our scheduled date that Keisha was a pretty solid young lady. She was twenty-two years old, single with no kids, and lived with her older sister and two nieces. Without being asked, Keisha told me she had finished one year of community college in Brooklyn and that she was going back to finish up as soon as she saved enough money.

Instead of battling mid-day traffic in Manhattan, where I wasn't likely to find a parking place, I hopped the subway, which deposited me on 135th Street station, near the legendary Harlem Hospital.

Walking toward Keisha's apartment building on 135th and Fifth Avenue, I passed a multitude of people scurrying to and fro with their own agendas. Inside her building's lobby, I asked the doorman to buzz her. Ten minutes later, the elevator door opened and out walked Miss Dixon sporting a beige blouse and an awesome black mini-skirt that showed off her shapely legs. She was a sight to behold. When she turned around to hold the elevator door open for an elderly resident who had just returned from shopping, I stole a glimpse of her cupped rear end. *Damn, Smokey!* I thought to myself as she approached me with a smile.

"I see you know how to be somewhere on time."

"My only regret is that I didn't get here sooner."

"Very funny, Mr. Collins."

Silenced by her beauty, I beheld the gorgeous sight in front of me. Keisha eyed me curiously.

"What?" she asked.

"I was just thinking, if you look this good for lunch, I can't wait to take you out to dinner."

"Aren't we putting the cart before the horse?"

Damn. Girlfriend had checked me. I made a mental note to myself to cool it down. Way down. Keisha must have picked up on my vibes.

"So, where are we going to dine at this afternoon?" she asked, flashing her dazzling smile.

"How about Delroy's? Have you eaten there yet?" I asked.

"No, I haven't."

"Great. You'll love it."

We strode onto Fifth Avenue, where I hailed a gypsy cab. A brother could hail a gypsy cab without fear of being profiled as a criminal and passed up. The yellow taxis were a different story.

Delroy's Café was full of scenic photos of Jamaica, the proprietor's birthplace. Music from the reggae master himself, Bob Marley, flowed through hi-fi speakers that were placed strategically throughout the establishment.

Besides being distinguished for its decor, Delroy's Café was renowned for its authentic West Indian cuisine. Delroy's favorable review in the *New York Times* increased business greatly, with patrons coming in from New Jersey and Connecticut to dine.

"So, what are we having?" I asked as we gazed at our menus.

"I don't know," Keisha answered with a slight frown. "Everything sounds so good on here."

"I'll be honored to pay for anything you order, Sister, as long as it's not chicken." She looked at me curiously.

"What do you have against chicken?"

"I have nothing against it. It's just that when most of my friends and family go out to eat dinner at a new restaurant, they always play it safe and order the chicken."

Keisha began cracking up with laughter.

"We sure do that a lot, don't we?"

Our first dining experience together was a total success. We laughed hysterically at each other's jokes, which clearly annoyed some of the other diners.

After pigging out on curried goat, plantains, and rice, we decided to take a stroll in nearby Central Park. Springtime had summoned out of doors and into that expansive park the roller-bladers, joggers, cyclists, sunbathers, and dog-walkers.

"Are you into any sports?" I asked Keisha as we strolled by the Harlem Meer, a small pond where dozens of people, both young and old, were scattered along the water's edge, fishing.

"I do a little running every now and then."

"Is that how you stay in such marvelous shape?"

I could have sworn I saw girlfriend blush.

"Please, don't even try to go there."

"Go where?" I asked innocently.

"Flattery will get you no-wheres, okay? Now, let's just enjoy this moment, huh?"

"Can't a brother give a beautiful young lady a compliment?" (Sure, it was a tired line, but I had to see what I was dealing with.) Keisha stopped dead in her tracks and looked me straight in the eye.

"The only reason that I chose to go out with you, Javier, is because you didn't strike me as the average brother out here shooting shit to every girl that he happens to pass by. However, if that is not the case, you can rest assured that this will be the only time that you and I ever hook up."

The girl ain't no pushover. I thought to myself. I threw both of my hands up in the air innocently.

"I'm sorry if I offended you, Keisha, but I was just speaking from the heart. Is it a crime?" I asked, riffing on that hit from Sade, my favorite rhythm and blues singer. There's something about the sexy way she croons that just drives me bananas.

"Nobody said that you committed a crime, Javier. I'm just letting you know what the deal is."

"Well, consider the deal known," I conceded.

Keisha gently took me by the arm.

"Now, shall we continue?"

With that, we strolled further into the park.

"So how did it go, Loverboy?" Tucker inquired when I ambled into our apartment later on that night.

"Everything was cool," I answered as I made a beeline straight to the bathroom. (From Harlem down to Brooklyn on the subway is a seriously long ride when you have to piss.)

"So, are you two going out again?" nosy ass Tucker continued.

"I believe so," I answered as I flushed the toilet.

After washing my hands, I walked back into the living room and joined Tucker, who was on the couch preoccupied with watching the New York Knicks play the Miami Heat.

"You believe so?"

"Yeah, we'll be going out again."

There was silence for a few seconds as we both watched the game. The Knicks' point guard was stripped of the ball and an imaginary foul was called on the Heat player who did it.

"Look at that bullshit!" I exclaimed.

"What are you talking about?" Tucker asked innocently.

"You know that was a clean steal!"

"Negro, please," Tucker sucked his teeth in disgust. "You better get you some glasses."

"You and the Knicks ain't shit," I countered.

"So, tell me about your date. What's she about?"

"What can I tell you? She's cute, she's fine, and hopefully she'll be mine."

"So you didn't hit the puddy yet, then?"

I stared at the fool in disbelief.

"What kind of question is that?"

Tucker smiled at me.

"I'm just asking a question. You left out of here on a lunch date, and here you are returning home damn near ten o'clock at night. The service at Delroy's can't be that damn slow."

"If you must know, Your Honor, we went to the park for awhile and then we caught a movie."

Tucker was silent as he eyed me closely.

"What?" I finally had to ask him.

Tucker remained silent as he continued to stare at me.

"What?" I demanded.

"You sure seem to be spending a lot of time with this GED."

My roommate has this very perverted philosophy concerning women. (Like I stated earlier, his ex-wife really messed his head up when she tipped out on him.) According to Tucker, there are only two types of women, or, as he states it, 'booty' out there on the singles scene in New York City: 'GED' and 'Ph.D.'.

GED booty refers to the women out there who usually do not possess a high school education. Therefore, these sisters dress in hoochie mama clothing to reveal their body because that's basically all they have to offer a brother. According to Tucker, if these women do not have a child or two already, they will have one shortly and therefore you should take the necessary precautions so that the kid won't be yours. And since these women, by the way they dress and act, obviously have no self-respect, you shouldn't bother to respect them either. GED booty is cheap and usually pretty convenient. Not too demanding, not too expensive. They are good if you want to have some fun, but that's about it.

Ph.D. booty, on the other hand, refers to the sisters that you may eventually want to marry one day (should you be that stupid). These are the sisters, according to Tucker, with a decent job and who are looking to move further ahead in the world. Ph.D. booty dresses tastefully, speak properly, attends various cultural events, so on and so forth. According to Tucker, you usually have to spend some quality time with and some quality money on these sisters, but that is okay as long as they don't take too long to express their 'deep appreciation' in return.

Before you make a final assessment on Ph.D.'s, please note that, according to Tucker, Ph.D.'s are not the end-all-be-all. They tend to be testy at times, and have been known to cause some serious drama. Therefore, it is up to a brother to decide how much he's willing to take off them before he goes out on the prowl for some GED booty, instead.

"Why you gotta call Keisha that?" I asked angrily.

"Keisha?" Tucker laughed softly. "Her name is *Keisha*? Boy, if that don't sound like GED booty to me, then I don't know what does!"

"Sometimes your ignorance amazes me."

"Alright, Bro, I see that you're taking this personal so I'm going to lay off. Just don't spend too much money on the girl. That's all."

At that moment, Miami's star point guard hit a three-pointer at the buzzer, winning the game for his team in Madison Square Garden.

"Yesss!" I shouted.

Tucker shot me a foul-ass look.

"Screw you, J.C."

CHAPTER FIVE

B ack at the office on Monday, I was actually humming as I worked on my cases.

"What's your problem?" Mandy asked, suspicious.

"Can't a black man be happy at his job?"

"In this place? No."

Mandy started walking back toward her desk when she suddenly stopped in her tracks.

"Wait a minute! The last time you were this chipper at work was when you and Juanita first hooked up." Mandy stepped back over to me.

"Who is she?"

"Who is she?" I echoed.

"Don't play games with me, Javier. You know what I'm talking about."

"I'm afraid I don't, dear."

Mandy frowned. She stepped away from my desk in a huff. I actually felt a little bad about not filling her in on the details since we were cool. But then, on the other hand, the grapevine in my office was a motherfucker. If I were to tell Mandy anything about my personal life, I would do just as well to stand on the top of my desk and shout it out to the entire office myself because everyone would eventually find out.

I took an early lunch that Monday so that I could dine with Keisha. We met at Junior's, Brooklyn's famous Flatbush Avenue restaurant.

"So, how's your day going so far?" Keisha asked before digging into her chicken salad.

"Not bad," I replied. "I only got cursed out three times today so far." We both laughed.

"You've got issues."

"I think I'll take that as a compliment," I replied before biting into my cheeseburger.

"You know what?" Keisha asked.

"What?" I inquired in a seductive voice.

"You sure do talk funny."

I was immediately offended. Ever since I'd migrated up North I had been trying my best to suppress my Southern accent. Even when I interviewed clients at my job, most of them would inquire as to where I was from originally, since I did not sound like a native New Yorker. Keisha saw the resentment in my facial expression.

"You're not mad at me, are you?"

"Naw," I lied.

"Actually, I think it's kind of cute, Javier."

"You do?"

"Yeah," Keisha smiled. "I bet you sound real sexy late at night, don't you?"

The intonation in her voice automatically required a positive response.

"I reckon so," I answered, sounding just like a Georgia hick.

Keisha began to playfully rub her foot up and down my left leg underneath the table.

"So, Javier, what cha doing today after work?"

"Well," I hesitated, "I'm supposed to go help a friend do some painting."

"Painting?"

"Yeah, that's my hustle on the side."

"Oh yeah, you did tell me that," Keisha recalled.

I read what looked to me like disappointment on her face.

"What's the matter, Keisha?"

"I was going to invite you over for dinner."

"Dinner?" I asked, slightly surprised.

"Yeah, my sister is taking her girls out to Jersey, so I'm going to be all alone this evening."

"Is that right?"

"Yes. I was going to let you sample some of my gourmet cooking tonight."

"Gourmet cooking? From you?"

"No. From KFC. Who the hell do you think from?"

We both fell out laughing. Keisha playfully kicked me on my shin.

"Believe it or not, Mr. Collins, I can throw down in the kitchen."

"I'm sorry I doubted you, Sister."

"So, what do you say, Javier?"

Now, I really enjoyed being in the company of a sister with a good sense of humor, and Keisha definitely had one. However, there was no way in hell that I was going over to eat dinner at this girl's house. Not yet anyway. Daddy always told me since I was a little pup, "Do not trust any woman's cooking but your mama's, and then keep an eye on her too, especially if she's pissed at you."

Now you folks can call me old-fashioned, country, backwards, whatever the case may be, but I don't take chances on stuff like that.

"I'm afraid I'm going to have to decline your invitation, Miss Dixon. I really need to go make some loot. You understand, don't you?"

I knew that I had her then. There wasn't a sister alive in Brooklyn who didn't understand about money, and the need to get more of it.

"I understand."

When Keisha started rubbing her foot up and down my leg again, I started to debate whether or not to let Daddy's advice take a back seat. The girl was really aggressive.

"Uh, you gonna eat those onions there?" I asked Keisha, trying to take my mind off the bulge that was straining to break through my pants.

"No. You can have them."

Never one to let some good food that I paid for go to waste, I piled Keisha's unappreciated onions onto my plate and began dining on them.

Looking across the table, I saw that Keisha was studying me. I began to panic. *Oh no,* I thought to myself, *not another psycho sister.* Almost as if on cue, Keisha began to grin again.

"Can I be frank with you?"

Here it comes. I took a deep sigh before answering.

"Of course you can." Keisha eyed me closely.

"You sure?"

"Absolutely," I responded. "What's up?"

She hesitated for a moment.

"Well uh, ever since that day you walked into the bank and gave me that bag with your lunch in it..."

Keisha floundered again.

"Go on, Miss Dixon."

"It's just that uh, ever since the first time I saw you in the bank and what not, I told myself that I wouldn't mind screwing you. That thought still lingers in my head."

My food slipped down the wrong pipe and I began choking. I knocked my plate onto the floor while reaching to grab my glass of water.

"You okay?" Keisha asked with genuine concern as I struggled to gulp down my water.

Our waiter rushed over to our table.

"Are you alright, Sir?"

"Does he look alright?" Keisha yelled. "He's damn choking!"

The waiter gave me two sharp blows to my back. Onion remains immediately spilled onto the table in front of me.

"Thank you!" I gasped.

"No problem," he responded with his Asian accent. "This happens all the time around here." The waiter then leaned over into my ear.

"She wanna go fucky-fucky now?"

The look of shock on my face confirmed his answer and he smiled as he walked away.

After finishing my lunch and tipping our waiter generously, I returned to work. This, I had to admit was a bit difficult to do considering every time I thought about Keisha, a bulge (rather huge I might add) immediately appeared on my person. This meant that I had to stay at my desk, which meant that I really didn't get much done for the rest of the day. However, I did manage to call my friend and tell him that I couldn't help him paint because I had something real important to go do.

That evening I rushed home from the job and hopped into the shower. I then changed into some leisure gear for my foray to Harlem. I figured that a pair of shorts and a T-shirt would suffice for the event. As I saw it, there was no need to get too dressed up to *maybe* eat dinner at Keisha's. And based on the deep confession that girlfriend told me earlier in the day at lunch, dinner wasn't the only thing that was going to get served.

I told Keisha that I would probably make it there around eight. That would allow time for me sitting in bumper-to-bumper traffic on the FDR Drive when I headed northwards along Manhattan's East Side.

Sure enough, I sat in Jada for almost an hour, creeping uptown to the 96th Street exit. It was a good thing that I had one of my Miles Davis CDs along with me for the ride. The soothing tones of his trumpet helped keep my frustration to a minimum. After finally finding a legit parking space, I strolled over into Keisha's building, where I was greeted by her doorman.

"Yes Sir, may I help you?" the elderly gentleman inquired.

"I'm here to see Keisha Dixon. Twelve C."

"One moment, Sir." The doorman reached over in his seat, picked up the phone receiver and buzzed Keisha's apartment.

"Yes?" an enticing voice answered.

"I have a..." the doorman looked over at me to help him out.

"Mr. Collins..."

"I have a Mr. Collins here to see you."

"Send him up, please," Keisha's sexy voice replied.

After signing my name on the visitors' registry, I slid into an elevator and rode up to meet with destiny.

Getting off on the twelfth floor, I was greeted by the latest hip-hop anthem that was being blasted from an apartment down the hall. How inconsiderate. I was quite sure that not everyone on that floor, myself included, wanted to hear that crap.

I rang Keisha's doorbell. There was a serious aroma wafting from under the steel door and into the hallway.

When the door swung open, there stood Miss Dixon dressed in a New York Giants football jersey that was way too big for her. The pair of black, spandex biker shorts that she wore under it seemed to be one size too small from the way they gripped her thighs. She held a glass of stout out to me.

"Welcome."

"Now this is what I call service," I joked as I took the glass from her and entered the apartment.

I took in the nice décor, while sipping my beer. Keisha's sister had a blue pastel thing going on in her home. Her carpeting, couches, and wallpaper were all some soft hue of blue. She even had blue pastel bulbs in the recessed lighting above us.

"This is nice."

"Thanks. My sister spent a lot of time hooking this place up."

"So I see."

I sipped on my brew and then strolled over to the entertainment center located at the far end of the room. I scouted out the CD collection, which was a diverse assortment of music. Hip-hop, funk, gospel, rhythm and blues, and even some jazz. I was elated that there were a couple of Miles Davis CDs in there also.

"I see you folks have good taste in music."

Keisha stepped up beside me smiling.

"We have good taste in everything."

"Modesty, now I like that in a woman."

"I made your favorite for dinner this evening," Keisha responded, choosing to ignore my little sarcastic remark.

"Gee, I wonder what that could be?"

On cue, Keisha grabbed me by the hand and led me into the kitchen area, where she had a small table laid out.

"Surprise!" Keisha sang as she revealed her meal of collard greens, corn muffins, and of course, some barnyard pimp.

"Chicken," I laughed. "How unexpected."

"The bathroom's straight down the hall to your right. Go ahead and wash your hands while I fix your plate."

I made my way down the hall wondering to myself if I was doing the right thing. I was always one for heeding Daddy's advice, but girlfriend looked so damn good in those biker's shorts. Also, the last thing that I wanted to do was to insult Keisha in her own house.

I glanced at myself in the mirror and smiled as I washed my hands in the sink. I thought to myself, *Here I am with a fine sister who took the time to prepare for me a home-cooked meal and I'm having second thoughts about eating it? Shit, you don't find too many sisters doing that these days anymore. Anyway, I'm sure that Daddy would probably break his own maxim if he saw how beautiful Keisha is.*

A rather large cockroach crawled across the mirror, interrupting my thoughts. I wasn't too alarmed by it, though. Lots of people mean

lots of food and lots of roaches. Harlem was jam-packed with bodies.
I mashed the bug, once it cleared the glass, with a piece of toilet
paper. Sometimes it doesn't pay to be too bold.

I returned to the kitchen and stood before the plate that Keisha
had lovingly prepared for me. The come-hither aroma from those
steaming collard greens commenced my stomach to growling. The
fried chicken wasn't smelling too bad either, and the muffins were all
nice and fluffy-looking. *This girl really knows her stuff.*

"Damn, I forgot the napkins," Keisha remarked, as I was about
to sit down at the table with her.

"I'll get them. Where are they?"

"In the cabinet above the sink. On the left-hand side."

I walked over to the sink and opened the cabinet. Two roaches
dropped down into the sink below. *This don't look too good, kid.* I
thought to myself as I retrieved several napkins from the opened
pack that sat before me. I returned to the table and placed them
between us.

"Thank you," Keisha said.

"You're quite welcome."

Then, I noticed another cockroach stealing along the edge of the
table. I assumed that Keisha must have noticed it as well, because
she knocked it off the table as she reached over to get a napkin for
herself. Wouldn't you know that as soon as she did, another one
scurried down the side of the wall beside us? I gathered that it must
have smelled those tempting collards. Keisha peeped it, too. She
gave me a little awkward smile as she smashed the insect with the
napkin she held. She then looked over at me.

"Well, dig in and tell me how you like it."

Needless to say that by this time I was second-guessing my rather rash decision to disregard Daddy's advice.

"Uh," I started, "shouldn't we uh, at least say grace first?"

"You're right. Sorry."

We both bowed our heads as Keisha mumbled a quick invocation to the Supreme Being on High and then looked over at me.

"Is that better?"

"Yes," I answered.

With much hesitation, I took my fork and began stirring the food around on my plate. As I did, I could hear Daddy's voice inside my head: "*You big dummy!*"

To make matters worse, I then had the misfortune to observe a dark object mixed amongst my collard greens. I didn't know if it was a piece of burnt food, a big flake of seasoning, or what. It was too damn close to call.

I had to think fast. I couldn't very well afford to embarrass Keisha, but I sure as hell wasn't going to eat any of her cooking either! During my glory days of quarterbacking at State, coach liked the fact that I could think fast in a jam. That was one of the reasons he picked me to start my second year on the team. I was used to getting rid of the ball whenever I was in a tight spot. Now I had to get rid of this damn food. I looked up to find Keisha smiling at me.

"What's the matter?" she inquired.

"Nothing," I lied as I eyed my now refilled glass of stout.

"I'm just savoring this moment. How about a little toast?"

"Sure," Keisha said as she picked up her glass.

As I retrieved mine, I 'accidentally' spilled it into my lap. Jumping up quickly from my seat, my plate of food was somehow accidentally knocked from the table as well. It crashed onto the floor.

"Crap!" I exclaimed.

Keisha immediately rushed to my side.

"Are you okay?"

"Yeah. Sorry about the dinnerware," I said as I bent down and began cleaning up my mess.

"I'll get that."

"No, Keisha. I made this mess; I'll clean it up."

"Okay, then. I'll go fix you another plate of food while you're doing that."

"No!" I exclaimed without thinking. Keisha looked over at me in confusion.

"What's the matter?"

Think fast boy!

"I need to go home and try to soak this stain out of my favorite T-shirt."

"Nonsense, Javier. I can wash it downstairs in the basement. You can wear one of my sweatshirts in the meantime. I have lots of extra-large stuff in my closet."

Crap!

"Keisha, darling," I started, "I think it's a little too early in our friendship for you to be washing any clothes for me. I appreciate the offer, though."

I stroked Keisha's hair playfully with one hand, as I dropped the broken plate pieces into the trashcan with the other. I then picked up the nearby dustpan and broom and began sweeping up the scattered food.

"Do you really have to leave now?" Keisha asked dejectedly.

"I think I'd better," I sighed, sounding disappointed myself. "I'll tell you what, though, how about we go out this weekend? Anywhere you want to go to." Keisha smiled slightly.

"Anywheres?"

"You name it."

"Okay then, bet."

I turned around to continue sweeping up when I felt my ass being pawed. I spun back around to see Keisha grinning at me wickedly.

"Can't you at least have a little dessert before you go, baby?"

As if on cue, my manhood immediately jumped on hard. (I swear sometimes I think the thing has a mind of its own.) I, on the other hand, knew better. The last thing that I needed to feel on me was a roach crawling across my bare, black ass.

"I really need to run, baby. Just save whatever it is you had in mind until this weekend. I promise you, I'll leave plenty of room for it."

I felt a little guilty as I climbed into Jada and cranked her up. Keisha was no doubt upset that our date turned out the way it did. I promised myself to make it up to her. I placed the wrapped up plate that Keisha had prepared for me in the seat behind me and then reminded myself to throw that crap away when I got home.

CHAPTER SIX

Under the luminance of a full moon, I slowly cruised Jada down my block looking for a legal parking place. It was half past one in the morning and Keisha and I were returning from a flawless Friday night on the town. After dining on some scrumptious Italian food at a restaurant in Times Square, we made our way to the Village for a little bar hopping. I must say that I was a bit taken aback at the large quantity of alcohol that Miss Dixon consumed.

At the first two bars we visited, girlfriend held her own as she accompanied me in sipping down a few pints of Guinness. At our third pub of the evening, a hole-in-the-wall on West Fourth Street called The Erogenous Zone, Keisha casually let it be known to me that drinking tequila made her somewhat horny. I declined her offer to drink some liquor. But I did graciously inform Keisha that I would pay for as many shots as she would require. So while Keisha progressed to the hard stuff, I slowed my pace down and nursed a couple of bottles of Coors Light.

Knocking back her fourth shot, Keisha swung around on her stool and seductively smirked at me. I knew then it was time for us to leave.

Finally parking three blocks away from my home, Keisha and I got out and began hiking back to my place. I thought that I detected a slight stagger in her gait, but I wasn't quite sure.

"You know you in some serious trouble now, right?" Keisha asked me with a crooked smile.

"Oh am I, now?" I asked with mock alarm.

"You sho is."

Her grammar is slipping as well. I thought to myself as we reached my doorsteps.

"Here we are," I announced.

Keisha gave our brownstone the once-over, stopping when she eyed the row of tulips that aligned our walkway.

"Hey, those are pretty."

I silently thanked Tucker for going ahead and getting permission to plant the flowers over my objections. His whole argument was that women liked to see a little sensitivity in their men, and shit like flowers did the trick. I guess he was right.

"Thanks. Shall we go inside, now?"

"Of course, Javier."

Her first few steps were wobbly, but Keisha regained her composure when I threw her a puzzled look.

"Are you going to be okay, Keisha?"

"I'm fine," she grinned. "You need to be more concerned with the job ahead of you."

"I like it when you talk dirty. I just hope that you can back it up," I whispered softly into her ear.

As soon as we entered my living room, Keisha grabbed me by the hand.

"Which way is your bedroom?" she asked.

"Follow me."

Boy, I hope I haven't bitten off more than I can chew? I thought to myself as I led Keisha down the hall. I opened the door to my bedroom, which of course was immaculate after the thorough cleaning I had given it earlier that morning. Keisha gave my room the once-over as well.

"This is nice."

"You like?" I asked.

"Yeah," she said and then turned to face me. "You're not doing too bad for yourself, are you? Nice ride and nice crib."

"You're about to see what else I have that's nice, Keisha."

I picked up the remote to my stereo system and clicked on some pre-programmed smooth jazz music from my man, Euge Groove. Keisha closed her eyes and began swaying in rhythmic time with his saxophone. She kicked off her heels, took a seat on my bed and began unbuttoning her blouse. When I saw her two proud C-cups standing up at attention, I instantly became excited myself.

Keisha then stood up, turned around, and slid out of her Levi's, pulling her panties down as well. I stared in awe at her picture-perfect ass. In fact, I almost had an accident right then and there. I hastily excused myself to the bathroom.

"Hurry up, baby," Keisha moaned as she began removing her bra.

In the bathroom, I took a mental assessment of my situation while I quickly brushed my teeth and reapplied both deodorant and some sandalwood body oil to my person.

Fact one: you have a fine-ass sister in your bedroom getting undressed for you! Fact two: you have a fine ass sister in your bedroom getting undressed for you! And last, but not least, fact three: you have a fine ass sister in your bedroom getting undressed for you! I gave myself a devilish grin in the mirror as I placed my deodorant and oil back into the medicine cabinet.

When I walked back through my bedroom door, I was harder than Chinese arithmetic. The sight that I saw before me stopped me dead in my tracks; Keisha was lovingly sprawled out across my bed, butt-naked and fast asleep.

"What in the...?"

"Keisha?" I called out in near panic as I leapt on the bed beside her.

"Wake up, baby...baby, please. Wake up!"

Keisha rolled over groggily and faced the other way on the bed still dead to the world. A small river of drool flowed out from one corner of her mouth.

"Keisha?" I called out, now on the verge of tears.

I made sure that the water wasn't too frigid before I stepped under the shower spray with my head hung down low, in sorrow.

The cold water pummeled my body. Twenty minutes later, I returned to my bed feeling hard and frozen, just like an iceberg. I sighed to myself as I gazed upon Keisha's fine body lying beside me, looking so beautiful, smelling so pleasant, and snoring so loud. Damn!

Waking up later on that morning, I found that Keisha had altered her position in my bed. Nevertheless, she remained fast asleep. After eating a large bowl of cereal, I reclined on my couch in the living room and clicked on the television to CNN. (Daddy always told me to keep abreast of what's happening in the world.) Looking at the sports ticker flowing across the bottom of the television screen, I saw that the Knicks had lost again over in Philly.

"Good," I sighed before dozing back to sleep.

I was rudely awakened when someone began fondling my family jewels.

"Not now Beyonce'. Cut that out…"

"Beyonce'!" Keisha demanded as she gave me a shove. Suddenly, I was wide-awake.

"I…must have been dreaming about her new video I saw recently."

"It better be just a dream!" Keisha scowled.

I raised myself up on my elbows and gave her the evil eye.

"Now I know that you aren't up in here calling yourself being mad at me?" Miss Dixon looked apologetic.

"I'm so sorry about last night."

"You got that right," I continued as I sat up on the couch.

"Let me make it up to you?" Keisha said as she gently took my hand and pulled me up from the couch.

"Didn't we go through this last night?" I asked half-gruffly as I followed her back towards my bedroom.

(Hell, I couldn't stay mad at her for long. Girlfriend was still butt-naked underneath my robe.)

Words cannot describe what took place in my bedroom for the next three hours. (That's right, three.) Keisha and I went at it like two horny lovers on a deserted beach at night. Whenever one partner would slow down, the other would gladly take up the slack. In the space of an eighth of a day, we learned every crack and crevice of each other's body.

When we finally called a truce, everything was hurting on me except my pride. To be honest with you, I was even craving a cigarette, something that I hadn't done since my junior year in high school. Keisha heaved a deep sigh before snuggling up against me.

"Was that good enough for you?" she cooed.

I painfully grinned in her direction.

"Girl, if it was any better we'd be on our way to the chapel right now."

"I'll keep that in mind," Keisha said with a laugh.

"You uh, do know that that was a joke, right?" I asked uneasily.

"I knew that. I was joking as well."

There was a brief moment of awkwardness before both of us started giggling. Even though I was playing the macho role and ridiculing the idea of Keisha and me marrying on the outside; in the back of my mind, 'The Question' was forming yet once again. *Could Keisha Dixon be the one meant for me?* I logically decided not to do anything rash, like catch any feelings for Keisha just because she was spectacular in the bedroom.

I was drawing my decision from a saying that Daddy told me when I first went off to college, where I'd be interacting with a vast array of beautiful people of the opposite sex.

"Son," he told me, "love is just like being in a boxing ring. You gotta keep your chin down and your eyes wide open so you can see what's coming, cause if you don't, you're gonna be flat on your ass real quick!"

My thoughts on love were interrupted when Keisha began to rub on me underneath the covers.

"Well?" she asked.

"Well, what?" I asked back.

"Are you?"

"Am I what?" I asked, still confused.

Evidently, I had been so deep in my own thoughts that I had missed a question that she had posed to me.

"Are you ready for round two?"

An ice-cold chill quickly shot down my spine. *This girl couldn't be psychic could she?* This was the question that I pondered in my mind as Keisha and I went toe-to-toe again.

Driving back home from the mall the following evening, I was greeted by a familiar sight. Tucker was in a heated argument in front of our brownstone with one of his 'clients', as he often referred to his numerous female companions. Luckily, I was able to secure a parking space directly across the street from him, thereby allowing me to view the entertainment at close range.

"What's your problem, girl?" Tucker demanded.

He was obviously peeved that he was being confronted with drama outside of his residence.

"You!" the young lady responded.

I recognized the sister that he was quarreling with as a young lady from Long Island. She was a frequent visitor to our crib the previous winter. I was almost certain that her name was Lori something. She was quite a looker too. Tall, dark, and lovely. I shook my head in wonderment. Why do some brothers think it's so important to run through as many women as they could during their time here on Earth? I was quite sure that this was one of the reasons for the animosity that some sisters were openly displaying towards us.

"You're the damn problem!" Lori repeated. "Why are you trying to screw me over?"

"Nobody's screwing you over, Lori!"

"Then what the hell do you call what I saw in your store earlier today?"

"I was just talking to that girl about a job, if you must know!"

"Do you always hold hands and rub on potential employees like that? Or was it a blow job that she was going to apply for?"

When I heard that, I doubled over my steering wheel in laughter and honked my horn in the process. Tucker glared across the street at me with a look of annoyance. He then turned back to Lori.

"Hey, like I told you before, I'm not the only game in town. You know what you can do if you don't like it."

Tucker folded his arms across his chest as he eyed Lori, who exhaled a huge sigh of defeat.

"You know what? You're right. You're not the only game in town!"

With that, Lori turned around and started walking off down the block. However, after about ten paces she suddenly stopped and picked up a nearby brick. Lori turned around and hurled it through the driver's side window of Tucker's cherished Range Rover. The girl's accuracy was uncanny. Lori slowly smiled as she walked off.

I tried to control my laughter as I got out of Jada and crossed the street. Tucker was steamed. This would be the third window that he would be replacing in as many months. It seemed that most of the clients that Tucker chose to deal with had a fondness for brick-throwing.

Now the appropriate thing for me to have done in this situation would be to enter my home in silence and leave my man alone in his moment of anguish. And that was exactly what I was going to do, until I remembered that little episode I had with the toilet bowl two months earlier.

"Another one of your satisfied customers?" I asked as I passed by my roommate.

"Forget you!" Tucker growled as he began cleaning up the shards of glass from the inside of his ride.

Later that evening, as I was getting ready to meet Keisha down in Lower Manhattan, Tucker knocked on my bedroom door.

"You may enter."

He opened the door and walked in carrying some folders under his arm. Seeing me lacing up my boots, he frowned.

"Don't tell me you're going out with that same ass chicken-head again?"

"What did I tell you about calling Keisha that?" I was not in the mood for any of his foolishness.

"I'm sorry," he said. "You're right. I shouldn't have called your new girlfriend a chicken-head to your face. That's disrespectful."

Tucker eyed me with a malicious grin.

"She is your new girlfriend, isn't she?"

"What's it to you?"

"Look at my little roomie, getting all bashful about his new girl! Where are you two going tonight? If I might ask?"

"I'm meeting her at The Well. If you must know."

"That's right. It's ladies night tonight, isn't it? Gonna be a lot of fine females down there, my man. Don't let your eyes get you in no trouble."

"What do you want, Tucker?" I asked through clenched teeth. My patience was wearing thin. Tucker sat down on the bed next to me and gave me a serious look.

"Actually, I wanted your thoughts on this new product that I was thinking of introducing over at The House of Pork."

"What's it called?"

"Pig on a Stick," Tucker answered. "Catchy, ain't it?"

I had to laugh at that one.

"I'll look at it in the morning."

"Thanks," Tucker said as he sat the folders on my desk and left.

For those of you out there who don't know, that Pig in a Cup idea? Mine. Tucker had been racking his brains trying to figure out some fancy name to call his creation, and I advised him to do what Daddy always told me. Keep it simple. Ever since then, Tucker liked to run various ideas and concepts by me before implementing them in his business. The only reason I don't charge my man for my wisdom is because I eat there for free. Well, most of the time, anyway.

Taking the subway into Manhattan, I reflected upon the question that Tucker had asked me earlier. Was Keisha my new girlfriend? If not, then what were we actually? It seemed to me that whenever I was without a special female in my life, well one that I could get serious about anyway, I was always wishing for one. Whenever it seemed as if I might possibly have my goal in sight, I felt a little uneasy. The thought of dealing seriously with Keisha reminded me of something that I always seemed to forget before making such decisions: having a lady in your life meant that you automatically give up certain privileges.

There would be no more going out where and when you wanted to. Being committed romantically also eliminated the spontaneity of, say, solo trips out of town, hanging out at one of your boy's cribs, or going out to shoot some ball. You couldn't stay out all night barhopping with the fellas anymore, either. (Actually you could, but it wouldn't be advisable.)

Having a steady girlfriend meant also that you had to check in with her at least twice a day on the phone to see how she was doing. Not doing this would be a big mistake. These reservations and more were on my mind as I got off the subway at Fourteenth Street and walked the two blocks over to The Well, one of New York City's biggest nightclubs.

When I saw Keisha sitting at the bar waiting for me, however, all of my uncertainties about getting serious with her went out the window. She was draped in a strapless red dress with matching pumps and a pair of black fishnets that accented her muscular calves. Like the singer Morris Day once crooned, I too, was a sucker for those fishnet pantyhose. Keisha was wearing a pair of designer frames that gave her that sexy intellectual look. When I crept up behind her and tapped her on the shoulder, Keisha spun her head around quickly.

"Excuse me, but don't I know you?"

Without saying a word, Keisha smiled as she got off her stool and gave me a kiss. She was undoubtedly glad to see me. However, I wasn't quite sure if I could say the same for the gentleman sitting next to her. From the disgruntled look I saw on his face, he had most likely just been getting to the gist of his rap and was not too pleased about my arrival. As Keisha and I embraced, I gave her would-be suitor the official take-a-damn-hike nod.

At that moment, the house deejay threw on the late Notorious B.I.G.'s hit, '*Hypnotize*'.

"Let's dance, Javier."

Keisha grabbed my hand and led me onto the crowded dance floor, where it was hotter than July. In no time at all I was dripping in sweat as Keisha and I got into a syncopated grind and kept in perfect rhythm with Biggie's thumping bass line. With sweat dripping in my eyes, I beheld the enchanting creature in front of me. Keisha looked so alluring in that tight red dress. (I won't even mention what those fishnets were doing for me.) I was ready to take her home, where we could dance together more intimately.

I mentally chided myself for hesitating about making a serious commitment to Keisha. Of course she was my girlfriend. That is, if she wanted to be.

After dancing to about six more songs, we both called a truce and retired to a cozy booth in the far corner of the club. I ordered two overpriced Coronas with lime and we then sat back to enjoy the atmosphere.

"This place is pretty nice," Keisha said.

"There sure are a lot of people in here."

"You mean women, don't you?"

That was exactly what I had meant but I wasn't about to concur with Keisha.

"Naw, I meant people in general. Both sexes," I said with a weak smile.

Keisha grinned at me before giving me a peck on the cheek.

"Yeah, I bet."

It was right then and there that I decided to take the initiative and ask Keisha in what direction did she think our intimate friendship was heading.

"Can I ask you something, Keisha?"

"Can it wait until I come back from the restroom?" Keisha asked as she got up from her seat.

"Do I have a choice?"

"I'll be right back. Don't let me catch you staring too hard at any of these other *people* in here either."

I watched Keisha work those fishnets as she made her way to the restroom. *Yep, I am definitely going to lock that down.* I thought to myself as I picked up my bottle of Corona and drained it.

Keisha was livid when I saw her returning to our booth about ten minutes later. I tried smiling at her as she neared me, but she apparently wasn't in the mood to do likewise.

"What's wrong, baby?" I asked when she reached our table.

"Nothing," she mumbled. "Are you finished with that?" she asked, indicating my empty bottle of Corona.

"I believe so," I answered, still trying to grin some pleasantness back into the sister.

Without uttering a further word, Keisha picked up my bottle and trotted back over towards the direction in which she had just returned. My eyes trailed her as she stole up behind a brother, whom I immediately recognized as the same guy who was sitting at the bar with her when I first walked in. Keisha slowly raised the empty Corona bottle and then thoroughly clocked homeboy across the back of his head with it. The poor fellow had no choice but to slump to the ground in agony. Keisha then stood directly over him.

"DON'T YOU EVER PUT YOUR HANDS ON ME AGAIN!!!"

My eyes and mouth opened wide in astonishment as Keisha returned to our table, took me by the hand, and then quietly led us out the exit door.

Riding back home underneath Brooklyn in the subway, I was still a bit unnerved by the incident that I had witnessed. Miss Keisha Dixon seemed totally nonchalant after we had left the place.

"Sorry that you had to see that, Javier," Keisha had told me as we held hands and walked towards Seventh Avenue.

"That dumb-ass motherfucker back there thought that he could squeeze on my ass when I walked past him from the restroom and get away with it. I had to set him straight. You know what I mean?"

(I was hoping that I was wrong, but a gut feeling told me that that wasn't Keisha's first time in straightening a motherfucker out.)

"Yeah," I had responded weakly. "I know what you mean."

"Dammit!" Keisha exclaimed as we continued along the street.

"What's wrong?"

"That nucca made me break a nail!"

After we had walked down into the subway station, I had glanced at my watch and saw that it was a quarter to twelve.

"You sure you're going to be okay, Keisha? Why don't we go back up top and let me get you a cab?"

"Don't even waste your money like that, Javier. I wish somebody else would fuck with me tonight while I'm on the train."

Once again, a gut feeling had told me that girlfriend would be quite okay during her train ride back up to Harlem.

"Oh, what was it that you wanted to ask me about earlier, Javier?"

Oh crap!

While I was pondering some good plausible lie to tell to Keisha, a computerized voice announced to everyone that an uptown train was approaching the station.

"That's you," I had informed her with a sigh of relief. "We'll talk tomorrow."

We then exchanged a brief, yet passionate kiss before Keisha headed to the uptown platform.

Damn. Girlfriend definitely has a little street in her. I thought to myself as I stood up to exit the train while it was pulling to a halt at my station. *I wonder if I can deal with it?*

CHAPTER SEVEN

"**S**he did what?"

Lance was laughing so hard that he almost rear-ended the Saab convertible stopped at the traffic signal in front of us.

"Look where the hell you're going, Lance!"

Lance sneered at me.

"It's my van. Let me do the driving!" I rolled my eyes at him.

"Did she really hit him in the head with the bottle?"

"Dropped him just like Mike Tyson used to do."

Lance shook his head in amazement.

"You know, I'd be careful if I were you."

"Man, am I ever."

We both looked at each other and started laughing again. Lance picked up the burning spliff out of his overloaded ashtray and offered it to me.

"Quit being funny," I replied as I pushed the joint away. "You know I don't smoke that stuff."

"Just testing you, mon, only testing."

My painting partner, Lance Brown, is the only person that I know of who can drink beer, smoke weed all day long, and still do quality work. A twenty-eight year old West Indian from the Jamaican paradise of Ocho Rios, this six-foot tall, dreadlocked brother and I have been working together for the past three years.

Lance also is the most laid-back brother I've ever encountered. For a guy living in a place as frenzied as Brooklyn, nothing ever seems to faze him. He always remains his same easy-going self. Lance Brown is also an extremely sagacious brother. My man is exceptionally shrewd when it comes to problem solving. Financial difficulties, family relations, job situations, he has them all covered.

His specialty, however, is female troubles. Whenever I need some sound advice on women and I don't want to bother Daddy, Lance is my go-to guy. He constantly tells me that he gets his knowledge from smoking the weed of wisdom. I say that he gets his knowledge from the four women that he previously lived with.

"So, what did Tucker say when you told him?" Lance asked, still smiling.

I tapped my man on the shoulder to get his attention. He faced me.

"Do I look that stupid to you?" I asked him. "The last thing I need to do is to give him some more ammunition to rag on Keisha about."

"Yeah, I see your point."

Lance was silent for a moment as we continued along Utica Avenue. It was a Saturday morning. He had driven over and scooped me up from my house to go on another gig, as we called our painting jobs. I barely had time to take off my gym gear and shower before he was outside my place blowing his horn.

"Knocking people out with bottles is definitely not a good sign, mon," he said. "Let me ask you this?" I looked at him questionably.

"Do you love this girl?"

"Come again?" I asked him, knowing full well what he had asked.

"I asked you, do you love this girl?"

"She's nice."

"But, do you love her?"

"What do you mean, when you say love?"

Lance slowed down the van and looked me straight in the eye.

"Evidently, you enjoy this girl's company and she enjoys yours in return. Keep it like that and you won't go wrong."

With that being said, he took another long pull on his joint before continuing.

"Too many people try to make things complicated when they needn't be. You like her, she likes you, fine. Leave it that way. In the meantime though, don't piss her off when you two are out drinking together." Lance looked over at me and cracked a sly smile.

"Yeah, whatever," I answered as we pulled up into the lot of the apartment complex that we were looking for.

As I stood in my shower scrubbing off the paint that accumulated on the uncovered parts of my body earlier in the day, I couldn't help but wonder what type of special surprise it was that Keisha had in store for me. My cell had gone off earlier while I was busy working. When I retrieved the voicemail Keisha had left for me, she said she'd planned a surprise for me and that I was to pick her up at seven.

I decked myself out in jeans, a dress shirt, and a tie. I slipped on a pair of loafers and headed out the door. I drove up to Harlem in a little less than forty-five minutes *and* parked right in front of Keisha's building.

Just thinking about Keisha as I walked across the street towards her building was getting me excited. I didn't know exactly what my baby had planned for me, but I hoped that it included her wearing another pair of those fishnets.

"Coming!" Keisha announced after I buzzed her apartment.

The doorman must have been off somewhere making his rounds throughout the building. I smiled to myself because I knew with her coming down that we wouldn't be trying to do the dinner thing upstairs. To be frank about it, I was beginning to run out of credible excuses for not eating with her and her family.

I'd met Keisha's sister Rochelle and her two cute daughters over a month ago. Keisha had brought them to Brooklyn with her one weekend to dine at The House of Pork. They all took a pretty good liking to me. (Eating for free might have helped things a bit.) Ever since that day, however, Rochelle had been inviting me to come over and have dinner with them. Between the two sisters' constant requests, I had to constantly lie my ass off to keep from dining again in that infested apartment.

We wound up at a damn Equalizer concert! To say that I was disappointed is an understatement. I could've easily listed about ten other things that I'd rather have done on a Saturday night than to sit in the Paramount Theater at Madison Square Garden and watch a group of grown men prance around on stage in sagging jeans yelling obscenities.

The concert was over around eleven thirty. Keisha and I decided to stop in at Larry's Lounge before calling it a night. Larry's was an afterhours spot just off Bergen Street. Its main appeal is the showcase of the area's up-and-coming musicians. I especially like the fact that it's also one of the few black drinking joints in Brooklyn that had brew on tap. (Paying six or seven dollars for a bottle of beer could break your behind real quick if you kept it up.)

When our waitress returned with our drinks, I grabbed my pint of Guinness and took a sip. Feeling good and in a laid-back mood, I decided to probe the inner workings of Miss Dixon's mind.

"Tell me something, Keisha...do you like children?"

Keisha looked at me real funny before answering.

"Why did you ask me that?"

"I'm just curious, that's all."

"Of course I like children. I mean, who doesn't?"

"So...how do you feel about the current epidemic of single black mothers that's going on today?" Keisha eyed me closely.

"Are you about to start with your job again?"

I looked at her and smiled. On more than one occasion, I've not only given her the low-down about the problems of the welfare system, but on the problems of working for it as well.

"You're right," I said. "Let's talk about something else."

"Let me ask you a question, Javier?"

I raised my eyebrows as I sipped my brew.

"What's the deal with you and me?"

I unintentionally spat my drink back into my glass.

"Uh, what was that again?"

"What's up with you and me? Where do you think we're going with this relationship thang that we're doing here?"

An image of Lance laughing his ass off at me appeared in my mind. He had been cracking up as he offered me a hit off his joint again. This time I took a big toke.

"Well, I say that we take it one day at a time and see where we end up."

I gave her my famous cheese-eating smile. Keisha frowned at me.

"What's the matter?" I continued. "Does that sound like a bullshit answer?"

"It sure does."

"Well, at least you're honest," I said.

"You can't tell me anything better than that, Javier?"

I suddenly found the bluish flame atop the candle on our table most fascinating. She was having none of my faked distraction.

"Well?" Keisha continued. "What's up?"

I gazed directly into Keisha's mahogany-colored eyes.

"You want the truth?" I asked.

"I would appreciate it, yes."

"Well, to be honest about it, I think I've fallen in love with you, Keisha."

Elated, those same mahogany-colored eyes lit up. Keisha slid over to me, and we had a long, delicious kiss.

That night we made love in every way imaginable. We did it in the bed, off the bed, and even under the bed. The morning sun was just peeking through the curtains of my bedroom window when Keisha decided that she'd had enough. It took me all of sixty seconds to crawl onto my mattress and fall fast asleep.

I woke up later that morning to the sweet essence of breakfast being prepared in the kitchen. Still tired and sore as hell, I climbed out of my bed to investigate. In the kitchen, Keisha was standing at the counter by the sink, opening a bottle of syrup.

"What's all of this?" I inquired with a smile.

I walked up behind Keisha and kissed her on her left cheek.

"Morning, baby. Did you sleep well?" she asked with a malicious grin.

"For all of about three hours, yes."

At that moment, Tucker chose to make his grand entrance into the kitchen.

"Morning, folks."

"Morning, Tucker."

I gave him the evil eye as I greeted him. I wanted him to know from jumpstreet that I wasn't in the mood to take any crap off him, especially with Keisha there with me.

"Morning," Keisha replied as well.

"How have you been, Keisha? I see you're still looking good as usual."

"I'm okay, Tucker. Thanks for the compliment."

Tucker remained in the doorway and examined the scene. A stupid smile slowly spread across his face.

"I just had to get up and see who it was that had this whole house smelling so good. What are you cooking there anyway?"

"Nothing," I answered. "Go on back to bed."

There was no smile on my face at all. Keisha playfully tapped me on the arm in annoyance.

"Don't be so rude, Javier!"

"Yeah," Tucker piped in. "Don't be so rude."

"I've made some scrambled eggs, French toast, tuna patties, and home fries if you want some, Tucker. There's more than enough here."

Tucker immediately walked over to the cabinet and retrieved a plate for himself. I made a mental note to myself to kick his ass later in the evening.

"I'd be delighted to dine with you fine folks this morning," Tucker said as he sat down at the table.

"Say, by the way," he continued, "did either of you hear that thunderstorm that came through here last night?"

"There wasn't any thunderstorm last night," I told him gruffly.

"Oh, then it must have been something else I heard making all that loud noise."

Tucker slyly winked at Keisha. It was time to kick his ass now. I angrily lunged for him, but was restrained by Keisha.

"Quit playing, Javier," Keisha said as she held me back.

"Yeah, Javier, quit playing," Tucker echoed. His grin disappeared when he saw the gleam of anger in my eyes.

"Uh, you know what Keisha? Maybe I'll just fix my plate and take it back to my room. I think it'll be a little more peaceful there."

Tucker quickly loaded his plate with food and left. After fixing our plates and saying grace, Keisha and I dug in. Girlfriend's cooking was on the one.

"Baby, you can throw down better than those folks at the Waffle House!" I exclaimed.

"I think I'll take that as a compliment. Thanks," Keisha answered with a laugh.

We ate in silence for the next few minutes, gazing lovingly at one another across the table in between bites. Our nirvana was interrupted by a loud crash coming from the apartment beneath us.

"What was that?" Keisha asked with alarm.

I dropped my head in disgust before looking up into her inquisitive eyes.

"That's just the Jenkins acting up again. Don't mind them none," I answered with an awkward smile.

"The Jenkins?"

"They're the elderly couple that resides downstairs. They're just having one of their occasional spats."

"Occasional?"

"Yeah, they fight all the time. Never on Sundays, though. Unless Mr. Jenkins is just now getting his tail in from last night." We heard another loud crash below us.

"Shouldn't you be calling the cops or something?" Keisha asked with a worried look on her face.

"The police don't even bother to come out here anymore. Rumor has it that those two have been going at it like that before both of us were even born. They're just blowing off a little steam. Married too long, I say."

At that moment, we heard a high-pitched shriek from underneath us.

"Oh snap! She must have landed a good punch," I thought out loud. Keisha looked at me oddly.

"You mean that she..."

"Yeah," I cut in. "Whips him every time."

"You are kidding me!" Keisha began, trying hard to restrain from laughing.

"I wish I was," I sighed. "I remember last summer when she threw him into a rose bush after she caught..." I stopped in mid-sentence.

"You know, I really shouldn't be talking about other people's business."

"Yeah, I think you're right," Keisha said.

We then continued to eat our breakfast in silence, ignoring the disturbance occurring below us.

During the week that followed, all I could do was think about Keisha. Nothing else even seemed to matter. The irate clients I encountered at the office, the two parking tickets I received while hanging out in Manhattan in Jada, the rude elderly woman at the gym who tried to jump in front of me on the treadmill, not even the embittered sisters that I passed during my travels to and from work. I was above it all. I was in love with Keisha, and she clearly felt the same way about me.

That following Saturday morning, as I was returning from yet another strenuous workout over at Bronze's, I was greeted by my cell phone ringing when I walked through my bedroom door. I reluctantly picked it up and flipped it open.

"Hello?"

"J.C., what's up, mon?"

"Lance. What's going on?"

"What you got planned for tomorrow afternoon?"

"Nothing really. Why, you got another painting gig for us?"

"Nah, mon. I'm throwing a big get-together out at Prospect Park. We going to be doing some serious cooking and I want you and Tucker to come out."

"I'm good to go, but I can't speak for Tucker."

"That's cool. Just give him the invite. Oh yeah, I want you to bring that roughneck girl of yours with you as well. The one that knocks motherfuckers out."

"You mean Keisha?"

"You have more than one?"

"I don't think she can make it."

"What's the matter? You scared she might start an altercation or something?"

"No, Lance. She already told me that she'd probably be over to her mother's this weekend."

"Well, if she can come, bring her along. If she can't, no problem. I'll see you tomorrow. We'll be starting around three. Peace..."

"Peace," I echoed before hanging up.

Right away I began debating on whether or not to call Keisha. She had told me previously that she would most likely be going out to Jersey. I really wanted to show her off at Lance's cookout. (I know that sounds a little bit chauvinistic, but that's how some of us brothers think when we have a woman that we're proud of and want the whole world to know it.)

I decided to try my luck and see if she was in Harlem. I picked my cell phone up and dialed Keisha's number. A little boy answered the phone on the first ring.

"Hello?" he asked rather tersely.

I wondered to myself who the heck he was.

"Yes," I began, dismissing the kid's rudeness to youth. "May I speak to Keisha, please?"

"My mama ain't home."

The phone clicked dead in my ear. I had obviously dialed the wrong number. I looked closely at my cell this time and made sure that I had retrieved Keisha's home number from my phonebook feature. (There was no need to dial her cell phone until she was caught up on her payments for service.) The same little brat answered the phone. I was therefore confused.

"May I please speak to Keisha Dixon?"

"I *said* my mama ain't home!" The phone clicked dead in my ear again.

I was totally lost. Some little boy was implying to me that Keisha was his mother. I angrily hit the call button on my phone again.

"Who is this?" I barked when the same kid answered.

"Quit calling here, dummy!" Dial tone once more.

I showered and changed into some comfortable clothing. I was definitely going up to Harlem to see what the hell was going on! I laced my brand new pair of running shoes, sprinted downstairs and out the door.

An hour and fifteen minutes later, I was turning the corner from 135th Street onto Fifth Avenue when I suddenly froze in my tracks. Less than a hundred yards away from me was Keisha. She was pulling a shopping cart full of groceries behind her as she headed towards her building. Trailing behind her were two little boys that looked exactly like her. For about five seconds I was speechless. I then hastened after her.

"Keisha!"

Miss Dixon abruptly turned and looked in my direction. Now it was her turn to be speechless.

"Javier?"

As I continued toward, her, she hurriedly went into the lobby of her building. The two boys were not far behind her. By the time I entered the lobby, she was just stepping into an overcrowded elevator.

"Keisha, what's going on?" I implored.

I will never forget the look of regret and humiliation that was on Keisha's face as the elevator doors closed between us. I dejectedly turned around in my tracks and walked out of the building. The last thing that I needed to do at that moment was to create another public spectacle in New York City.

CHAPTER EIGHT

There was only one word that could accurately describe the way I felt after that startling revelation. Broken. For the life of me, I couldn't understand why Keisha had chosen to lie to me about having children. All of my calls to her cell phone went straight to voicemail. (After she paid her bill and had it turned back on.) And whenever I called for her at her house, I was told that she wasn't there.

Her sister did grant me the courtesy of informing me that Keisha had given birth to twins during her junior year in high school, and that their mother had demanded that she raise Keisha's children herself until Keisha finished her education and was able to support them on her own. That was the reason she was always going over to visit her mother in Jersey. Rochelle swore to me that she didn't know that her sister had not divulged that information to me. She even apologized for her sister's lapse.

After about three futile weeks of trying to make contact with Keisha, I finally gave up. I seriously considered going to her job at the bank to confront her, but eventually I thought better of it. I was not one for bringing drama into somebody's place of employment, and I certainly didn't want anyone bringing any over to mine. Besides, I remembered a serious lesson about love that I'd learned the hard way back in high school.

It was my sophomore year at Springs Valley High and I had called myself madly in love with me some Nicole Harper. Nikki, as she was called, was a brainy, cute, curvy little sister who also happened to be on the varsity cheerleading squad. She was a year older than I was, but I got away with it since, I myself, was on the varsity football team. I didn't start, but I was the second string quarterback and I did get some playing time.

Now, anyone who ever attended high school knows that dating a cheerleader or a football player automatically gives you some serious status on campus. Nikki and I played it for all it was worth. We were like the perfect Negro couple back then and made all the appropriate social rounds together. We did the hanging-out-at-the-mall scene, went to all the major school sporting events, and of course, attended all of the major parties.

Nikki was one of the first sisters that I went with who knew how to really get down on the dance floor. Back then, we used to jam non-stop to whatever song the deejays played. Nikki and I would even appear at some of the 'white-boy' parties, as we used to call the get-togethers thrown by our Caucasian counterparts. Their affairs were notorious for the numerous kegs of beer they always had on hand.

Nikki and I were a serious item all through that fall, winter, and well into the spring. With the prom approaching, I didn't even bother to ask Nikki if we were going to be attending together because I already knew we were. Until I started hearing rumors that Nikki was also dating some senior from Richland Southeast High, our rival school on the other side of town. I asked her once about it, she denied it, and that was the end of the story. I attributed those lies to folks who were jealous of the type of relationship that we had going on.

Lo and behold, a week before the big event, Nikki called me to say that something had suddenly come up. Breaking our date, she apologized repeatedly and asked me to find someone else to go with since I had already reserved a tux, limo, and a room at the Red Roof Inn.

Of course, I told my baby not to worry about it because if she couldn't go to the prom, then I wouldn't be going either. But when Nikki insisted that I go with somebody else, I got a little suspicious. It then dawned on me that Richland Southeast's prom was the same night as ours. I got scared as hell. The thought of Nikki, the love of my life, stepping out on me was just too much to bear. There was only one thing for me to do.

The night of the prom, I dressed in my tux and swung by Tucker's house in the limo. (There was no need to waste my deposits.) We rode across town to where Richland Southeast High's gala was happening. I breezed through the doors of the Fine Arts Center, and immediately spotted Nikki, splendidly dressed in a fabulous lavender gown, being twirled lovingly around in the arms of some big, steroid-laden brute.

Due to the nature of this brother's size and build, I had to go back outside to the limo for reinforcements. After leaving my tuxedo jacket behind in the limo for safekeeping, Tucker and I went inside and rolled up on homeboy like the police!

I'll never forget the look on Daddy's face as he drove me home from the hospital later on that night. He just gazed at me and shook his head in disgust as he observed my bandaged forehead and the neck brace I wore below it.

"You should see the other guy," I told him with a weak smile.

"I can't believe I did this," he replied softly.

"Did what, Daddy?"

"Raised a moron."

My feelings were crushed.

"Why you wanna say that, Daddy?"

"Cause you going around here letting folks kick your damn ass for free. You should at least get paid like those wrestlers on television."

"Nobody kicked my ass," I informed my father as I adjusted my neck brace. (It was starting to make me itch.)

"I guess you must have beaten this guy's fists up with your face then?"

Daddy could be cruel sometimes when he was trying to make a point.

"By the way, did Tucker regain consciousness yet?"

"He woke up briefly about thirty minutes before you got there. I think they're keeping him overnight for observation."

My father suddenly pulled our car over to the side of the road.

"J.C., if you never remember anything else I ever tell you, I want you to remember this. If a girl doesn't want you, she doesn't want you. Running after her and getting your ass kicked over her isn't going to help matters any. Okay? You have to let it go. Do you hear me, boy?"

"Yes Sir," I answered humbly. "I hear you."

I officially gave up on Keisha Dixon. Needless to say, I needed some therapy. I bought a cold case of Guinness Stout, locked myself into my room and clicked on my stereo system. After searching for a few seconds, I located my *Best of The Whispers* CD and put it on. I selected '*And The Beat Goes On*' and cranked the volume up as loud as it would go.

In the weeks that followed, I was still a mess. I wouldn't eat much, I couldn't sleep, and I was more disinterested than ever in my job. My situation was truly sad. Even Tucker was feeling a little pity for me. He approached me one evening while I was sulking in the kitchen.

"Me and Lance are going over to Larry's for a few brews. You wanna hang?"

We rolled up into Larry's around nine o'clock that evening. The place was packed as usual; so we had to stand around the bar for a few minutes and sip on our beers before getting a table near the back. As Tucker, Lance, and I took our seats, I couldn't help but reflect upon the last time I was in Larry's. That was when I had first told Keisha that I was in love with her.

On the stage in Larry's, a brother recited poetry while beating on a pair of elegant bongos. He was soaked in sweat as he hung his head low and banged away on his instrument, riffing about the virtuous black woman. What he spoke was so profound that a few sisters scattered throughout the audience began moaning in agreement and excitement.

"Damn, sounds like a couple of these girls in here are going to cream on themselves if my man don't ease up with that erotic wordplay," Tucker remarked as he observed the mostly female gathering that was present.

The three of us exploded with laughter. A waitress came over to our table and Lance ordered another round of beer for us. After paying his tab, Lance peered over at me.

"J.C.?" he began.

"Yeah?"

"Are we good friends?"

"As long as you keep buying the brew, we are."

"I'm serious, mon."

"You know we're tight. Why you wanna ask me a dumb question like that?" Lance took a sip from his beer before answering.

"I need you to do me a really big favor."

"What is it?" I asked warily.

"I want you to take a girl I know out to dinner next weekend. I'll pay for the meal."

Lance pulled out a hundred dollar bill and handed it to me.

"If this isn't enough, let me know."

"Who is she?"

"My cousin, Sheila. She just moved down here from Toronto. I want her to get out and see the city a little."

"Then why don't you do it?" Tucker interjected.

I turned to him.

"Would you mind your own business?" I then turned back to Lance. "So why don't you do it?"

Tucker sucked his teeth at me in contempt while Lance threw his hands up innocently.

"I got too many other females to attend to. Besides, she tells me that she's looking for a good brother, so here I am asking you."

"Why me?"

"I just told you. She's a nice girl; you seem to be a pretty decent fella. I'm just trying to be a love broker."

"Then you're too late, Lance. His heart's already broken because of love."

"What does she look like?" I inquired, ignoring my obnoxious roommate.

"She's my cousin. I don't look at her that kind of way, you know."

"What does she look like, Lance?" I repeated.

Tucker started humming the tune to George Clinton's hit, '*Atomic Dog*'.

"She's cute, mon. You'll be alright."

Something still wasn't adding up in my book. A cute girl here in New York City who couldn't find a date was an anomaly.

"Okay, Lance, what's the catch?" I asked.

"Hey, this is Lance that you're dealing with."

"You'll be sorry..." Tucker sang out in a low voice.

"She's a nice girl, got a good job. I wouldn't steer you wrong. You know that."

"Does she come with any accessories?" Tucker asked.

Both Lance and I shot an icy stare at him.

"No, she doesn't have any children," Lance answered. "You'll be fine, J.C. Trust me..."

My Daddy always told me that if something seemed too good to be true, that was because it probably was. Most of the things that Lance told me about his cousin Sheila turned out to be accurate. She was quite friendly and she did have a good job as a lab technician somewhere in Manhattan. However, he did fail to inform me that his cousin looked exactly like him, except that she had breasts and longer hair.

It was the spookiest crap that I had ever seen before in my life! It took me at least twenty minutes before I was certain that Lance wasn't trying to play some sick, perverted prank on me. (I called him on his cell and when he answered, I quickly hung up.) The only way that I could make sense out of the whole scenario was that those two were more closely related than what their parents told them. Needless to say, I was not a happy camper.

Of course, I didn't let my disappointment show on my face when I met Sheila in front of her apartment building. She lived off Beverly Road in the Flatbush section of Brooklyn. I got there at eight o'clock sharp as planned. I helped him, I mean her, climb into Jada, and then we headed to Cafe Saint Felix, which was one of the prevailing restaurants in the borough.

The smell of West Indian cooking hit us as soon as we walked inside. The place was lit dimly and a nice crowd was already on hand. The reggae booming throughout the building had everyone there in a festive mood. Due to my visual dilemma with Sheila, my plan was to eat dinner and then take her back home straightaway. As soon as we took a seat at a nearby table, a young waiter approached, carrying some menus.

"Good evening, folks. My name is Mitchell. Welcome to Cafe Saint Felix." Mitchell smiled charmingly at us as he handed each of us a menu.

"I'll be right back to take your orders," he informed us before he scurried off.

"He seems pretty friendly, don't you think?" I asked Sheila.

(I was briefly entertaining the idea of fixing Sheila up with him, so that I could leave earlier than planned.)

"I guess he's okay," she answered nonchalantly.

So much for that idea! I thought to myself as I began scanning the menu. Our waiter quickly returned.

"Are you two ready to order?" Mitchell asked.

I looked over at Sheila.

"I'll just have a salad and some water for starters," she uttered.

That was only her snack. The damn girl ate just like Lance after he'd smoked a few joints. Both cousins had voracious appetites. Sheila was incredible. She put away two house salads, a whole jerk chicken with an extra side of rice, a double order of dumplings, and a large plate of plantains. I'm not even going to go into what she ate for dessert! If I had not been there to see it for myself, I would have never believed it. I kept shaking my head in wonderment as I watched him, I mean her, put away her food.

"What's wrong?" Shelia asked me after she had come up for air and caught me staring at her in awe.

"Nothing," I said with embarrassment. I began toying around with my red snapper to play it off.

"So, how do you like New York, Sheila?"

"It's alright," she said nonchalantly.

Sheila didn't appear to be a heavy conversationalist. She went back to work on her meal.

"Do you have any hobbies, Shelia?"

Was there anything, besides consuming food, that you enjoyed?

"Not really, no," she said between bites.

"You, uh, follow any of the sports teams around here?"

"No."

"Then what is it that you like to do in your spare time?"

"Not too much. I do love dining out though."

Out of the corner of my eye, I caught our waiter passing a few yards away from us.

"Mitchell?"

"What else can I do for you?" he asked, also perplexed by Sheila's gluttony.

"Could you get me a Guinness when you get a chance? Better yet, make that two of them, please?"

As soon as I dropped Sheila off in front of her apartment building later that evening, I picked up my cell phone and began dialing. Lance picked up on the fourth ring.

"Hello?"

"Are we friends, Lance?"

"Yeah, mon."

"Good friends, Lance?"

"Yeah, mon."

"Then could you do me a favor?"

"Yeah?"

"Don't ever fix me up with any more members of your family!"

"Sorry, mon."

"Oh yeah, before I forget, you owe me another sixty bucks."

"I got you, mon."

I hung the phone up.

When I returned home, I sat on my bed with a cold Guinness in my hand ready to drink and sulk. I was just about to open the can when I heard a knock at my door. I picked up the remote next to me and turned the Miles Davis song I was listening to down a couple of notches. I heard the knocking again.

"Come in, Tucker."

Tucker opened the door and swaggered in.

"Yo, what you up to?"

"I'm trying to get drunk."

"How did your date with Lance's cousin go?"

"I don't wanna talk about it."

"That bad, huh?" he asked as he threw some type of ticket onto my lap.

"What's this?" I asked as I picked it up to examine it.

"It's a ticket."

"Fool, I know that! A ticket for what?"

"You know, they do say that reading is fundamental."

I rolled my eyes at him as I read the printing on the ticket. It was to an art show that some sister was having over in Park Slope.

"No, thank you. I've got better things to do," I said as I held the ticket back out to Tucker.

"Like what? Sitting around the house moping?"

I rolled my eyes at him again.

"The last thing that I need to do is to pay money so that I can stand around a bunch of uppity, pretentious Negroes, who shell out exuberant amounts of money for overpriced artwork simply so they can brag about it to others."

"Ain't nobody said anything about buying any art, fool. Read the bottom line of that ticket."

"Buffet dinner and open bar..."

"These tickets are complimentary, dude. One of the sisters involved with this event frequents my store. She hooked me up with them."

"Well, now," I said with a slight grin, "that's a different story."

I figured that I could stand to tolerate one of those art shows if there was free grub involved.

"Tucker, do you think they'll be serving any Guinness?"

"Take ya sad ass there and find out for yourself," he answered as he left my room.

CHAPTER NINE

True to habit, Tucker and I arrived at the art show an hour late. I was a bit surprised that a crush of people already was inside the brownstone when we walked in. I was even more surprised at the number of sisters of all shades, shapes and sizes who were in the house, which was doubling as an art gallery. The nice spread at the buffet table included a few dishes from Tucker's restaurant. I fixed myself a generous plate of food, selected a brew from the imported beers and commenced doing the 'art thang'.

The artwork was not cheap at all. The collection was impressive, so were the prices. Making my rounds to admire the remarkable talent, I listened in on snatches of conversations here and there. Folks held forth about fishing at Martha's Vineyard, buying property in the Pocono Mountains, vacationing in Europe, finishing up advanced degrees, and the amazing amount of income one could earn by owning your own personal online travel agency.

Two hours later I was stuffed, a little tipsy, and bored. It was time to go home. I looked around for Tucker and spied him standing in the far corner of the room, next to a beautiful sister dressed in jeans and a dark blazer, chatting away. I caught his eye and signaled him, pointing to my watch. His sorry behind only smiled and waved for me to come over. I made another mental note to strangle him later, as I crossed the room. The woman next to him smiled as I neared them.

"Good evening," I said to her.

"Hello," she replied with a blinding smile.

Tucker stepped over to me and grabbed me by my shoulder.

"This is my roommate, Javier. Javier, this is Yolanda Meetze, one of the co-sponsors of this event."

We shook hands. Reflexively, I checked for a wedding ring. There was none.

"Nice to meet you, Javier. Did you see anything here tonight that caught your eye?"

I was mesmerized by the beauty of this woman.

"I'm not sure," I answered, gazing at Yolanda absentmindedly.

Tucker elbowed me gently in the ribs.

"She's talking about the artwork, you moron."

There was an unmistakable edge in his voice, hinting for me to back off.

"No, not really," I responded.

Yolanda appeared to be genuinely disappointed.

"Maybe next time?" I added.

"Okay," she answered with a grin. "Next time."

With his finger, Tucker impatiently stirred the contents of the drink that he was holding.

"I've enjoyed myself here immensely, but I really do need to leave now," I said.

"Do you really have to go?" Yolanda asked.

"Yes, I'm afraid so."

I looked directly at Tucker as I spoke. He swiftly reached into his pants pocket and retrieved a twenty-dollar bill, which he handed to me.

"What's this for?"

"Cab fare. Leave my change on my dresser."

I was still steaming when the gypsy cab pulled up in front of my place. I handed the driver the money that Tucker had given me.

"Keep the change, Sir."

"Wow! Thanks brother!"

As soon as I got inside, I took a hot shower, crawled into bed, and then dozed off. My ringing phone jolted me awake the following morning. I slowly dragged myself across the bed to retrieve my handset.

"Hello?" I answered groggily.

"Is this Javier Collins?" a perky female voice asked.

"Yes, it is."

"Good morning. How are you?"

For the life of me, I couldn't place the person who was on the other end of the line. I sat up in my bed.

"Who is this?"

"This is Marcia Freeman," the voice answered pleasantly.

I was totally lost.

"Who?"

"Marcia Freeman. I was at the art show last night."

I scratched my head. I was certain that I hadn't met anyone by that name the night before, and I knew for sure that I hadn't given my phone number to anyone.

"Excuse me, but uh...how did you get this number?"

"I got it off the mailing list that we both filled out. I was going to ask you for it personally, but you left kind of early."

I did recall putting down my home phone number when I filled out the mailing list that was passed around.

"Uh…what can I do for you, Ma'am?"

"Please, don't call me Ma'am. I don't think that I'm that much older than you," she giggled.

"Okay, Miss Freeman, what can I do for you?"

"I was wondering, if it would be possible for the two of us to get together sometime in the near future?"

"And uh, why would I want to do this?" I asked, trying not to sound too snobbish.

"If anything, the question that should be asked is, why wouldn't you want to do this?"

(Girlfriend was on the phone talking shit! At seven in the morning!)

I still didn't have a clue who she was though, so I had to keep my guard up.

"Perhaps you could refresh my memory a little, Miss Freeman? Did we speak to each other last night?"

"No, we didn't. I arrived while you were talking to Yolanda. When I looked over there again, you were gone before I had a chance to introduce myself to you."

"So you decided to copy my number down and just call me up?"

"Once I found out your name and saw it on the list, yes. I believe in taking chances. You only live once."

"How do you know that I'm not married, or engaged, Ma'am?"

"If you are, then I apologize for wasting your time. However, my sources told me that you lived with a roommate, a guy. And please, don't call me 'Ma'am' again."

The sister definitely had my curiosity piqued, but I certainly wasn't going to get suckered into another blind date that easily. I figured that I'd ask Tucker to get me some details from Yolanda.

"Uh, Miss Freeman, it's kind of early right now. Can I reach you back at this phone number? I would like a little time to contemplate your proposition."

"I take it that you're not married then, Mr. Collins?"

"No Ma'am. I mean, no. I'm not."

"Okay. Go ahead and ask my girl Yolanda about me. Just don't take too long with responding."

The woman had read me like a book. Whoever Marcia Freeman was, she was unquestionably self-assured to say the least. I said goodbye to her, and went back to sleep.

I woke up later that morning and went directly to Tucker's room. I rapped lightly on the door. I would have opened it and walked in, but there was no telling who, or what, Tucker might have had in there sleeping alongside him. After a minute or so had passed, he opened the door and stepped out into the hallway clad only in a pair of purple boxer shorts. The smell of alcohol reeking from him was nauseating. Tucker closed the door softly behind him. He wasn't alone.

"Yeah...what's up?" he asked, half-asleep.

"Do you know a sister named Marcia Freeman?"

"Why, did she call here for me?" he whispered.

"No, Romeo, she called me. She said she was a friend of Yolanda's, and that she saw me at the art show last night."

"And she called you?"

"Yeah, she got my number off the mailing list that was passed around."

"I can't say that I recall that name off the top of my head."

"Gee...I wonder why?" I remarked sarcastically.

Tucker scowled at me.

"Could you do me a favor? Check with your girl Yolanda for me and see what's up with her friend?"

"No problem," Tucker replied. "Are we done here?"

"Bye, Romeo."

Tucker turned around and went back into his bedroom without another word. I went into the kitchen and fixed myself a large bowl of cereal. I checked the clock on the microwave as I ate. If I hurried up, I still could catch The Truth at the gym before she left.

As I opened the door to walk into the gym, I spied The Truth walking toward me up the corridor with her gym bag slung across her shoulder.

"Damn, you're too late!" I thought out loud. Girlfriend heard me.

"What was that?" she asked cheerfully as she stopped in front of me.

"I said, damn...you look great." The Truth stood there and smiled.

"Thanks," she said. "You don't look too bad yourself." She then strolled out through the exit.

All during my workout, I couldn't help but think about my unusual phone call that morning. Who in the heck was this Marcia Freeman? And more importantly, what was the catch with her? Even in Brooklyn, a sister didn't just cold call a brother up and ask him out. The way I figured it, a woman had to be mighty desperate to do something like that. Yep, mighty damn desperate.

That following Tuesday night, as I was returning home from another painting gig with Lance, I found Tucker sitting in the living room when I walked through the front door. He was dressed in his 'ho-hopping' gear as he called it: a pair of black baggy jeans, a dark blue New York Knicks T-shirt, and a pair of half-laced boots. Tucker was buffing those boots with a rag when I walked in on him. He greeted me with a silly grin on his face when he finally looked up.

"What's up?" I greeted.

Tucker looked at me and shook his head in astonishment.

"My man, my man..."

"What?"

"Some guys have all the luck."

"What are you talking about Tucker?"

"I talked to my girl Yolanda today."

"And?" I asked, feigning disinterest as I continued into the kitchen and grabbed a cold bottle of beer from the refrigerator. I really didn't have time for one of Tucker's long, drawn-out narrations. I popped the top off my brew and started down the hall to my room so that I could get out of my clothes and shower.

"She reminded me who that Marcia person was!" Tucker yelled after me. My interest was suddenly piqued. I stopped and spun around.

"Is that right?" I asked with a slight grin on my face.

I walked back up the hall toward him. Tucker nodded his head in affirmation. I looked at him, awaiting some info on girlfriend, but he only stared at me with that stupid grin.

"Well?" I asked.

"You wanna know what Yolanda told me?"

"What do you think?"

"I wasn't too sure if you wanted to hear it from me or not. You know how I sometimes have a tendency to give long, dragged-out narrations and make a story too..."

"Tucker! Tell me what's up!"

"I only have one word for you...B-A-D."

Once again, I found myself waiting for more information from my roommate.

"Bad what?" I asked, trying to be polite. A slight edge was still in my voice, though.

"Marcia has got it going on, my man."

"Is that right?"

"Most definitely."

"So uh, what does she look like?" I asked, not at all sure that I was concealing the enthusiasm that churned inside of me.

"That's for me to know and for you to find out," Tucker stated flatly.

I couldn't believe that he had just told me some kiddie crap like that. It took all the restraint I had to keep myself from going upside Tucker's head with my beer bottle. Evidently, he had forgotten that I used to roll with Keisha!

"What kind of shit is that?" I screamed at him.

Once again, Tucker had plucked my nerves.

"I don't want to ruin it for you, J.C. Call Marcia up and ask her out. You'll be alright; trust me."

Tucker sauntered out the front door. I guzzled the rest of my beer and then got another one from the refrigerator.

"Shoot...we ain't going to be the same fool twice," I laughed out loud to myself as I opened the beer and took a swig from it.

I walked into the living room, turned on the television, and began surfing the channels. Nothing drew my attention. I clicked on the local news but quickly turned the broadcast off when it showed police dragging yet another handcuffed brother out of his house.

My thoughts turned instead to Marcia. *Heck, the girl really couldn't be all that flawed if Tucker said she had it going on.* But then again, I didn't trust Tucker any further than I could throw his butt when it came to women. They all looked good to him, especially when naked. *She did sound kind of sexy over the telephone, though. Of course, any girl sounded sexy on the phone when you're horny.*

I finished dialing the number and listened for her line to ring. My heart was beating fast. I felt like a high school kid all over again. After five rings, I got Marcia's voice mail.

"Hello, Marcia. This is J.C., I mean Javier. Could you give me a call when you get a chance? I look forward to talking with you. Bye."

My cell phone rang as soon as I ended the call.

"Hello?"

"Javier?" a familiar perky voice asked.

"Marcia?"

"Yes."

My heart began to pound faster.

"Uh, how are you doing?"

"Fine. And you?"

"I'm okay."

Suddenly, I didn't have anything else to say. There I was, a grown man intimidated by some sister I'd never even laid eyes on. There was nothing but gut-wrenching silence on the line between us.

"I take it that you've talked to Yolanda about me, then?" Marcia asked.

For some reason, she sounded to me like a schoolteacher who was helping a slow student solve a difficult math problem on the blackboard, in front of the rest of the class.

"Actually, a friend of mine talked to her."

"And?" Marcia coaxed.

This is getting ridiculous. I thought. I reflected back to my high school football days. "Never let someone talk you out of your game," Coach Fogle had instructed me. "And never, ever let your opponent intimidate you!"

The only difference between love and football is that love hurts more when it hits you, usually from behind.

I took another swig of beer and my anxiety subsided some.

"He told me that you were a pretty solid sister; so that's why I'm calling you back. When can I take you out?"

"If I'm not mistaken, I believe it was *me* who called to take you out."

My anxiety returned. This woman sounded like a real piece of work.

"I hope you're not a black man who has problems dealing with a sister who's self-confident?"

"Uh...no, not at all," I answered rather meekly.

"Great, now when can I pick *you* up?"

"Pick me up?" I asked.

"Yeah, I'm asking you out. Remember?"

"I'm good to go any day of the week, Miss Freeman."

Talking shit ain't nothing but something to do. I thought to myself as I drained the rest of my beer.

"Is that right?" Marcia countered.

"You didn't hear me stutter, did you?"

"Actually, I didn't. How about this Friday night?"

"Friday night it shall be."

I gave Marcia my address. She then told me that she didn't need directions, as she knew her way around the Clinton Hill area. We said goodbye to each other and I closed my phone. As soon as I did, I couldn't help but second-guess myself.

For the next three days, my pending date with Marcia troubled me. I couldn't believe that I was going to be on another blind date so soon. Of course, Tucker was no help at all. After I informed him that Marcia and I had set a date for that coming Friday, he merely looked at me oddly, shook his head, laughed, and then once again walked off. I begged him for some information on Marcia, but that sorry bastard steadfastly refused to give me any.

CHAPTER TEN

Lo and behold, Friday night arrived. I didn't have a clue as to where I was going, so I played it safe, dressing up slightly. I picked out a nice pair of black designer jeans, a black sleeveless silk shirt, a matching black blazer, and a pair of black Italian loafers. Miss Marcia Freeman wanted an un-intimidated black man. I decided to flip the script on her and give her an intimidating one instead.

After getting dressed, I went into the bathroom, gave myself the once-over in the mirror, and then rubbed a little sandalwood oil on myself for good measure. Marcia told me to expect her at eight o'clock sharp. I had fifteen minutes to kill so I went into the living room to watch some television. The distraction would calm me. No sooner than I sat down in front of the tube did Tucker ease himself through the door carrying a bag of groceries. He quickly gave me the once-over.

"Who died?"

If looks could kill, Tucker would have dropped dead right then and there.

"Forget you," I snarled.

"You going out dressed like that?"

At that moment, a car horn blared outside. I rolled my eyes at Tucker as I walked by him and looked out of the window. Outside, on the street below, was a candy-apple-red Lexus Coupe. Marcia did tell me that she would be driving a red car, but she neglected to tell me the make of it.

Without a word to Tucker, I proceeded outside, skipped down the steps, and stood on the curb as I tried to peer into the Lexus. (Now keep in mind that in Brooklyn one would not exactly be advised to roll up on an unfamiliar car that happened to be out in front of one's house.) The tinted windows blocked my view. After standing there for a few seconds, the driver side window slowly eased down and a cute little face appeared.

"Are you coming or what, Javier?"

So...a pretty little thing with a Lexus, huh? I thought to myself as I crossed the street with a grin ear to ear. I went to the passenger side of Marcia's ride and she clicked the door open for me. I gently lowered myself into her car. Of course I had disposed of my smile by then. I looked her dead in the eye as I closed her door.

"So...we finally meet face to face."

Marcia looked at me for a brief second or two.

"Are you okay?" she asked innocently. Her question baffled me.

"I'm fine. Why?"

"I thought that you might be in mourning or something."

Tucker would have gotten a serious chuckle out of her statement. I immediately fell in love with Marcia's Lexus. The leather seats were butter-soft and the ride was smooth as silk; I felt as if I were riding on air. I couldn't see where it was placed, but a strawberry air-freshener was definitely somewhere in Marcia's car. A Jill Scott CD played softly in the background as we made small talk.

"Nice car."

"Thanks."

"Good on gas?"

"It's okay, I guess."

"How about the insurance?"

"Actually, it's kind of high."

"Yeah, mine too."

Marcia looked at me as if she were trying to make up her mind about something. I wondered what was her dilemma.

"What part of the South are you from, Javier?"

I laughed at Marcia's question.

"What makes you think I'm from the South, Miss Freeman?"

"Because you sound like it. I thought I detected an accent when I talked to you over the phone earlier, but now I'm certain."

"South Carolina."

"South Cakalacky, huh?" Marcia teased. "What part?"

"Columbia."

"My grandmother's from Elloree."

"Is that right? One of my partners in college was from there."

Marcia and I hit it off instantly and continued a lively conversation as we wove our way out of my neighborhood and headed toward Flatbush Avenue. As we were crossing the Manhattan Bridge, Marcia slammed on the gas to go around a slow-moving truck. The sudden acceleration threw me back into my seat as the car flew over into the left lane around the vehicle.

After we made the pass, I was alarmed to find that we were rapidly approaching the rear of a city bus. Marcia quickly darted out and around the bus as well without even batting an eye. I was speechless.

"So, where were we?" she asked casually.

"I...I forgot."

My heart was still in my throat. I now could see why girlfriend's insurance was a little high; Marcia was a speed demon! All during our trip through Chinatown, she zipped in and out of traffic. It was hard for me to hold a steady conversation with Marcia because I kept bracing myself for sudden impact. She looked at me and laughed as she continued whizzing across Manhattan. She obviously got a kick out of scaring me.

The ride into New Jersey was no better! Heading into the Holland Tunnel, Marcia once again opened up her Lexus. We roared through the tube weaving in and out between cars on our way to Jersey City, though it's illegal to change lanes in the tunnel. She had to know that she was breaking the law.

Now under normal circumstances, I would have asked Marcia, or whoever it was driving crazy like that to please slow down, or even better, to let me the heck out of the car. Yet, for some strange reason I was determined to show Miss Freeman that if hauling ass in and out of traffic didn't faze her, then it didn't faze me either.

Finally, we made it safe and sound to Jersey City's famous Roof Top restaurant, where diners were always guaranteed a magnificent view of the Manhattan skyline. We sat on the restaurant's terrace sipping drinks while our food was being prepared. I had my usual stout while Marcia sipped on wine. A slight breeze blew in from the Hudson River below us.

I mentally gave my girl an 'A' in the courtship category, because she certainly knew how to choose a romantic setting. I also mentally kept a tab on how many drinks sistergirl was having. There was no way that she was going to drive me back home feeling tipsy. It was hectic enough riding with her sober.

Marcia could have easily passed for a model. She had flawless skin. She stood about five-five, weighed about a buck and a quarter, and wore her hair cut in a low buzz. Needless to say, I was instantly attracted to her. (There's just something about a woman with little hair on her skull that gives me goose bumps.)

Miss Freeman looked snazzy in her navy blue, pinstriped, linen suit. She wore some expensive looking pumps that matched her outfit perfectly. Marcia exuded self-assurance as she sipped her wine with her back to Manhattan's majestically lighted skyline. She was indeed a sight to behold.

With the exception of her hazardous driving, Marcia appeared to be perfect. As a matter of fact, she seemed *too* damn perfect. My suspicions began to go to work. *There has to be a catch to this woman. This has to be a set up.* I began to chuckle to myself lightly as I vowed not to get caught up in somebody's twisted charade. Marcia caught me grinning.

"May I ask what is it that's so funny?"

"Nothing. It's nothing important."

"So why can't you share it with me?"

I sat my glass down and looked her straight in the eye.

"Did Tucker put you up to this?"

Marcia looked totally baffled.

"Tucker? Who is that?"

"You mean you don't know my roommate, Tucker? He's the one who knows your girl, Yolanda."

I detected a trace of recognition in Marcia's eyes.

"Is he the brother who owns that rib place? The uh, Pork House?"

"The House of Pork."

"Yeah, that's it. As a matter of fact, Yolanda did introduce me to him at the art show last weekend. Why would he put me up to do something?"

Either the sister was a damn good blactress, or she actually didn't have the slightest clue as to what I was talking about. I decided to give her the benefit of the doubt.

"Uh, please disregard that question, would you? Sometimes my imagination gets the better of me." Marcia looked at me slyly.

"You have a vivid imagination, huh?" she asked seductively.

"Very."

A sinister smile appeared across her luscious lips.

"Let me ask you a question, then?"

"Go ahead...shoot," I answered in my best Mack Daddy voice.

"If I was to take off my underwear right now and hand them to you, what would you do?"

I almost choked on my Guinness. Marcia's question had taken me totally by surprise.

"Eat," I slowly answered.

"Really?" she asked with a devilish smile.

I pointed to our waiter, who stood behind Marcia with our food on his tray.

"Food's here," I announced smugly.

"Oh," she uttered in complete embarrassment.

"Sorry to disappoint you, Miss Freeman."

"Very funny, Mr. Collins."

The waiter served us our meals and we immediately dug in. The food was splendid. Marcia dined on lobster tail while I kept it real with a large sirloin and a side of smashed potatoes.

With that question, Marcia had inadvertently told me that she was a freak. I was elated about that, though it wasn't exactly the type of information that I looked for on a first date. I decided to be direct with my questioning. That way, I could know immediately whether or not there would be any possibility of us making some kind of connection. (Notice that I didn't include the word *love* in that last sentence?)

"So, Marcia, tell me three things about you that I don't know?"

She cleared her mouth of food as she contemplated an answer.

"Let's see," Marcia said with a small sigh. "I'm recently divorced, I'm the mother of a five-year-old son, and I'm a Republican."

Oh well, I thought to myself, *it was fun while it lasted.* Divorced with a crumb-snatcher and a black Republican? Even though she was up front about her child, I knew that Marcia wasn't the move for me. It was such a shame, too. A nice smile, a nice body, a nice car, and obviously a nice job as well. It was all for naught. Before I knew it, Marcia was holding out a photo of her son for me to take a gander.

"His name is Brandon. Isn't he adorable?"

Out of courtesy, I took the picture from her and glanced at it. The boy was the spitting image of his mother. Even without his two front teeth.

"Yeah, he is quite handsome."

I quickly handed Marcia back her son's photo. It was time for us to finish our meal so that I could get back home. Hopefully there was a ball game on television.

I slowed Jada down as I peered out of my window. It was drizzling outside and I wasn't doing too good a job making out the addresses on the buildings that I'd already passed. Marcia had told me that she lived on Henry Street, in Brooklyn Heights. I was going to help her hang some of the artwork she'd bought at her friend Yolanda's show.

It seemed like only yesterday I was telling myself that there was no way in hell that I would ever deal with her. But that was before Marcia mentioned to me that she had made the mistake of getting married one time, and that she wouldn't be doing that again. Marcia also stated that she had no plans of becoming involved in a serious relationship anytime soon.

Of course after hearing something like that, the green light automatically clicked on in my mind's eye. The way I figured it, I had nothing to lose. If girlfriend wanted to kick it with me for awhile and not get serious then I was definitely game for that.

We had called each other a few times after our date in Jersey, and one night Marcia asked me if I wouldn't mind coming over. "Sure," I told her. "As long as some cold Guinness was waiting for me when I arrived."

I re-checked the address I'd scribbled down on a piece of paper against the numbers on the building in front of me. Right address. I stared from Jada in awe. From the looks of Marcia's building, she really did have it going on. The front yard was magnificently landscaped, replete with two miniature statues of harp-playing cherubs.

An elderly white doorman greeted me as I walked inside. Now I was *really* impressed.

"Good evening, Sir. May I help you?" he politely asked me.

"Yes Sir. I'm here to see Marcia Freeman."

"Go ahead up. She's been expecting you."

"Thank you."

I gave the man a fifty cents tip and then strolled off as proud as a peacock for the elevators. The walls glistened, spotless. I could just about see my reflection in the freshly waxed floors. *So this is how the other half lives, huh?*

A middle-aged white woman, who stepped off the elevator with her poodle in tow, interrupted my thoughts. One look at me and she clutched her handbag tightly to her side. To make matters worse, her mutt began yapping, straining desperately to take a bite out of me. I secretly prayed she'd let the dog charge me so I could kick it across the lobby one time. Since I didn't have any bail money on me at the time anyway, I decided to let the matter go and proceeded into the elevator.

Marcia opened her front door with a wide smile.

"What kept you so long?"

"You guys really don't have the ideal parking situation around here," I explained.

Marcia stepped back from her door and I entered the foyer. To say that she lived in a real nice apartment would have been an understatement. Marcia had plush, burgundy carpet running throughout the dwelling, which complemented her off-pink walls. Those same walls were covered with numerous pieces of art and pictures of her family as well. I spied one photo of Marcia holding her infant son in her arms with a gentleman, probably her ex, standing behind her. The fellow looked a bit older than Marcia and was rather muscular.

Marcia had an off-pink leather couch set. A huge fifty-inch, flat screen television sat in the far corner of the room. It was surrounded by an array of high quality audio speakers. Plants were hanging everywhere throughout the room as well. Looking out onto her patio, I made out the illuminated top of the Brooklyn Bridge, spanning the East River.

"This is pretty nice," I said, nonchalantly. I was determined not to let Marcia know how impressed I really was with her obvious display of wealth. Being a computer programmer apparently paid nicely in the NYC.

"I'm glad you like it. Sit down while I get you something to drink."

I sat down on her soft couch as she went into her kitchen.

"I have your Guinness for you, but would you like a mixed drink instead?" Marcia asked from the sink, where she stood rinsing some glasses.

"Thanks, but beer would be fine," I called back into the kitchen. I decided she didn't need to know about my liquor handicap.

"I'll be right out. The remote to the entertainment center is on the table in front of you. Feel free to turn on some music."

I picked up the remote and turned on the stereo. I then tuned it to the local jazz station. Some group was playing the instrumental version of Bryan Adam's '*Everything I Do*', and was doing a pretty good job of it. I slouched down further into Marcia's couch as I listened to the song.

My serenity was shortly interrupted by a whooshing sound that was coming from down the hall. As I turned around to look for the origin of the noise, I spied a young boy running up the hall toward me, carrying a toy rocket ship in his hand. He was dressed in a red Power Ranger's uniform. I was about to meet the adorable Brandon Freeman.

When he saw me relaxing in his living room, the boy stopped abruptly. He then looked over to his mother as she was entering the room with my stout.

"Who is this, Mommy?" the young boy asked her.

I smiled awkwardly at the child while I waited for his mother to introduce me.

"This is a friend of mine, Brandon. Say hello to Mr. Collins."

Brandon looked at me for a second before contorting his face into a frown.

"No."

It was apparent to me right then and there that the adorable Brandon and I would not be getting along together anytime in the near future. Marcia was livid.

"Brandon! What did I tell you about being rude to people? Go back to your room!"

The little kid glared at me one more time and then rolled his eyes at me in disgust before flying his ship and himself back to the galaxy in his bedroom.

Marcia could not conceal her embarrassment as she handed me my stout. We both smiled at each other awkwardly.

"I'm sorry about that, Javier. Brandon's still upset about me and his father splitting up."

"You don't have to apologize. That's quite understandable."

(I also wanted to add that a little ass-whipping might help Brandon respect his elders, but I didn't.)

After downing my brew, I proceeded to help Marcia hang her artwork. She had bought three pieces from the show, dropping over twenty-five hundred dollars in the process. They were limited-edition pieces that were quite impressive, a shrewd investment. Once we were finished with the job, Marcia and I sat down in the living room and began to chat quietly.

Little Brandon was apparently jealous of his mother's new focus of attention, for he called out for her every ten minutes. Of course, Marcia would instinctively go and cater to her son's needs. A glass of cold water, something to snack on, help brushing his teeth in the bathroom, Brandon kept his mother busy.

Marcia finally succumbed and gave her son permission to come out of his room. Brandon promptly joined us in the living room. There, he insisted on sitting in his mother's lap. After snuggling up in his mother's arms, he then turned his little apple-shaped head in my direction and proceeded to glare at me. His mother was unaware of her son's antics because he had prudently positioned himself so that only I could see his face.

Naturally, it was hard for me to carry on my conversation with Marcia with her son eyeing me down. After a few more minutes of this treatment, I conceded defeat to little adorable Brandon and decided to take my butt home. His glare turned into a smirk after I had announced my intentions to leave.

Marcia got up and walked me to the door. She thanked me for coming and helping her with the artwork. Marcia then surprised me by giving me a quick peck on the lips before she opened the door for me. I looked at Brandon and saw that he was even more surprised than I was. His cute little mouth was opened wide in astonishment. Now it was my turn to smirk.

"See you again soon, Brandon," I sneered at him as I walked out the front door.

Tucker was at my bedroom door early the next morning knocking. I stirred awake.

"Come in."

He walked in grinning from ear to ear. He was still dressed in the same outfit that I had seen him putting on last night before I left to go over to Marcia's.

"Well?" he asked.

"Well, what?"

"Did you hit it?"

At six-thirty in the morning, I really wasn't in the mood to discuss my sexual exploits, or lack thereof. I decided to change the subject.

"You just getting in?"

"Don't try to change the damn subject, Javier. And yeah, I am just getting in. I ran across a little something at this new club I went to. Now, what did *you* do last night?"

I ignored Tucker as I walked past him, headed for the bathroom. He trailed right behind me.

"So, what did you do, Javier?"

Once again, my roommate was getting on my nerves. I spun around in the hallway and faced him.

"I helped her hang up some pictures. Alright?"

Tucker looked at me impatiently as he waited for me to tell him more.

"Is that it?"

"Yeah, that's it."

Tucker then stared at me as if I had just grown a third eye.

"You mean to tell me that a fine sister like Marcia, who happens to be some real serious Ph.D. booty by the way, invites you over to her house and you didn't even push up on her?" Tucker reached out his hand and began to feel my forehead.

"What's ailing you, boy?"

I snatched his hand away from me and then proceeded into the bathroom, closing the door firmly behind me.

"You know, sometimes I really don't get you," Tucker called from the other side of the door. "If I didn't know you any better, I'd swear that you were scared of getting booty."

Now I had to defend myself. I could not let Tucker insult my manhood and get away with it. I finished my business in the bathroom, washed my hands, and then stepped back out into the hallway.

"I could have gotten the draws, but her son was in the way," I lied.

"Is that all?" Tucker asked.

"What do you mean is that all?" I countered. "I don't know about the hootchie mamas that you deal with, but this woman has respect for herself and her child. Besides, the kid wouldn't let us be alone together."

"Wouldn't let y'all be alone together?"

"Yeah, he doesn't like me."

"Do you plan on marrying this Marcia person?"

"No."

"Then what the hell does it matter whether her kid likes you or not? You ain't trying to sleep with him! At least I hope not."

I chose to ignore Tucker's chiding. I also had to admit to myself that every now and then, my roommate did pose a good logical question.

"I see your point," I told him. "What do you think I should do?"

"There's only one way to deal with her kid."

"What's that?"

"You gotta bribe him."

"Bribe him?"

"Either that, or snatch his little ass up when his moms ain't looking and show him who's the boss."

"I'll opt for that first suggestion, if you don't mind."

"Good choice."

"What should I bribe him with?"

Tucker looked at me funny.

"Don't you know anything? Geez! Give the kid some candy, or some toys or something. If all else fails, just give him money."

"You sound like an expert, Tucker."

Tucker smiled proudly as he puffed out his chest.

"Trust me brother, I gets mine by any means necessary," he stated as he walked off toward his room.

CHAPTER ELEVEN

Marcia and I continued to call each other that following week. During one of our conversations, I brought up the idea that maybe she, Brandon, and I should all go out one weekend. Marcia instantly agreed to the suggestion. We arranged to meet at Junior's the following Saturday for lunch and then maybe take in a movie afterwards.

I showed up at the restaurant at two o'clock on the dot. Marcia and her boy had not yet arrived. I fetched myself a cold beer from the bar, where a group of fellas already were watching the New York Yankees (another team that I didn't care much for) play the Baltimore Orioles on a gigantic television. I looked up at the game just as one of the Orioles smacked a home run, scoring three runs in the process.

"Alright!" I yelled out loud without thinking.

Suddenly, all the chattering around me ceased. All eyes were on me. I hurriedly paid for my beer and disappeared.

On my way back toward the front of the eatery, I spied Marcia and an irritated-looking Brandon walking through the door. They made their way over to where I stood.

"It's about time," I said with a smile as I looked at my watch.

"Sorry, I'm late," Marcia said.

We hugged briefly.

"Hi there, little fella," I said to Brandon as I rubbed the boy's head playfully.

The kid only looked up at me and rolled his beady eyes. Just as I was about to ask Brandon's mother what his hang-up was, a hostess walked over and offered to show us to our seats.

The hostess sat us not too far from the bar area. Once we were seated, I could sense some kind of tension between Marcia and her son.

"So, how is everybody?" I asked, making small talk.

"I'm okay, but I don't know about you know who here," Marcia answered, pointing to her son, who slouched in his chair with his bottom lip poked out. I leaned over toward the boy.

"What's the matter, Brandon?" I asked as nicely as I could.

Brandon rolled his eyes at me again.

"He's mad, that's all," Marcia informed me.

"Why?"

"He doesn't want to eat here."

I leaned in closer to Brandon.

"You'll love the food here Brandon. The shakes are delicious."

"I want McDonald's!" the boy declared.

"You're not getting McDonald's; you're eating here," Marcia told him. Brandon stuck his bottom lip out further. At this moment, our waiter approached our table.

"Hello, everybody," the waiter greeted us as he passed out our menus.

"Is there anything I can get you folks right now?"

"I want McDonald's!" Brandon demanded again.

Our waiter was taken aback for a brief second. Then he too leaned over towards Brandon.

"You like McDonald's?" he asked.

Brandon shook his blockhead vigorously in agreement.

"Our burgers taste way better than theirs do, son. Would you like to try one?"

"I want McDonald's!"

A few of the other patrons began to look our way. I was so damn embarrassed that I crouched down as low as I could in my seat. I didn't want people to think that I was Brandon's father and that I didn't know how to control my son. I also prayed to God that there was no one in there that I knew. I looked over at Marcia and saw that she was just as embarrassed as I was. She took a big sigh before she spoke.

"Brandon, for the last time, you are not eating at McDonald's. You eat there too darn much as it is already. Now either you eat here or you don't eat at all!"

It made my heart glad to see Marcia checking her son's behavior. My happiness was short-lived. Her ultimatum provoked Brandon, who began to wail uncontrollably. More people began to look over in our direction. I wanted so bad to snatch that little joker up and put him across my knee that I had to sit on my hands to contain myself.

Our waiter looked over at me, expecting me to do something. I looked over at Marcia, waiting expectantly for her to act.

"Cut it out now, Brandon!" Marcia commanded.

The boy only cried louder. I looked around and saw that a few of the fellas over at the bar were shooting icy glares in our direction.

Apparently, they couldn't hear the game over Brandon's wailing. I had to act fast.

"Look, why don't we go to McDonald's, Marcia?"

"No. We came here to eat and that's what we're going to do."

Brandon's wailing climbed two octaves higher.

"Can't we eat at McDonald's?" I pleaded.

"No. He'll stop crying when he gets tired."

The boy showed no signs of letting up to me. The kid had a damned good set of lungs on him. I again looked back over at the bar area. Everybody over there was now glaring at our table.

"Marcia, I beg of you...let's go to McDonald's. Please?"

Marcia, evidently frustrated with the whole scenario herself, agreed.

"Oh, alright. Come on!"

She stood up, grabbed her son's hand, and then helped him out of his chair. As we were walking away from the table, a huge cheer went up behind us. I turned around to see the clowns at the bar giving each other high-fives in celebration of our departure. It was a lucky thing for them that Marcia and her son were present at the time. Otherwise things may have gotten real ugly!

Little Brandon's performance at Junior's canceled his trip to the movies. After getting him his damned McDonald's, I followed Marcia back to her place. Once there, Brandon went straight to the kitchen and began devouring his meal. Marcia and I took a seat in the living room. I could see by the stress lines on her face that she was still pretty upset with her son's earlier antics, as was yours truly.

"You need me to help you lighten up some?" I slid closer to her on the couch, cracked my knuckles, and then began executing one of my famous country-style back rubs on Marcia.

"Ooh," she moaned with delight. "Where did you learn how to do this?"

"If I told you, I'd have to kill you, Ma'am."

"Is that right?" Marcia asked with a giggle.

She leaned back further in my arms. I could feel the tension being released from her body. I could also feel some other things on her body as well. Marcia was indeed fine.

"Yes, that's right," I reassured her.

"Then do what you must," she sighed with contentment.

Marcia turned around in my arms and then wrapped hers around my shoulders. I leaned down and zeroed in on her luscious lips.

"I'm finished, Mommy!"

Brandon jumped up in the chair next to his mother as Marcia and I quickly broke apart.

"Uh, Brandon, don't you want to watch that new video your daddy just bought you," Marcia said, more as a statement than a question.

"No," Brandon answered flatly. He then turned and stared directly at me.

"What about playing that new game daddy gave you, then?"

"That's okay, Mommy."

At that moment, I assessed the entire situation with Marcia as being hopeless. It would be better for me to quit while I was still ahead. I faked a yawn and a stretch as I looked at my watch.

"Gee, will you look at the time?" I got up from the couch.

"Do you really have to go?" Marcia asked, dejectedly. I nodded my head in the affirmative.

"Time to take it on in. I have a long day ahead of me tomorrow."

As Marcia followed me over to the door, she spoke in a hushed tone.

"I'm sorry about today, Javier. I really am."

"Forget about it," I said, half-seriously. I wasn't in the mood for hearing another song and dance at the moment. While waiting for her to open the front door, Marcia must have read in my eyes that I had no intentions of ever seeing her or her spoiled son again.

"No, I am not going to forget about it. I know how patient you've been with my son." With that, Marcia stroked her hand across my crotch playfully. "I'm going to make this up to you big time. Trust me."

"Uh, when will this be taking place?" I pried.

"Next weekend?"

"And...what about Junior over there?" I directed my eyes towards Brandon.

"He'll be at his father's next weekend."

I banged my head in the doorway when I jumped for joy.

"You've got yourself a date then, Marcia."

"Good. I'll be anxiously waiting for you to come over. I hope you don't let me down," Marcia said slyly as she closed her front door behind her.

I walked out of Marcia's building as happy as a pig in a pile of fermenting acorns. It seemed as if my attempt to win Brandon's favor had paid off after all. It wasn't exactly what I had planned but hey, you gotta take 'em any way you can get 'em.

The next Saturday night was D-Day. I had on my funky pair of black Bermuda shorts and a beige paisley silk shirt. A pair of black leather sandals completed my wardrobe. It was the middle of August, and the nights, as usual, were extremely humid.

Marcia and I had elected not to do anything too extravagant for our date, just dinner and a movie. It was up to me to pick the restaurant for the occasion and I went with a new seafood joint, The Shrimp Shanty, which had just opened on the corner of Fourth Avenue and Flatbush. Of course, I had already scoped the place out and found it to my liking. They had an impressive selection of beers on tap.

I double-parked in front of Marcia's place ten minutes ahead of schedule. I took a quick scan up and down the street for police and traffic cops before jumping out of Jada and darting into the building. I certainly wasn't in the mood to donate any more money to the New York City Department of Finance. The doorman let me in and buzzed Marcia for me. I thought I noticed a slight look of apprehension on his face as he pressed the button to her apartment.

"Uh, you have a gentleman here to see you," he informed Marcia when she answered.

"I'll be right down," I heard Marcia's voice say over the intercom.

"She'll be right down," the doorman repeated to me.

I thanked the man and then stepped back over to the front door, where I could keep a watchful eye on Jada. New York City police and traffic cops were merciless when it came to handing out tickets. They always materialized when you least expected them. I turned around when I heard the elevator bell ding. The door opened and out stepped Marcia followed by Brandon.

Bringing up the rear was the same muscular gentleman that I had seen in the portrait that hung in Marcia's living room. The expression on everyone's face told me instantly that everything wasn't quite that kosher.

Damn! I thought to myself as the cheerless trio approached me. The last thing that I felt like doing at that moment was becoming involved in some drama. Besides, I definitely wasn't wearing the right kind of shoes to scrap in; not to say that I would have to fight, but you never knew in Brooklyn. Marcia made a half-hearted attempt to smile at me as she drew near.

"Hi?" she asked.

"What's up?" I replied while looking directly at her ex-husband.

"Nothing, I'm just seeing Brandon and his father to the door."

I looked over to little Brandon, who was in the process of gazing upon me with a malicious grin on his face.

"That's nice," I lied.

Marcia could tell by my response that I wasn't being honest. She turned and smiled awkwardly at her son's father.

"Craig, this is my friend, Javier."

Something about the weak way that Marcia said 'friend' didn't sit with me too well, but I chose not to address that issue at the moment. Craig shot me a look of contempt when I held out my hand to him. He declined to shake it. (I knew then why little Brandon was so screwed up.)

"Just a *friend*, huh?" Craig asked suspiciously.

I drew back my outstretched palm and formed a fist with it instead.

"I see that you're growing them younger now, Marcia."

"Beats sticking with something that's old and used up," I said.

There was no way that I was going to sit quiet and take shit off of Mr. Craig, muscles or not. Marcia looked as if she wanted to curl up in a corner somewhere and die. Craig looked at me with a sneer on his face.

"You know, where I come from, children were taught to respect their elders," Craig said.

"Well, where I come from, you gotta earn your respect, Pops."

I could see the rage instantly appear on Craig's face. I shifted my stance to the right and leaned back in my sandals. Craig appeared to be a lot stronger than I was, but I was betting on the fact that I could move a lot quicker than he could. If he charged me, I was going to roundhouse-kick the shit out of him before he knew what hit him. I'd practiced that move ever since I was a small kid watching Bruce Lee movies on videocassettes back in the day.

"You know what son? Maybe you're right about that."

I had squatted down slightly when Marcia stepped in between us. Her back was to me as she faced Craig.

"Have you lost your mind, Craig?" she hissed. "I can't believe that you're behaving like this in front of our son!"

Either Marcia had talked some sense into my man's head, or he saw that I wasn't going to back down from him. Whatever the case, Craig took his son by the hand and exited the building with him. I glanced at the doorman, whose earlier look of apprehension was now replaced by one of dismay. He had thought for sure that we were going to give him some free entertainment. I was so mad that I felt like going over to him and providing him with some at his own expense.

Marcia still had her head down in her hands when I looked at her. Fine and cute as she was though, she wasn't worth all the trouble that came along with her. That was exactly what I was planning on telling girlfriend, too. When Marcia looked up at me, I saw that she was on the verge of tears. It didn't matter to me though, because I was history.

"Uh, Marcia..." I began before she cut me off.

"I'm sorry about what happened just now, Javier."

"Forget it. Marcia, I..." She cut me off again.

"Could we just go to dinner? I really don't feel like sitting through a movie right now."

I opened my mouth to tell her that *we* weren't going anywhere, but those weren't the words that came out.

"Okay."

I guess I must have felt guilty about abandoning the sister when she was feeling down. I sighed to myself as I held the front door open for her. She slowly walked out, with me following behind. When I looked across the street, I almost snapped. A traffic cop was just pulling away from my ride, leaving a bright orange-colored ticket pinned underneath my windshield wiper.

"Dammit!" I mumbled.

All indicators were pointing to the fact that Marcia needed to be left alone. Plain and simple.

"What's wrong?" Marcia asked before seeing the ticket herself. I angrily snatched the piece of paper off Jada.

"I'll pay for it," Marcia offered. "You got it waiting for me."

Even though Marcia was right, and I didn't have money to throw away, I had to play the role and decline her offer.

"That's okay," I said with a sigh.

This crap won't happen again. I thought to myself as I cranked up Jada and pulled off.

On the ride over to the Shrimp Shanty, Marcia constantly kept apologizing for her ex-husband's behavior. She quickly got on my nerves with explaining to me all of Craig's shortcomings.

"He's been that way ever since I met him. At first I used to enjoy his jealousy, but then it only got worse."

"I see," I said, unenthused.

"That was the main reason Craig and I got divorced. He was too damn possessive."

"Is that right?"

"Tonight he wanted to know where I was going, and who I was going with. It was ridiculous."

"Isn't that something?"

I was so uninvolved in Marcia's lame conversation that I began reminiscing about Keisha.

Both of our moods picked up a little once we were inside the over-crowded restaurant. We had to take seats at the bar while waiting for a table to become available for us. Of course, we took advantage of the situation. Marcia's disposition perked up after she gulped down two large White Russians. My spirits heightened when Marcia insisted on picking up the tab for the night, since I wouldn't let her pay for my parking ticket. I didn't object one tiny bit. Our bartender returned to us just as I was draining the remnants of my second pint of Guinness.

"Another round?" he asked Marcia as he took her empty glass away from her.

"Sure."

Marcia then turned to me.

"You wanna try one?"

It was plain to see that the alcohol was doing its job on her. I knew better than to put some liquor in myself, however.

"I'll take another Guinness, please."

"Ah, come on, Javier. Be a man."

"I already am."

"Is that right?" Marcia asked seductively.

"I can show you better than I can tell you, sister."

At that moment, our hostess came over to us.

"Are you two ready?"

Marcia and I merely looked at each other and smiled.

I had never eaten a meal so fast in my life. You know, it's amazing how the prospect of sexual gratification can erase one's memory. Thirty minutes earlier, I had been ready to cut Marcia Freeman loose and go about my business. With a couple of brews in me, and a little word play, I was ready to explore every inch of Marcia's sensuous body. Well, most of it anyway.

Marcia had ordered a serving of steamed clams and a side of fried oysters, while I had settled on a plate of fried shrimp and scallops. To make the story brief, the food was superb, the service was excellent, and we were ready to go within twenty minutes.

Marcia paid the bill while I went out and pulled Jada in front of the restaurant. Six minutes later, we were on our way back to her crib. I pulled up to Marcia's building and was surprised to find a parking spot available in front of it.

"Well...this is a nice surprise," I remarked as I parallel parked.

"You ain't seen nothing yet," Marcia replied lustfully.

"Is that right?"

"I can show you better than I can tell you, brother."

The doorman was not at his desk when we stepped to the entrance door. Marcia let herself in, and we held hands as we strolled over to the elevators. When we got to her apartment's front door, Marcia turned abruptly and faced me.

"I hope you'll still respect me in the morning?"

"Heck, that all depends on what you do tonight."

Marcia rolled her eyes at me playfully before turning back around and opening her door. We entered her apartment and immediately began kissing each other all over. When we finally came up for air, Marcia grabbed me by the hand.

"This way, baby."

"Whatever you say, boss."

"Remember that."

She grinned at me devilishly before leading me to her bedroom. I picked up the scent of burnt frankincense as we stepped into the darkness of her sleeping quarters. I was curious as to how the place looked, as I had not seen it on my previous visits. When the lights clicked on, I was surprised to find myself standing before a king size brass waterbed. The waterbed sat in the middle of Marcia's spacious room. It was surrounded by a pair of oaken nightstands, upon which sat a pair of brass lamps. The girl was certainly coordinated. A few pieces of artwork hung on the walls, and another wide screen television and stereo combination sat directly across from the foot of her bed.

Marcia remained silent as she stripped off her jeans and blouse. She looked absolutely ravishing standing in the soft, pastel pink light that emitted from the dimly lit lamps. Marcia saw that I had not yet begun undressing.

"What's the hold-up, Javier? You're not nervous now, are you?"

"Not hardly."

"Good."

I slipped out of my shirt and shorts, folded them up neatly, and then placed them on top of Marcia's solid oak bureau. I was in the process of pulling my T-shirt over my head when I was flying-tackled onto the bed.

"Hey!" I shouted. "I'm not ready yet!"

"All's fair in love and war!"

Marcia pinned me down on the bed and we rocked back and forth on the mattress for a moment. I could feel the beer that I had guzzled earlier rocking back and forth inside my stomach. Now keep in mind that I couldn't see a thing due to my T-shirt still being pulled over my head. It was kind of hard to breathe in that predicament, also.

"Let me up Marcia!"

"What do I get if I do?"

Marcia began bucking on top of me, which created even more wave motion in the bed. I felt myself becoming nauseous.

"I'm sick," I warned her.

"Not sicker than me..." Marcia said lovingly, as she began bucking even harder and then started nibbling away on my navel, which was not a very good idea. I had heard before that waterbeds could cause seasickness. That night I had proof.

I wound up throwing my T-shirt away. Trying to get the huge stain out of it would not have been worth the effort. After apologizing profusely to me for the second time in one night, Marcia provided me with a washcloth and led me to her shower. I took my time in her huge walk-in shower and scrubbed myself down thoroughly while Marcia changed the green satin sheets on her bed earlier than she had planned to.

Marcia had some peach body wash that smelled real good and created a rich lather. I went to town with it. I was in the middle of rinsing my face clean when I suddenly felt a cold draft blowing on my skin. Next, I felt someone's hand pinching my rear.

"Guess who?"

"Lisa?"

Marcia popped me hard with the towel that she was holding.

"Yo! That hurts!"

"That's what you get for being such a smart-ass."

"Wait 'til I get a hold of you," I warned.

"I've been trying to."

I finished rinsing and began drying my face with the towel Marcia had furnished me. When I opened my eyes and focused them, I found Marcia standing butt-naked in front of me. She held out a baby's bib in her right hand to me.

"What's that for?" I asked.

"You. I can't afford to mess up any more of my good sheets."

Marcia dropped the bib on the floor when I chased her out of the bathroom. I caught up with her in the bedroom and playfully threw her down on her bed. And then we went on a long fantastic voyage.

CHAPTER TWELVE

They say that life is full of surprises – some of them good, and some of them bad. The last time that my toes twinkled during sex was ten summers ago. It was my birthday and my fine next-door neighbor, LaShonda Cunningham, had decided to give me the ultimate birthday present. We both skipped school that day and met over at, oh yeah, I almost forgot, I promised LaShonda not to reveal that little escapade to anyone. Sorry, folks.

Anyway, Marcia had me twinkling that night. Needless to say, I was addicted, hooked, sprung, whipped, whatever you want to call it. My mind was completely blown. I now understood why Marcia's ex-husband was so jealous of her. If I were married to a woman that could ring my bell the way Marcia did, I would want to keep an eye on her all the damn time too!

When I rolled over and looked at the digital alarm clock on the nightstand next to me, I saw that it was already seven in the morning. I lovingly tapped Marcia, who was resting peacefully on her shoulder. She stirred slowly.

"What?" she asked groggily.

"Morning."

"Morning. Now can I go back to sleep?" Marcia pulled her blanket over her head.

"Wait a minute."

"Now what?" Marcia mumbled from underneath the cover.

"What do you want for breakfast?"

"You going out somewhere?"

"No, I plan on cooking for you myself."

Marcia's head popped back up from under the blanket. She looked at me with astonishment.

"Are you serious?"

"You think I'm not?"

Marcia had one of those fancy kitchens that most black folks only see in the movies. A large island design that was equipped with high end, stainless steel appliances. She also had every little gizmo for cooking or baking something that you could think of. I fished out some eggs, bread, cereal, milk, and grits. I couldn't find any meat though; so I returned to the bedroom. Marcia had fallen back to sleep.

"Marcia?"

"Yes, Javier?" she mumbled.

"I hunted all over for some bacon, but I didn't see any."

"Did you look on the lower, right-hand shelf in the fridge?"

"Yeah, but I only saw a pack of turkey strips."

"That's it."

"Uh...turkey ain't really bacon."

"Just pig, huh?"

"It's been like that for years."

"I'm sorry, but there's no pork in this house. We don't eat it."

"Oh well, nobody's perfect."

I went ahead and prepared the turkey strips the best that I could. I sampled a piece to see how it tasted. I'd chewed on paper bags as a little kid that had more flavor.

Nevertheless, Marcia was quite appreciative of the meal that I had prepared for her, and she expressed it to me with another bout of intense, toe-twinkling sex after breakfast.

I swear that was the first time in years that I was actually disheartened to leave a woman's bed and return to my own home. Most of the time, I'd have to explain to a sister that I had to go to the gym, wash my ride, help a friend move, feed my goldfish, anything to be able to leave without hearing static. But Marcia Freeman was different. I wanted to hang around her some more, but I didn't want to seem too pathetic. I reluctantly wished Marcia a good day and made my way outside, where Jada was waiting patiently.

I got home right before eleven o'clock. Tucker had already left for work, so I had the whole place to myself. After fixing myself a real bacon and egg sandwich, I stretched out on the living room couch and clicked on the television.

By sheer coincidence, I found a very interesting documentary on public television that discussed the secret life of pigs. I took a bite on my sandwich and sat back on the couch captivated. The narrator was right in the middle of pointing out the multiple varieties of pigs found throughout the world when the phone rang. I picked the nearby handset up.

"Hello?"

"How's it going?" a familiar voice asked. I sat up straight on the couch. It was Daddy.

"I'm okay, Sir. How about you?"

"Hell, I won't complain; wouldn't do no good anyhow."

We both laughed lightly. Daddy never called me unless something was wrong.

"Is everything okay, Sir?"

"Why something's gotta be wrong? Can't I call you if I want to?"

"Sure you can."

"Something told me to check up on my boy, that's all. How's all them fine women up there treating you?"

"Pretty fair, I reckon."

"You reckon? What kind of dumb ass answer is that?"

(Daddy always did have a penchant for being rude.)

"I'm doing alright in that category."

"Business that slow, huh?"

I ignored Daddy's last question. He figured that out after a few moments of silence between us.

"When you coming home, son?" he asked, switching subjects.

"Tucker and I will be down for homecoming."

"Is he still an obnoxious pain in the ass?"

"Come on, now. Tucker's not all that bad," I said with a laugh. (I couldn't believe that I was actually defending that jerk's character.)

"Well, tell him I said hello."

"Will do, Sir. Everything's alright down there?"

"Yeah. It's hot as hell, but that's about it. Oh yeah, Myra Cooper's still asking about you." I cringed upon hearing that name.

"Oh, really. How's she doing?"

"Fine."

"That's good. And her kids?"

"They're fine, too," Daddy conceded.

"That's nice. Tell her I asked about her."

"You know she's getting divorced?"

"No Sir, I didn't know that."

"Well, you do now."

It was time to change the subject again.

"Is there anything that I can do for you, Sir? Anything you need?"

"I would ask you to send me a woman down here, but it sounds like you ain't doing so hot yourself in that area," Daddy said with a chuckle.

"Doing better than you, I bet," I retorted without thinking.

"You getting smart with me, boy!"

"Sir! No Sir!"

"I'll take your ass out!"

"Sir! Yes Sir!"

"You better recognize!"

"Sorry Sir! Won't happen again, Sir!"

"Alright then," Daddy concluded. "I guess I'll talk to you later on. Goodbye."

"Bye, Sir," I said humbly.

Right then and there I sent up a silent prayer for Lawrence Xavier Collins. I gave thanks to the Lord above for making only one of him! I hung the phone up and reclined on the couch. Just as soon as I was once again focused on the documentary divulging the mysterious ways of the pig, a loud racket going on downstairs disturbed me. My neighbors were at war again.

If you ever saw the couple that lived below me when they were out in public together, you would never believe that such an angelic-looking twosome as Mr. and Mrs. Jenkins could raise so much holy hell.

The gray-haired couple always seemed so loving and adoring whenever they stepped outside of their apartment. Whether accompanying each other to church, or walking side-by-side during one of their occasional strolls, the couple was the emblem of happily married soul mates.

Flora Jenkins had worked for thirty years as a librarian. Her husband, Harry, had put in nearly forty years as a bus driver for the city. The couple never had any children. This most likely added to their frequent discontent with each other. (That and whenever Mr. Jenkins got caught cheating on his wife again.)

When Tucker and I first moved into the apartment above them, the duo made us feel as if we were their children. Mrs. Jenkins used to bake all sorts of goodies and bring them up to us. Cookies, pies, cakes, you name it; she could hook it up.

Mr. Jenkins, on the other hand, used to invite us constantly to baseball games. I must admit that he wasn't exactly too thrilled when he paid for Tucker and me to attend a Yankees' game and I cheered for the visiting team, which happened to win that day.

So, for the first three or four months, my roommate and I thought the Jenkins were the perfect neighbors. Our positive perspective of them changed late one Friday night. It was around midnight.

I had just returned home from a meaningless date with the acquaintance of a friend from back home. We had gone to the movies and had eaten a late dinner. After sitting around and making small talk at the restaurant for a while, we called it a night. No sooner had I returned home and stretched out in my bed did I hear a loud commotion coming from downstairs. I immediately jumped up from my bed and ran to get Tucker, who was occupied at the moment entertaining one of his clients in his bedroom.

I urgently banged on his door, ignoring the soft moans and groans being projected from his bedroom. After a few seconds, an irate Tucker threw the bedroom door open.

"What?!" he demanded.

"The Jenkinses are being robbed!"

"How do you know that?" he inquired.

As soon as he asked that question, we heard a loud crash come from below us.

"Hold up," Tucker said before closing his door in my face.

He re-emerged two minutes later wearing his pajamas and toting a Louisville Slugger baseball bat.

"Let's go," he commanded.

I grabbed a butcher knife from the kitchen drawer and we rushed out the front door. When we started down the steps we saw Mr. Jenkins racing out of his front door as if his life were in jeopardy. (It probably was at that moment.) Unfortunately, he was not able to outrace the pot that soared through the air after him as he tried to unlatch the entrance door in the hallway. It was a direct hit. Mr. Jenkins dropped to his knees momentarily, but continued his quest to open the door from a kneeling position.

Tucker motioned for us to retrace our steps up the stairway as the situation before us became quite evident. It was a domestic squabble, one of the most dangerous occurrences in the city. Even the police around here dreaded getting involved in such matters. Mr. Jenkins skillfully dodged a second flying pot. He then succeeded in opening the entrance door and scrambled outside to safety.

The following morning, I encountered Mr. Jenkins as I was heading out to the gym. He had apparently ventured outside to retrieve the morning paper and did not expect to see me on his way back in.

"Morning, Sir."

"Morning to you, too."

Though Daddy had taught me better, I couldn't help being nosy, so I inquired about the previous night's occurrence.

"Did you, uh, hear that commotion that took place last night, around twelve?"

"Commotion? What commotion?" Mr. Jenkins asked me with a poker face. The man was in complete denial.

"I thought I heard an argument last night."

"That's funny. I didn't hear a single thing. Maybe it was my television set that you heard. Flora does tend to play it too loud sometimes."

I studied Mr. Jenkins for a few seconds to make sure that he was being serious. He was.

"Yeah, that must have been it," I said.

"I'll make sure it doesn't happen again," Mr. Jenkins stated.

"It's no big deal," I told him as I continued towards the sidewalk.

"That's okay. I'll go in there and straighten Flora out right now about that shit."

I couldn't help but notice the enormous knot on the back of Mr. Jenkins' skull as he walked by me.

"Have a good day," Mr. Jenkins instructed me as he stepped inside the vestibule of our brownstone.

"Thanks, you do the same, Sir."

I hurried up the street to Jada. I didn't want to be anywhere in the vicinity in case my neighbors started fighting again.

Ever since that eventful night, Tucker and I have known better than to grow too alarmed whenever we heard a disturbance happen downstairs.

So, with that thought in mind, I picked up my remote, drowned out the uproar below, and learned about the clandestine activities of swine.

CHAPTER THIRTEEN

The next time Marcia and I got together she had a pleasant surprise waiting for me. She had come to an earlier conclusion that for the time being, it was best for me to come over to her place only when Brandon was not going to be around. (I made no objections about her plan.)

When I walked into her apartment, Marcia kissed me passionately, then handed me a wrapped package that had my name written across it.

"What's this?" I asked in wonderment.

"A little something I picked up for you."

I sat down on the couch in her living room and instantly tore the wrapping off the package. It was a shoebox. Marcia had bought me a pair of black, genuine leather, cowboy boots. I was totally surprised because I knew those boots had easily set her back at least four C-notes.

"Yo, these are funky."

"Try them on," Marcia said lovingly.

I put the boots on and they were a perfect fit. I stood up and began strolling around the room.

"You like?" Marcia asked.

"Yes, I do. Thank you."

That was the first time that a sister had ever bought me a gift without it being some kind of holiday or other special occasion that necessitated it. Marcia didn't know it, but she had just earned herself some serious brownie points.

"Good. They're yours to keep...on only one condition."

"What's that?"

Marcia sashayed over to me and then pulled me close to her.

"That I be the only girl you ride with them."

Ten seconds later, I felt a bulge in my pants. Marcia noticed it as well.

"What's that?" she asked innocently.

"Come on," I said in my best western drawl, "let's go and knock some boots." (Yeah, that line was kinda corny now that I think about it.) Marcia began laughing as I swept her up effortlessly into my arms.

"What about the movie? Aren't we going to go?" she asked with a chuckle of delight.

"That's okay. I already read the book."

I carried Marcia back into her bedroom and once again she catapulted me to the stars.

"Uh, is there anything else I can do for you before I go, Marcia?"

It was the next morning. I had already cooked breakfast, taken Marcia's Lexus to the carwash, purchased a few items at the grocery store, and picked up her dry-cleaning. I was eager to please that woman in every possible way.

"No, Javier. You go on home. I'll call you later."

"Okay..."

We exchanged kisses and I reluctantly departed for home.

Tucker was thrilled when he saw the present that Marcia had bought for me. He was sitting at the kitchen table reviewing some employee applications when I walked in the house wearing my new boots.

"You sure wouldn't get nothing like this from any of them GEDs. Dealing with Ph.D. women definitely has its advantages."

"You might actually be right for once, Tucker."

"What kind of work does Marcia do again?" Tucker asked, putting his papers aside.

"She works with computers."

That was putting it lightly. Marcia had graduated from Columbia University with a degree in computer science and in no time at all found employment as a programmer for a brokerage firm down on Wall Street. She let it be known to me that she was compensated quite generously for her skills.

Marcia also did some consulting work on the side. Add to this the fact that she received a hefty amount of money for child support from Craig, who worked as an administrator for the Borough of Queens, and one could see how Marcia could afford to live as luxuriously as she did.

"That's alright, man. I wish I'd met her myself," Tucker replied.

"I'm sure you've got your hands full already."

Tucker smiled to himself.

"Yeah, I do."

I headed for my room when Tucker stopped me.

"Wait, roomie, let me run something by you?"

I sat down at the table with him.

"What?"

Tucker handed me a folder. I opened it and saw that it was plans for another addition to his store's menu. I certainly had to give my man proper credit. Even though he fooled around a lot with his womanizing, when it came down to his livelihood, Tucker was always looking for ways to improve it.

With my input, his 'Pig on a Stick' promotion was a documented success with impressive sales. Once again, Tucker was looking to try something new. I briefly scanned his proposed idea and had to fight myself to keep from laughing in front of him.

"This one might not be a good idea," I said with a straight face.

"What's wrong with Sow Chow?" Tucker asked defensively. "I'm gonna give folks their choice of pig, plus fries and a soft drink for under five bucks! That's not a good deal?"

"It is a good deal, but the crap sounds too funny."

I handed Tucker's folder back to him.

"You need to change the name."

"Then what do you suggest?"

"You should name it something catchy. Something that the folks can remember."

"Like what?" Tucker implored.

"How about the uh...Squeal Meal?"

"Squeal Meal?"

"Yeah."

"Hmm, that does have a nice ring to it. Thanks."

"Anytime, Tucker."

I got up to go to my room.

"Javier?"

"*Yes,* Tucker?" I was beginning to lose my patience.

"Why won't you come and work with me? Aren't you tired of getting your ass cursed out at work?"

"Evidently, you've forgotten what happened the last time I was down at your store."

An elderly woman had cursed Tucker out badly because she thought that he had cheated her out of her change. In actuality, Tucker had called himself being generous and had undercharged the woman because of the two malnourished-looking grandchildren that she had with her. That old lady had called Tucker everything but a child of God that day.

"Yeah, we do get cursed out every now and then down there, but then so does everybody else in Brooklyn. I really would love to have you working with me. Seriously. I plan on expanding within the next year and I know that you've got the right head for this business. I could really use you."

"I don't think so, Tucker."

"I guarantee you that you'll make much more money than you're earning now."

I was indeed tired of my job, but I still viewed working with my roommate as jumping out of the frying pan and into the fire.

"I'll keep that in mind," I told him before walking off.

That following Tuesday morning at the gym, I noticed that The Truth looked a little despondent as she conducted her workout. Being in a state of bliss myself after a few trips to Shangri-la thanks to Marcia, I decided to see if I could spread a little happiness to others. I ambled over to the unoccupied abdominal machine next to the one she was using.

"Good morning," I said with a smile.

"Hi," she answered without missing a beat on her machine.

Just as I was about to sit down on the available machine, a short, stocky brother rudely went in front of me.

"Yo, my man...I was about to use this," I informed the interloper.

"That's too bad now, ain't it?" he replied.

Since it was not yet seven o'clock in the morning, the last thing on my agenda was a possible ass kicking for breakfast. I was thinking of something diplomatic to say to the rude brother when The Truth finished her set and moved to another machine. I followed behind her. A half scowl appeared on her face after she turned around and found me standing behind her.

"Are you following me?"

"Not really," I answered.

She climbed onto a stationary bicycle. I hopped on one beside her.

"So this is only a coincidence?" she said, obviously miffed.

"Something like that, yeah."

(Evasive answers were my specialty back in college. They helped me to graduate.) The Truth ignored me and began programming her machine. I did likewise.

"You seem to be in a bad mood today. Wanna talk about it?"

"You wanna mind your own business?"

I was completely taken aback. *Maybe this was girlfriend's time of the month?* I thought to myself.

"My bad. It won't happen again."

The Truth stopped pedaling and turned towards me.

"I'm sorry for that last remark. I am in a really bad mood right now and I don't feel like being bothered." With that, she resumed exercising.

"I know how you feel, gurl."

I phrased the sentence just like I'd heard hundreds of females do whenever they got together with each other and 'exhaled'. I saw that The Truth had cracked a little smile out of one corner of her mouth. A chink had appeared in her armor.

"I got upset myself just yesterday when I chipped a nail opening a can of stout. Talk about being pissed?"

"You've got issues," replied The Truth, laughing.

"See there? Laughing won't kill you."

The Truth studied me for a few seconds as we pedaled merrily away on our machines.

"Can I ask you a question?"

"Shoot," I told her.

"Why are all of you brothers so full of shit?"

Once again, The Truth shocked me.

"What was that?"

"I'm not talking about you, because I don't know you, but the rest of these brothers around here ain't nothing but dogs!"

I knew better than to fall into an early morning debate with a sister concerning the infidelity of us brothers; so I elected to answer her question with a question of my own.

"I sense a lot of anger coming from you. Am I correct?"

"Yes, you are. I caught my boyfriend cheating on me."

"How do you know he cheated on you? It could just as well be a big misunderstanding."

(What I really wanted to ask her was how did the fool get busted?)

"I saw on his credit card statement where he paid for a weekend in Atlantic City."

"Is that all? He could have been hanging out down there with the fellas."

"Would any of the fellas you hang out with purchase some hair from The Weave Warehouse?"

I couldn't argue with that one.

"I, uh, I see your dilemma."

"As soon as you think you've finally found yourself a decent black man, and you start to trust him, he goes and fucks around on you! Why is that?"

I brainstormed quickly to come up with a suitable answer for her.

"Well, I'll tell you, Truth..." I started and then caught myself.

"What did you just say?"

"What I said was, to tell you the truth, some brothers out there, excluding myself of course, view women somewhat the same way that a farmer would view tractors. You always want to have the latest model with all the bells and whistles on it, but after a few years of wear and tear, you feel the need to upgrade. You know, get yourself something new."

The Truth eyed me in serious contemplation for a few seconds and then burst out laughing.

"That's the biggest crock of country shit I've ever heard!"

"Hey, you asked me a question..."

"And I got a bullshit answer."

The Truth got off her machine and wiped her tantalizing body down with her towel. I had never so wanted to be a piece of woven cotton before in my life.

"Thanks for cheering me up, though," she added with a smile.

The Truth then sauntered off toward the treadmills.

"Glad to be of service!" I called after her.

CHAPTER FOURTEEN

It was the middle of October. Homecoming time. It was my turn to drive down to South Carolina since Tucker had driven in his ride the year before. After I finished loading the rest of my bags in the back of Jada, I turned around and looked for Tucker. He was nowhere to be found. I gave a deep sigh as I checked my watch; it was two o'clock in the morning.

I wanted to leave in time to pass through Washington D.C. before the morning rush-hour traffic began backing up there. I closed the rear hatch and turned around to go fetch my roommate. As soon as I started up the steps of our brownstone, Tucker appeared at the top of them with his bags in tow.

"Will you come on, Tucker?"

"Hold your horses, dude."

We went through the same routine every time we traveled together. When Tucker had finally stowed his belongings and climbed into the seat beside me, I turned to him.

"Okay, what did you leave this time?"

I knew better than to just up and pull off because just as soon as we got a little distance between us and Brooklyn, Tucker would suddenly remember something that he had meant to bring along with him. He would then demand that we turn around to retrieve it.

"I didn't leave anything," he said defensively.

I wasn't buying that so easily.

"You got your wallet?"

Tucker felt the back pocket of his jeans.

"Yeah."

"You brought along your money and credit cards?"

Tucker pulled his wallet out from his pocket and flipped it open.

"I got all that," he answered with a slight edge to his voice.

"What about your cell phone...and its charger?"

Tucker glared at me.

"I'll be right back," he hissed.

Twelve hours later, we were rolling through the outskirts of Columbia, South Carolina. I dropped Tucker off at his mother's house and proceeded to Daddy's. He was sitting on the front porch smoking a cigar and reading the newspaper when I pulled into the driveway. Daddy smiled as he stood his six-foot-three, robust self up and walked over to greet me. He had served most of his thirty years in the army as a drill sergeant; so he was still in pretty good physical shape.

"How long did it take you?" Daddy asked as he snatched one of my bags from me.

"A little over twelve hours."

"You got the tickets to the football game?" Daddy asked, changing the subject.

"I'm picking them up from Cheese tonight."

I followed Daddy into the house. My father had bought his house in one of the numerous subdivisions that were being developed around the perimeter of Fort Jackson in the early eighties. My mother had just given birth to me, and the two of them decided that they needed more space than their one-bedroom apartment could provide.

The house they purchased was a two-garage, bricked, split-level number with an adequate number of pine trees in both the front and back yards. Growing up as a child there, I had plenty of room outside to run around and act a fool.

I was an only child. I never knew if it was because my mother had decided to continue her education and had gone back to school to become an attorney, or because Daddy kept getting transferred to other military posts. Hell, it could have even been the fact that I did give my parents quite a run for their money during my formative years, and they decided to quit while they were ahead.

I didn't mind all that much being the only child because I basically got what I wanted as long as I stayed out of trouble, which I managed to do usually. I did, however, try the teenage rebellion thing, which included cutting school, smoking weed, and dabbling in shoplifting. Thanks to the many lectures from my mother and the far more numerous ass whippings I received from Daddy, I was able to eventually straighten myself out.

After one excruciatingly painful encounter with Daddy, when he found a large bag of weed under my mattress, I realized there had to be more to life than hanging out late and getting high with my friends. That night, I promised myself that I would straighten up so I could go on to college and make both of my parents proud.

Sadly, things did not turn out as planned. The week after I graduated from high school, my mother was diagnosed with breast cancer. She died less than a year later. I felt guilty about being away in college and not at home with Daddy, so I asked him if it would be okay for me to take some time off from school and come back home for awhile. When Daddy told me he'd kill me first, I decided to stay put in the safety of my dorm.

After dropping my bags in my old bedroom and taking a quick shower, I went back outside and began washing Jada thoroughly. (You'd be surprised at the amount of dead bugs a windshield collects after charging hundreds of miles down the highway.)

Daddy stepped back onto the porch and proceeded to read his newspaper again.

"You plan on seeing Myra while you're down this time?"

"Sure," I lied. I had no intentions of looking that sister up.

"I told her that you were coming."

"I figured as much."

Once Jada was clean it was time to hit the streets.

"Where are you running off to?" Daddy asked when he heard me crank my engine.

"Tucker's house," I yelled as I drove out of the driveway.

Tucker's mother was backing her red, Toyota Sequoia out of the garage when I pulled up in front of her house.

"Leaving so soon?" I called out to her.

Mrs. Tucker let her window down. I used to have a secret crush on her when I was growing up. In fact, Mrs. Tucker was the main reason that I played with her spoiled son as much as I did back then. She was still as fine as ever, especially when she wore her nursing uniform.

"Got to go make me some overtime at the hospital."

"I heard that. Is your son still in there?"

"I think he's in the shower. Just ring the doorbell. Imani's home."

"Thanks."

Mrs. Tucker rolled her window up and continued backing out of the driveway. I strolled up onto the porch and rang the fancy doorbell that the Tucker family has had on their door ever since I could remember.

"Coming!" a female voice sang out after a few seconds.

The front door flew open and there stood Imani. She was wearing a pair of black, baggy jeans and a large, gray USC Gamecocks sweatshirt. I could still make out her entrancing figure underneath all of that excess clothing.

"J.C.!"

Imani gave me a tight, affectionate bear hug. She and I had always treated each other as if we were brother and sister when we were younger. All of that stopped the summer Imani's hormones began to sculpt her body into a masterpiece. I quickly broke our embrace.

"Come on in."

Hearing her Southern accent made me smile. It really felt good to be home again. I followed Imani into the living room.

"So, how's school?" I asked.

"School is school. All I do is eat, write, and study."

"You should have a pretty good grade point average then."

"A three point eight so far."

"Impressive."

"So, how's everything in Brooklyn?"

"Brooklyn is Brooklyn. All I do is eat, work, and pay for a lot of damn parking tickets."

"You're still crazy, J.C."

"No…not really."

We faced each other in awkward silence. Imani looked better every time I saw her. It was time for me to keep it moving before someone got in trouble.

"Excuse me, Imani, but your brother's gonna have me out here all day waiting on him."

"Be my guest. He's washing up."

I strode down the hall to the bathroom, where I heard the water gushing away in the shower. I was just about to knock on the door when I heard a horrible noise coming from the other side.

"IT WAS JUST MY IMAGINATION, RUNNING AWAY WITH ME!"

I banged hard on the door.

"Hannibal, you all right in there?!"

The water turned off quickly and a few seconds later, a still-dripping Tucker cracked the bathroom door open. Steam slowly crept out into the hallway from around him.

"What did you just say?"

For those of you who haven't guessed it already, Tucker goes by his last name. His real name is Hannibal Alexander Julius Tucker. (His father was a history teacher.) Now, of course you know we kids made fun of 'Hannibal the Cannibal' in elementary school. The boy had more than his fair share of fist fights back then and spent many hours in the principal's office. By the time Hannibal reached junior high, he hated his name so much that he dropped it completely.

"I asked if you were okay. You sounded like you were in a lot of pain in there."

Tucker glared at me.

"You're going to be in a lot of pain if you don't cut out the monkey business with calling me by that damn name."

"And you're going to be walking over to The Pub if you don't hurry your slow behind up."

The Pub was the legendary drinking establishment near the main gate of Fort Jackson. Even Daddy used to hang out there when he was a youngster. As soon as I opened the door, malodorous cigar smoke hit me in the face. The Pub used to be the spot where the older locals hung out back in the day, but the place was currently overrun with new jacks. Everywhere I looked, I saw young men wearing large, low-sagging, belt-less jeans, unlaced work boots, and oversized T-shirts.

For an instant, I thought that Tucker and I had accidentally walked into one of the many pawnshops that encircled Fort Jackson because everybody in The Pub had on gold jewelry. Each individual wore a golden accessory in their mouth, on their hand, or around their neck. The local, illegal economy was definitely booming. I headed straight to the bar, where the bartender was busy handing out brews and plates of hot wings.

"Hey! Can I get a damn drink in this place?"

My friend Cheese scowled as he quickly spun around to see who was shouting at him. A look of surprise then appeared on his face.

"What's up, partner?"

"You got it," I answered.

We clasped hands and gave each other a hearty handshake.

"What's up, Tucker?"

"Chilling, man."

"When did you guys get in?"

"A few hours ago," I informed him.

"Yo, what you guys drinking? It's on the house."

After a moment, Tucker and I found an empty table and sat down with our pints.

"Boy, it looks like the drug business down here is on and popping, Tucker."

"Tell me something I don't know."

The crowd was dotted with a few faces I recognized, former schoolmates who had stayed in the area like my friend Cheese had done. After graduating high school, Cheese had gotten hired at a new truck manufacturing plant that had just opened up outside the city limits. He has been there ever since. That allowed Cheese to buy a house, as well as a couple of nice cars. His part-time gig at The Pub was solely a little something for him to make a few dollars off the books.

Minutes later, Cheese strolled over to our table with another round of brew for us. He took the empty seat beside Tucker.

"How often does this place get raided?" Tucker asked him, trying to be a wise ass.

"Not as often as you'd think, Hannibal," Cheese said.

Tucker hushed up and sipped on his brew. Cheese then dug into his back pocket and pulled out three tickets to the upcoming football game. He handed two of them to me and the third one to Tucker.

"How much I owe you?" I asked him.

Cheese waved away the money I held out to him.

"Those are on the house. Your old man did me a solid not too long ago."

"Thanks."

"Yeah, thanks," Tucker echoed.

"Uh, not so fast there, Tucker. I'm afraid I'm going to need thirty-five dollars from you."

Tucker begrudgingly dug into his back pocket and fished out the requested amount.

"We're not exactly made out of money around here," Cheese told him.

"Ain't that a bitch," Tucker remarked as he paid up.

"So, how the women treating you guys up North?" Cheese asked.

Tucker and I looked at each other before answering.

"Okay," I responded. "What's the deal down here with you?"

Cheese grinned at us from ear to ear.

"Not bad at all. Actually, I might be getting married soon."

"You bullshitting!" Tucker exclaimed.

I was surprised also, but I managed to keep my astonishment in check. The Cheese that I knew ran the streets way too hard to get hitched.

"No, I'm not," Cheese stated calmly.

"Who is she?" I asked.

Cheese gave a delightful sigh before continuing.

"She's a sister who works down at the plant with me. Her name is Stacey."

I shuffled my chair around the table closer to my friend.

"So, you think that she's the one?" I inquired.

"Yeah, man. She's a keeper."

"Why?" Tucker asked.

Cheese sighed delightfully once again.

"Well, for starters, she doesn't care about how much money I make, or what kind of car I drive."

"That's all good, Cheese, but how does that still make her the one for you?" Tucker asked. He had taken the words right out of my mouth. Cheese eyed both of us briefly.

"I don't know about you guys, but I'm ready to settle down and have myself a family. The last thing that I want to be is some old motherfucker up in a club somewhere, still trying to prove that I can pull women and what not. I see enough of that sad shit up in here."

"I heard that," I said to no one in particular.

"But are you really ready?" Tucker asked. "Marriage is a big step there, homeboy."

My roommate was obviously referring to the sour experience of his own marriage and didn't want to see our friend go through the same dilemma as he had.

"I can't afford not to do it, dawg," Cheese explained. "Look, I've been through my fair share of sisters out there, and I know a good thing when I see it. Stacey is about as close to the perfect mate as I'm going to find. If it turns out to be a mistake, then I can say that at least I tried."

Everyone sat around the table in silence for a few seconds.

"Let us know when the big day is," Tucker smiling, told Cheese. "I don't give a damn about going to the wedding ceremony itself, but I loves me a good open-bar reception!"

"Ignore him, please," I said to Cheese. "Just let us know when the event is and we'll be there."

Cheese stood up.

"Sure thing," he said. "I got to get back to work. You guys enjoy the game and holler back at me before y'all break out."

"Bet," I told him.

"Oh, yeah, J.C.," Cheese said, "Myra's been asking about you."

"Thanks for the warning," I responded, weakly.

CHAPTER FIFTEEN

I hunted high and low to find a parking space in the vicinity of the football stadium. Even though it was only eleven in the morning and the game started at two, the lots were already congested. Conversion vans, luxury Mercedes, Acuras and Lexuses, and countless sport utility vehicles dominated the parking areas.

As soon as I stepped out of Jada, the sweet aroma of cooking barbecue hit my nostrils. A mixture of hip-hop and soul music filled my ears. Folks were getting their tailgating grooves on. Everywhere you looked there were grills, coolers, tents, tables, chairs and smiles.

All factions of the black community, young, old, rich, and poor had turned out to watch State go up against Grambling University, and the game promised to be a good one.

Besides the actual football game, the halftime show was also the reason so many folks had ventured down to Orangeburg, South Carolina. The Battle of the Bands was always a popular attraction at black college football games. Even if your team couldn't play football worth a damn, there was no excuse for your school having a weak band on the field.

"Boy, that barbecue smells good, doesn't it?" Daddy asked to no one in particular as we mixed in with the crowd.

"I've smelled way better," Tucker said, with a huff.

"Sorry about that, Hannibal. Your barbecue is the best there is." Daddy mockingly patted Tucker on the head as if he were still a child. Tucker sucked his teeth in protest.

Moving through the crowds, Tucker and I ran across a lot of our old classmates. I was pleased to find that most of them seemed to be doing well.

The Bulldogs had a new head coach who we didn't know, so Tucker and I didn't bother to go down on the sidelines and talk to the members of the team like we used to do whenever we came to watch them play.

Game time finally arrived and just as everyone expected, the contest was high scoring. Grambling's return man ran the ball back all the way for a touchdown on the opening kickoff and the Tigers' fans went berserk. State answered with a scoring drive of its own on the following possession. At half time the score was tied at thirty-five points apiece.

The halftime show was impressive. Both bands played and danced their tails off to the crowd's delight. As soon as they were both finished, arguments could be heard all around us as to which band was the best. I personally thought that Grambling's band had stepped just a little bit harder than our own; but, of course, I kept this opinion to myself.

Sitting in the stands during the second half of the game, I couldn't help but reminisce about all of the fond memories that I had experienced on the same field below me.

"Remember that Morgan State game, Tucker?"

"You mean the one I won for us?"

"If I'm not mistaken, it was *I* who scored the winning touchdown on a quarterback keeper."

"But who made the block that sprung you?"

"That was Reggie Bell, Tucker."

"Yeah, but who blocked his man?"

Daddy and I turned and stared at Tucker in unison. At that same moment, the Bulldogs' strong safety intercepted a poorly thrown pass and ran it back for a touchdown. The crowd was ecstatic! That touchdown turned out to be the last one of the game, and the Bulldogs won forty-nine to forty-two.

We made it back to Columbia by eight. I dropped Tucker off at his parents' place and went on home with Daddy. Once there, I jumped in the shower and scrubbed myself down good. I then went into my old room and picked out my sharpest outfit to step out in. It was time to hit the club.

Rumors Nightclub is in the middle of the section of Columbia known as St. Andrews. The area is predominately comprised of apartment complexes and condos. It residents mainly are college students, newlywed couples, and other young folks striking out on their own. Each in their own car. The traffic in St. Andrews is some of the worst Columbia has to offer.

"Damn," Tucker said when we saw the long line of people waiting to get inside the nightclub.

"This is ridiculous," I added. "Cheese said the place was jumping now, but this is off the chain!"

We cruised along the front of the club to observe the line at close range. After making a pass, I turned and faced Tucker.

"What do you think? You wanna queue the line here, or check another spot out? I think The Side Effect is opened back up."

Tucker looked at me as if I had lost my mind. He then placed his hand on my forehead.

"Don't you see all of those fine ass sisters standing out there?"

We stood in line for damn near an hour waiting to get in. Once we got inside though, we realized that the wait had been well worth it. Exquisite black women were everywhere. Even so, my mind was on Marcia. I wondered what she was up to at that moment. The thought of her made me smile.

A tapping on my shoulder brought me back. When I spun around, I almost pissed in my pants. Standing there was my ex-fiancée, Myra! Dumbfounded, I began calculating the odds of her finding me here at this club, on this night.

"Hey, J.C.!" she exclaimed. "I thought that was you over here."

I could only manage to flash an ambivalent, phony smile at her.

"What's going on?" Myra continued.

"Nothing much," I mumbled.

"So, how's everything?" she asked.

"Pretty cool. How's everything going with you?"

Myra gave a small sigh.

"My divorce will be final soon."

"Oh, really?"

We both remained silent for a few seconds as we watched the crowd out on the dance floor getting down.

"How's New York treating you?"

"I can't complain, except for still living with Tucker."

"You know, I thought I saw him sitting at a table across the way making out with some girl, but I wasn't too sure."

"That's probably him."

More silence, until Myra elbowed me.

"Will you buy me a drink?"

I wanted to tell her no, but looking into those hazel eyes of hers, I couldn't.

"What's your poison?"

"Don't you remember?"

"Gotcha..."

I fought my way through the ever-growing crowd to get to the bar. While standing in line to place my order with the bartender, I shook my head sadly. The last thing I needed that night was a painful trip back down memory lane.

Myra Cooper and I developed a relationship during our last year of high school. And I may as well be honest about it. At first, I was only interested in Myra because she was a cute, little, copper-toned honey who lived in the same community I did. All through grade school, Myra avoided talking to any of the local fellas because she thought that we weren't smart enough for her. Now mind you, that didn't keep me or all the other little nappy-headed boys in our neighborhood from constantly badgering poor Myra, steadily commenting about how beautiful she was. Nevertheless, Myra didn't give a rat's ass about any of us.

I decided to ignore her right back. While all the other guys kept sweating Myra throughout middle school, and on into high school, I paid her no attention.

Then one day, as I was walking home from football practice, she pulled up beside me in the little gray Mitsubishi truck that she drove back then.

"You wanna lift?" she asked.

I looked around to see who she was asking.

"You talking to me?" I asked.

"You see anybody else here?"

I got into her truck and by the time she dropped me off in front of my house I had Myra's telephone number. We began dating soon afterward. Eventually, I became infatuated with her. (That took me a little while to do because I had still not quite fully recovered from being dumped by Nicole Harper two years earlier.)

Myra had no problem winning my parents over either, since they had watched her grow up and knew her folks.

Since we would be heading off to different colleges that upcoming fall, we decided to see as much of each other as we could over the summer. Slowly, but surely, I fell head-over-heels in love with Myra.

I don't know who was more in love with her at that time, Daddy or me. He constantly warned me not to let a good girl like Miss Cooper get away. I believe his exact words were: "Myra is a nice girl. Don't fuck this one up, boy."

So, I did what any fool who didn't know any better would do: I asked Myra Cooper to marry me. She said 'yes.' We decided not to tie the knot until we both had completed college.

Myra went to a university in Charlotte, North Carolina, which placed us only a few hours away from each other by car. All went as planned during our first year apart. As the second year rolled around, however, Myra became more and more difficult to get in touch with.

I didn't know exactly what was going on, but I could sense that something wasn't right. When Myra gave me some lame excuse as to why she wasn't coming home for spring break, an alarm went off in my mind.

Borrowing a teammate's old car one weekend, I rolled up on homegirl unannounced. I had to sit in the car and wait outside Myra's dormitory when I got there because she wasn't home. About three hours later, a black, brand-new Chevy Tahoe pulled up in front of me. Myra slowly climbed from the passenger side of the vehicle after kissing the dude driving it. She was wearing a maternity dress.

I hadn't been intimate with Myra for damn near a whole year. It wasn't my baby. Rather than confront her, I simply drove off in misery.

Myra Cooper was the one and only woman who broke me down and made me cry. All the way back down the interstate, I bawled my head off. It took me quite some time to get over her.

Myra returned my engagement ring in the mail with a letter that I didn't even bother to read. She then married the father of her baby and stayed in Charlotte. I started hearing some gossip about Myra's marital problems after she had her third child.

Those thoughts raced through my head as I stood at the bar, ordering myself a Guinness and a banana daiquiri for Myra. After downing my beer I was going to the men's room and then I'd head home. That was my new plan. But Myra had miraculously found an empty table and was sitting at it, awaiting my return. I sat down and handed her the daiquiri.

"Thank you, kind Sir."

"Don't mention it."

This was the first time that I had seen Myra since that fateful day in Charlotte. I studied her on the sly as she sipped her drink. She was still beautiful. She looked up to steal a gaze at me as well, and our eyes met. When I turned away, Myra set her drink down beside her.

"Will you ever forgive me, Javier?"

"Does it really make a difference now, Myra?"

"To me it does, yes."

Since forgiving Myra didn't mean squat to me, I told her what she wanted to hear.

"Okay," I said with a sigh. "I forgive you." I kept my eyes glued to the participants on the dance floor as I spoke.

"You talking to me, Javier?"

"You see anybody else here?" I asked her smugly.

We both laughed upon hearing that old line again.

"Can we be friends again?" Myra asked cautiously.

"Why not?"

"When are you going back up the road?"

"Thursday."

"Maybe we can get together before you go back?"

"Who knows? Maybe."

I drained the rest of my beer and stood up.

"Where are you going?"

"I've got something to do with Daddy early in the morning. Enjoy yourself." I turned to walk away.

"You want my cell number?" Myra called out.

"I still know where you live."

"Right," Myra said, dejectedly.

I began the trek across the club. I located Tucker still on the dance floor slow dragging away with some cutie. I pointed to my watch and then to the exit. He gave me the thumbs up before waving me away.

Out in the parking lot, I laughed to myself as I cranked Jada up. I couldn't believe the set of balls that Myra had on her. Sure, I could forgive her, but there was no way I was ever going to forget.

For the next four days I made my rounds around the city visiting all of my friends and relatives. It seemed as if everybody wanted me to hang out for dinner and drinks and whatnot; so I tried to accommodate as many folks as possible. The night before I was to drive back to Brooklyn, I was pretty much exhausted. As I was casually packing my clothes away for my return trip, Daddy eased himself into the room behind me.

"I need to talk to you, son."

He had a serious look on his face. I stopped what I was doing and took a seat on my old bed.

"Yes, Sir?" I asked, giving Daddy his cue.

He sat down on the bed beside me.

"You know, ever since we lost your mama, I've done the best that I could to raise you right."

"Of course, I do."

"I can't say that I did the best job, but hell, I did keep you in school, out of jail, and off of drugs. So I guess I didn't do all that bad now, did I?"

"Not at all, Sir."

I didn't have a clue where my Daddy was going with this conversation. He leaned closer to me.

"You know, I was about your age when me and your mama got married."

Suddenly, I didn't want to know where Daddy was going with this conversation.

"I guess what I'm really trying to say is that I don't want to see you out there running the streets all your life. You need to find you a good woman and settle down, son."

"Does any of this have to do with Myra?"

"No, it does not. Since you refused to get in touch with the girl after she's come over here three times looking for you, and you wouldn't call her, I'm gonna let that be."

"Thank you."

"But, I still think you ought to give her another chance."

I didn't respond to his last comment. Daddy cleared his throat.

"Anyway, I want you to go to church, too."

"Church?" I echoed.

"Yeah, church. That way you can kill two birds with one stone. Get in touch with the Lord, and find yourself a nice, Christian girl to boot."

"But…you don't go to church, Daddy?"

"Don't do as I do! Do as I say do!"

(I had clearly pissed him off.)

"Sir! Yes, Sir!"

"Questioning me like that! Boy, you know I can still take your ass out, don't you?"

"Sir! Yes, Sir! It won't happen again, Sir!"

Daddy stood up from the bed.

"Now finish up your damn packing so you can get yourself some sleep. You've got a long trip ahead of you in the morning."

"Yes, Sir. Good night, Daddy."

CHAPTER SIXTEEN

My heart raced as I waited for Marcia to unlock her front door. She had been on my mind constantly while I was down South and we kept in close contact over the phone. As soon as I returned, we made plans to see each other the following weekend. Brandon would be with his father and we would have plenty of time to ourselves. Seeing her standing there in front of me, I thought of how lucky I was to be kicking it with Marcia.

"Hey, girl." I greeted her with a smile.

"Hey, yourself," Marcia replied, with a bigger smile.

I swept her off her feet and twirled her around in my arms while we kissed. Marcia felt and smelled so good wrapped in my arms that I wanted to hold her forever. But I decided to put her back down when I felt myself grow dizzy.

"You hungry?" she asked.

"Kind of."

"I'll order us some Chinese."

Marcia placed our order, hung the phone up and looked me square in the eye.

"We've got about thirty minutes before the food arrives. What do you suggest we do to kill time?"

She didn't have to ask me twice. We were still sailing along on our 'sea of love' in Marcia's bedroom when the door buzzer sounded. I dropped anchor.

"Don't stop," Marcia pleaded.

"Do you like cold Chinese food?"

I slowly unwrapped my body from hers and then rolled over by her side. Marcia leapt off the waterbed with a huge frown on her face.

"Aw, come on now, baby. Don't be mad."

"Screw you, Javier," Marcia said playfully as she pulled her robe around her sweaty flesh and left the room.

I stretched out on her waterbed, adrift in a sea of relaxation. Seconds later, I heard what seemed to be a heated exchange going on between Marcia and the Chinese food deliveryman. Now, I had known a few of those guys to get pushy when it came to how much a customer tipped, but this argument had clearly gotten out of hand.

I slipped into my drawers and left the bedroom. I headed up the hallway to show this fella Marcia was not alone.

"Yo, what's the problem in here?!" I boomed, approaching the end of the hall. Stepping toward the front door, I almost had an accident in those drawers I had just slipped on. Craig was standing in the doorway and he didn't look all that happy to see me.

"You laying up in here with *this* sorry motherfucker?"

Now since Daddy had never called me a sorry motherfucker (at least not to my face) there was no way that I could let Craig get away with that comment.

"I got your motherfucker right here, Pops!"

"Oh yeah? You think so?" Craig asked as he tried to push his way around Marcia, who stood defiantly in the doorway blocking his entrance. I raised my arms in front of Craig, indicating to him that I was game for whatever it was that he wanted to do. He tried to push his way by Marcia again.

"Stop it!" Marcia shouted to the both of us. "Do I need to get the police involved over here?" she asked, looking her former husband directly in the eyes. Craig was silent.

"I'm quite sure these nosy neighbors here would enjoy seeing that spectacle!" Marcia continued.

Her point evidently hit home. Craig deflated his puffed-up chest as he slowly stepped back out into the hallway.

"Thank you," Marcia hissed at him. "I'll be right back." With that, she closed the door hard in his face.

"Yo...what's going on?" I asked Marcia as she whizzed by me and headed up the hall. I followed behind her.

"He came by here to pick up a suit for Brandon to wear to church tomorrow. When I told him that he couldn't come in, he got upset and wanted to know why," Marcia explained, sighing heavily as she opened the door to Brandon's room.

"So where's Brandon now?"

"Craig's mother is over at the house watching him."

Marcia then turned and glared at me.

"Of course you coming around the corner in your underwear didn't help matters much."

I couldn't believe she was trying to go off on me.

"I thought you were having trouble with the delivery person!"

"Thanks a lot."

Now I was getting riled up but I caught myself. I inhaled deeply and made a conscious effort to slowly count to ten, but that crap didn't work. Marcia pulled a suit from Brandon's closet, along with a pair of shoes, and stomped back to the front door, swinging it back open.

"Here!" Marcia growled, shoving the items into Craig's mid-section. "See you Monday!"

She slammed the door in his face again. I strolled back into her bedroom and began gathering up the rest of my clothes, which were strewn about on the floor.

"You going somewhere?"

Marcia was standing in the doorway watching me.

"Yes. Home. I don't know whether I mentioned this to you before or not Marcia, but I don't do drama." I stuck my legs into my jeans and pulled them up around me.

"I'm sorry, Javier. I didn't mean to snap at you."

"Believe me, Marcia, it's no big deal," I said, fastening my belt. Marcia walked up to me and grabbed both of my arms.

"Look at me, Javier."

I stopped what I was doing and glared at her.

"I'm really sorry for going off on you. Please don't be mad. Stay?"

"I honestly think it best if I leave now."

Marcia released my arms and grabbed my crotch.

"You sure you want to leave?"

"Well...I guess I could hang around just a little bit longer..."

As I began unbuckling my belt, I heard someone knock hard on the front door.

"Let me handle this clown this time," I ordered Marcia.

I stomped off down the hall and into the living room before she could respond.

"Javier, wait!" Marcia cried after me.

"You want some of me?!" I yelled as I swung the front door open.

The small young Chinese man who stood in front of Marcia's door dropped the order of food that he was holding and made a mad dash for the exit stairs.

"Hey!" I yelled after the guy, realizing my blunder.

The deliveryman only ran faster. He threw open the exit door and was two levels below me before I could reach the stairway myself. I decided that it would be useless to pursue any further. I returned to Marcia's apartment feeling like a complete imbecile until I realized I had just obtained a free meal.

Marcia and I spent the rest of the evening making love to each other, while watching a Three Stooges marathon. After a peaceful night's sleep, I woke up around seven on Sunday morning and turned Marcia's giant television set on again. As I channeled-surfed, I saw every other station had some type of religious programming on. I then began to think about the conversation I had had with Daddy the last night that I was home.

"Marcia?"

"Yeah, baby?"

"Do you ever feel guilty lazing around on Sunday mornings?"

Marcia turned over in the bed to face me.

"Guilty about what?"

"About not going to church."

"What's there to feel guilty about?" Marcia was once again straight to the point.

"Don't you believe in God?"

"No. Do you?"

"Of course I do!" I exclaimed, amazed and appalled at the same time.

"Why?" Marcia asked matter-of-factly.

"Why what?" I asked, trying to keep my disgust from growing.

"Why do you believe in God?" Marcia was taking the offensive.

"Because...I just do." (That was the best answer I could come up with in the moment.)

"You *just do*, huh?"

"Yeah!"

Marcia shook her head in disappointment as she softly mumbled.

"Uh, what was that you just said, Marcia?"

"I said, another brainwashed Negro."

I sat up in the bed.

"What's that supposed to mean?"

There was a definite edge in my voice and Marcia detected it. She sat up in the bed as well.

"If you were well-read, you'd know that religion was a ruse used by the Europeans to help conquer other peoples."

I sensed an insult in Marcia's statement.

"Are you insinuating that I don't read?"

"I didn't mean it that way, baby," Marcia laughed. She reached over and gave me a peck on my cheek. It didn't help.

"All I'm saying is that the white man has been running that 'pie in the sky' routine on us since the beginning of time, while he robbed and killed to get what he desired right then and there. Be it land, gold, or slaves. Now, if you choose to believe that there is a Supreme

Being that sits around and condones that type of evil behavior, then good for you. I happen to be a bit more knowledgeable than to fall for that nonsense."

I sensed another insult in Marcia's statement somewhere.

"Yeah, Marcia, but how do you explain..."

Marcia put her right index finger onto my lips, effectively shutting me up.

"Let's not argue about religion?"

She then jumped out of the bed and found her slippers.

"How about I get started on some breakfast?"

"Alright," I reluctantly agreed. I still wanted to continue our discussion, but I figured that it was best not to force it. As Marcia left the room, I couldn't help but wonder about her. I mean, what kind of person didn't believe in God?

Feeling festive, I called Marcia the following week to invite her and Brandon out to a movie. Marcia stated that she had to go to Manhattan on Saturday to take care of a client she was doing some consulting work for, but that Sunday would be fine for her. We made it an official date.

I took Marcia and Brandon to see a new comedy about a kleptomaniac who found a fancy bottle on the beach in sunny California. When the guy opened the dusty bottle and polished it off with hopes of selling it for a few dollars, a genie popped out in front of him. That old genie was real resourceful when it came to helping his master steal other people's property. After the movie, which was quite entertaining, we had an uneventful meal in Mickey D's. This was at Brandon's suggestion of course. We also did a little window-shopping in Fulton Mall, and then I drove Marcia and Brandon home. I saw them into their building, gave Marcia a quick, sultry kiss, and left.

I was happy as a lark as I crossed the street toward Jada. I had spent the whole day with Marcia and her little brat and had emerged unscathed. During my drive back home, it dawned on me that little Brandon had been quiet the whole evening. I silently hoped that he stayed that way whenever I was around him. I parked in front of my place and hopped out of Jada whistling an old ditty from my high school days.

When I stepped to the back of my vehicle to retrieve a bag from the rear compartment, I froze. My jaw dropped in disbelief as I stared at my rear hatch door. The word '*Brandon*' was keyed sloppily across it!

"What's wrong? You sounded upset over the intercom," Marcia asked me when she opened the door to let me into her apartment.

"That little...your son carved his name on the back of my ride!"

"Brandon?"

"That's exactly what he wrote!"

Hearing his name, the little vandal strolled into the living room as if he didn't have a care in the world.

"Did you write your name on the back of Mr. Collins truck?"

Brandon nodded his head. Marcia walked over and squatted down in front of him.

"Why did you do it, son?"

The kid slowly hunched his shoulders up close to his ears, indicating he didn't know what had compelled him to be so devilish.

I knew that I couldn't snatch the boy up. One, he wasn't my child; and two, I couldn't afford to give Craig any more ammunition to want to do me bodily harm. I jammed my hands deep down in my jean pockets in frustration.

"Now what did mommy tell you about doing that?" Marcia asked. I shook my head in amazement upon hearing that this wasn't the first time he had done this sort of thing. Brandon didn't utter a word.

"Aren't you going to do anything about this?" I asked Marcia.

I was careful not to raise my voice too loud.

"Brandon, say that you're sorry to Mr. Collins."

Brandon remained defiantly silent.

"Say you're sorry, Brandon."

Even though there was a more threatening tone in Marcia's voice, that little squirt still didn't say shit.

"You're not going to apologize?"

Marcia's son shook his head.

"Very well, then. Young man, go to your room!"

Brandon turned around and skipped back down the hallway and into his room, slamming his door hard behind him. I stared at Marcia in disbelief.

"That's it?"

"No, that's not it," Marcia said with a sigh.

She then walked down the hall herself. I secretly began to hope that Marcia would give me the honor of teaching her son about the consequences for not respecting other folk's property when she came back with a belt. When Marcia returned to the living room, she handed me a signed blank check.

"What is this?" I asked.

"Just fill in the amount it costs to get your truck repaired."

There was a hint of impatience in her voice.

"Aren't you going to chastise Brandon? Give him a little painful incentive not to do this crap again?"

"I don't believe in hitting my child with a belt," Marcia informed me matter-of-factly.

"Can I do it for you?"

I automatically began to unbuckle the belt from around my waist.

"I don't believe in anyone else hitting on my child, either."

"So what are you going to do?"

"Brandon will get 'time-out' until he learns his lesson."

I glared at Marcia as if she was deranged.

"Time-out?" I repeated. "Y'all ain't even white!"

"Very funny," Marcia sneered.

"That's why he's so damn bad now," I continued. "You need to put the fear of God in him."

Marcia eyed me hard with disdain.

"Oh yeah, I forgot."

"Don't tell me how to raise my son. You're not his father."

"Yes, and I thank the Lord for that. But if he were my son, his ass would know how to behave, or else!" I tugged hard on my belt once for emphasis.

"So what are you trying to say, Javier? You think that my son has a behavioral problem?"

"Shit…you think he don't?"

I should have bitten my tongue, but I couldn't help it. I was that damn mad. Marcia was incensed also.

"I don't have to take this in my own house!"

"You're absolutely right, Marcia."

I stormed to the front door and swung it open. Marcia followed.

"Think you can just come here in my house and berate my child-rearing skills? I've been raising my son from day one!"

"Well, you'd better figure out how to do it right, before he gets locked up!"

"Fuck you, Javier!"

Marcia slammed her door shut so hard in my face that it sounded like a shotgun-blast going off in the corridor. Several of her nosy neighbors silently peered out of their apartments to see what all the commotion was about.

"You're kidding me, right?"

Tucker was dumbfounded.

I shook my head before taking another sip of my Guinness. I was sitting at the kitchen table trying to eat my fried fish dinner in peace, but Tucker insisted on interrogating me after I had foolishly mentioned my spat with Marcia to him.

"No, I'm not," I said.

"Did she get mad?"

"She almost broke her door when she slammed it in my face. I'd say she was upset a little."

Tucker slapped his hand to his forehead.

"You big dummy!"

In spite of the low spirits that I was in, I laughed at Tucker. He reminded me of Fred Sanford.

"What the hell's so funny?"

"Nothing," I said, still smiling.

Tucker walked closer to me and peered directly into my eyes.

"You smoking that crack, boy?"

"No."

"You sure?"

"I'm not on crack, nor any other type of drug, Tucker!"

He was getting on my nerves once again.

"Well, evidently you're on something! You don't go off on a Ph.D. like that, fool! Do you know how hard a successful single sister like Marcia is to come by?"

Tucker's point was a direct hit home. My smile vanished.

"Her son scratched up Jada. I was pissed."

"But you wasn't fucking him, you was boning her!" (Tucker always did have a blunt way of making a point.)

"It ain't like you two were ever going to get married!"

That was another valid point.

"Tell me this, Tucker, what would you have done if that kid had carved his name into your Range Rover?"

"I'd of knocked his little gangster ass out. But that's a moot point."

I finished the rest of my brew and got up to get another one.

"So, what are you going to do about the situation?"

I grabbed another can of Guinness from the fridge and headed down the hall to my bedroom. I would eat dinner later.

"I don't know, Tucker."

"Javier?"

I turned around in front of my bedroom door and faced Tucker as he approached me.

"If uh, you two don't work it out, would you mind if I gave it a go?" This time, I was the one slamming a door in someone else's face.

Mr. Jenkins was outside raking up leaves when I returned from my gym workout the following Saturday morning.

"How are you doing, Sir?" I asked him as I passed by.

"Mighty fine," he replied. "And you?"

"I'll be alright just as soon as I take a bath."

I made my way up the steps.

"Collins?"

"Yes, Sir?"

I turned around and hoped that he wasn't going to tell me that it wasn't him that I had heard the previous night around ten o'clock. Evidently he and the missus had another altercation and she had run him off again. He had pleaded and banged on their apartment door for damn near two hours before Mrs. Jenkins finally decided to let him back inside. Since I was funky and needed to bathe I decided that I would go along with anything that Mr. Jenkins told me. Instead, he reached his hand into his coat pocket and pulled out a white envelope.

"A young lady stopped by here about half an hour ago and asked me to put this in your mailbox. I guess she thought I was your landlord or something 'cause I was out front here cleaning up. I told her that I would hand it to you personally."

I wearily accepted the thick envelope from him. I could tell a card was inside.

"A real cute young lady..." Mr. Jenkins continued, winking at me slyly. "She drove a real nice car too. Kind of fast, though."

"Thank you, Mr. Jenkins," I said before jamming the envelope into my back pocket.

"Ain't you going to read it?" There was a hint of disappointment in Mr. Jenkins' voice.

"After I rest up awhile, I will. Have a good day, Sir. And thanks once again."

I went inside to my apartment. After running a tub full of hot, sudsy water, I sat my dirty behind in it and soaked. It felt like heaven. I had brought Marcia's card inside the bathroom with me to read, but nodded off once I had gotten comfortable in the tub. The cold water woke me up about an hour later. I reached over and turned the hot water on full force. As the water level rose, I stretched my dripping hand over onto the toilet seat and grabbed the envelope.

The card had an illustration of a sad looking puppy on the front of it. I laughed at the picture. Underneath the puppy was the caption, 'Missing You'. I flipped the card open and read the message that Marcia had carefully written:

Javier,

I'm sending you this card to let you know how I'm feeling right now. I hope that you will not remain angry with me for long. I know that my son is not the most well behaved child on this earth, but heaven knows, I'm trying my best to raise him right. Please don't let this misunderstanding be the end of us.

Love, Marcia

P.S. I have made several attempts to contact you by phone and you have chosen not to return any of my calls. Please be advised that this will be my last attempt at contacting you.

"This woman must think I'm some damn client or something," I mumbled to myself.

I angrily balled Marcia's card up and tossed it over into the wastebasket. It was time for me to move on. I sighed heavily as I slid back down into my bath water for a few more minutes of relaxation. After finishing my bath and changing clothes, I walked into the kitchen and grabbed a cold can of Guinness from the refrigerator. Retreating to my bedroom, I put my *Best of Luther Vandross* CD on and selected '*Wait For Love*'. I popped the top off my brew, took a swig, laid back on my bed, and waited for the therapy to begin.

CHAPTER SEVENTEEN

I had struck out for the last time. I was sick of love! Tired of the relationship game. I vowed to focus strictly on personal goals, which did not include interaction with the opposite sex. My main priority was to make and save more money, find myself a new career, and find a church to join.

Reflecting back, I realized that getting involved with Marcia had been a mistake from the start. It was virtually impossible for a man and woman to become sexually involved with each other without somebody catching feelings, and that was what had happened to me.

Even though I knew that Marcia and I would never have gotten married, and that our relationship would eventually amount to nothing, I had found it hard to get enough of her. Fortunately, Little Brandon had helped me out. True to her word, I did not hear from Marcia again. I had picked up my phone on more than one occasion to call her, but I never did.

For the next two months, I busied myself with work. I had no trouble staying occupied at the office, and all of my spare time was spent working with Lance. He had more jobs than he could handle, so he was glad to have me tag along.

One Saturday evening, as Lance and I were refinishing some hardwood floors in an apartment complex in the Midwood section of Brooklyn, his cell phone began ringing. He released the handles of his sanding machine and pulled his phone from his back pocket.

"Hello?" he mumbled after pulling off his dust mask.

Lance muttered a quick conversation into his phone and then hung up. He looked annoyed as he stepped back over to his sander.

"Everything's okay?" I asked.

"I have to pick my cousin up from her game when we finish. You don't mind, do you? She's not that far from here."

"I'm cool."

Lance had picked me up from my place earlier in the day in his van, so I really had no choice but to go wherever he was going. We finally finished our job, hopped into Lance's van and headed out to East Flatbush. There, we parked in front of a middle school.

"Damn netball," Lance grumbled to himself.

"Netball? What's that?"

"Come and see for yourself," Lance said.

I followed Lance out of the van and into the school, where we were guided straight to the gymnasium by the security guard stationed at the entrance door. Lance greeted a few familiar faces as he walked into the gym.

"Good, it's almost over," he whispered to me.

Lance and I found seats on the bleachers. After settling down, I directed my eyes toward the court to see what this netball thing was all about. There were seven female players on each team and each player had a designated area on the court. They could not dribble the ball; only pass it to each other in order to advance it.

Also, only two positions on each team were allowed to shoot at the opponent's basket. The number of nice-looking players astonished me, as well as the number of spectators cheering their team on.

And I had no difficulty discerning which of the players was related to Lance. The poor thing looked just like him, only heavier. Once again, I wondered what kind of family tree my man really had. When the match ended, Lance's cousin made her way over to him.

"Javier, this is my cousin Alice. Alice, this is Javier."

"Pleased to meet you," I told Alice, smiling as I extended my hand out to her.

From behind his cousin, Lance eyed me expectantly. I frowned at him and he quickly dropped any notions he might have had about hooking us up.

"Nice to meet you, too. How did you like our game?"

"To be honest with you, this was the first time I ever heard of or saw netball being played."

"We usually play outside and without a backboard. We're in here until the weather gets warmer."

"Come on, people. I gotta run," Lance announced.

Alice continued to give me the low-down on netball as we rode home. It seemed like a very interesting game.

All the time that I was busying myself with work to help keep my mind off members of the opposite sex, I was checking out different churches in Brooklyn, also. Most of the ones that I attended had beautiful worship services. A few of them, however, seemed to pass the collection plate around a little too often for yours truly. I didn't want to commit to any particular house of worship until I had visited a considerable number of them and could therefore choose wisely.

One bright Sunday morning, I was feeling adventurous so I decided to make the trek out to the Bushwick area of Brooklyn. I had overheard one of my co-workers speak passionately about the dynamic young pastor of a church there and so I made up my mind to investigate for myself. Since I wasn't too familiar with Bushwick, I left around seven in the morning. Also, I didn't know how the parking situation would be at the church so I gave myself some extra time just in case I had to hunt for a legal spot to leave my ride.

I got lost three times before I finally located the right street! I pulled up in front of the church and was surprised to find a line of worshipers waiting to get in. The line snaked around the corner of the building. You would have thought that folks were trying to get into a nightclub. I had to drive four blocks over to park before walking back and joining the queue.

The entire experience was well worth the wait. Walking into the sanctuary, I looked up and was awestruck by the gothic interior design of the building. I was shown to a seat in the rear of the church by an usher and sat down. I looked around at the huge congregation and was amazed to see so many young adults and young couples there. I was still scrutinizing the church membership when the choir began to sing, which was accompanied by a six-piece band that sounded pretty funky.

The entire congregation was soon on its feet praising the Lord, and I was right along with them. When the young pastor, Reverend J. W. Matthews, finally took the pulpit, the audience was more than ready to receive the word. He spoke eloquently, but his message was understandable to common folks like me. I enjoyed the church service so much, that when it came time to take up an offering, I put in two brand new, still crisp, dollar bills. No lie!

It was the first Sunday of the month and the church was holding communion. I decided to leave before this observance began since I wasn't a member in good standing anywhere, and I didn't want to press my luck. I was seated only two pews away from the exit door so I got up and dismissed myself. As I crossed the entrance hall and headed for the front door, I passed a sister who was stepping out of the nearby women's bathroom. I smiled sheepishly at her as I reached for the door handle.

"Excuse me, Sir, but haven't I seen you somewhere before?"

I turned and observed the woman more closely. She was kind of tall, and had a slender, yet curvy build. She wore her hair in braids that ran midway down her back. She was wearing a beautiful, yet simple, light-green dress that fitted her perfectly. This sister was easy on the eyes as she stood there smiling at me questioningly. I didn't have a clue as to who this woman was.

"Have you seen a recent FBI's Most Wanted list?" I joked.

The woman laughed.

"No, that's not it."

She began studying me some more. I didn't want to be rude to the sister, but I had to go.

"People often mistake me for other folks," I stated as I reached for the front door handle again.

"Aren't you a friend of Alice's?"

I didn't recall any Alice in Brooklyn. I slowly shook my head.

"You were at one of our netball games the other weekend."

"Okay, that must have been it."

The woman stuck her hand out to me.

"I'm Jeannette."

"Javier," I said, extending my hand likewise.

"Nice to meet you, Javier. Leaving so soon?"

A wave of embarrassment swept through me.

"Yeah, I need to go," I said awkwardly.

"Well, it was a pleasure having you here, Javier. Hope you come back and worship with us again soon."

"I plan to do that, sister."

Two weeks later, I was doing another job with Lance. This time we were up in the Bronx, not too far from Yankee Stadium. Some elderly woman, who was a friend of Lance's mother, wanted her house repainted. Her husband had recently passed away and I guess she was trying to change the scenery of her home, possibly making it easier to deal with her loss.

Lance had started on the project earlier in the week, but had called me in because he needed to finish up that weekend. The woman had new furniture scheduled to be delivered that following Monday. I was in the bathroom painting over the bathtub when Lance knocked impatiently on the door.

"Yes?"

"I need to get in there."

We both had eaten generous servings of spaghetti for lunch. I knew exactly what he meant.

"Give me one minute. I wanna finish this corner up in here."

"I need to get in there now."

There was a sense of urgency in Lance's voice.

"Alright, alright. I'm coming out."

I came out of the bathroom and Lance quickly dashed in.

"Light a match in there when you're done!"

"Fuck you, mon," Lance grunted from behind the bathroom door.

I went and found a seat on the floor as I waited for Lance to handle his business.

"J.C.?"

"What?"

"I just remembered something."

Whatever he recollected while sitting on the throne could not have been that important in my eyes.

"That's nice," I said nonchalantly.

"I hear you have a secret admirer, playa."

"Say what?"

Lance was quiet, preoccupied with his personal affairs.

"I understand that you've caught somebody's eye."

Lance was obviously up to some joke or something. I decided to play along.

"Is that right?"

"That's what they tell me, mon."

"You uh, wanna clue me in on who this person might be?"

"I believe her name is Miss Charles. You know her?"

"No..." I answered, prompting for Lance to continue. Another moment passed. He was preoccupied again.

"She plays with my cousin Alice on that netball team."

It was the woman from the church in Bushwick. My interest was now somewhat aroused.

"You mean Jeannette?"

"Yeah, she's been asking my cousin questions about you."

"Like what?"

"Let me finish up in here first? Then I'll tell you."

I wanted to strangle him. Lance emerged from the bathroom five minutes later. He picked up his roller from the paint tray and resumed his work. I still had to let at least another ten minutes elapse before I was going back into that bathroom.

"So?" I asked.

Lance turned around and looked at me funny.

"Oh, yeah. Jeannette wanted to know if you were married."

"If I was married?"

I beamed with pride as I asked that question. Like any other man, I was flattered that a nice looking woman had shown interest in me.

"You might wanna check her out."

"And why is that?"

"Alice says that she's a real nice sister. She don't drink, she don't smoke, nothing."

"Any kids?" I asked cautiously.

"Nope."

I arrived early at worship service the next time, and I didn't have to wait too long before I was able to get inside. The church was filled to capacity once again and the sermon was just as motivating as before. I scanned all the pews around me as best as I could, but I wasn't able to locate Jeannette Charles anywhere. I walked out of the church after service was over in high spirits regardless, since I had received another uplifting message. Once I crossed the street I heard an angelic voice call my name.

"Nice to see you again, Javier."

I glanced back behind me and there stood Jeannette Charles, smiling and looking radiant. She held a choir robe in her hands, which explained why I hadn't seen her inside earlier. I hadn't even thought about looking for her in the choir stand.

"Nice to see you, too," I replied as I crossed the street to greet her.

The January weather was still cold and breezy, so Jeannette and I chatted briefly while I walked her to her car. During that brief time, I learned that Miss Charles taught school not too far away from her church, and that she lived in Jamaica, Queens. She also drove a fairly new, silver Toyota Camry.

When Jeannette asked me if I would be returning to service soon, I told her that in all likelihood I would be. Even though I wanted to, I didn't feel that church was the right place for me to be hitting on Jeannette for her phone number. So I didn't.

I found myself thinking about Jeannette often during the next week in spite of my new mandate concerning women. I wasn't looking for another sister to become emotionally involved with. But since Jeannette was involved in the church I wondered if perhaps she was a gift from above?

After work that following Friday, I found myself driving about in Brooklyn with no particular place to go in mind. I decided to drive out to East Flatbush. Thirty minutes later, I was cruising by the middle school where Jeannette's netball team held its matches and practices.

Lance had told me what days of the week the teams practiced when we picked his cousin Alice up previously. I spotted Jeannette's car parked along the street. I parked Jada and went inside.

They were still doing stretching exercises when I walked into the gymnasium. If Jeannette was surprised to see me there, she didn't show it. She merely acknowledged me with a slight nod of her head and a little smile.

Jeannette didn't fare too badly in practice. Lance's cousin, however, dominated the court. During their scrimmage game, Alice made every one of the shots she took. I shook my head in pity for her lack of beauty again when she and Jeannette came out of the locker room after practice was over. They walked over to where I was still sitting, both with mischievous smiles on their faces.

"Hello. What brings you out here?" Jeannette asked. (She was still dripping in sweat, which turned me on.)

"I was kinda sorta in the neighborhood."

"Yeah, right."

"Hi, Javier."

"Hello, Alice."

"You seen my cousin lately?"

"As a matter of fact, I'm going to see him tomorrow."

"Tell him I said to give me a call?"

"Will do."

Alice then turned to Jeanette.

"I'll see you at the game tomorrow. Later, Javier."

With that, Alice left the gym. I didn't know exactly what to say to Jeanette, but I knew that I had to say something and quick.

"So...you guys have a game tomorrow?"

"Yeah. It's at three-thirty. You can come out if you want to."

"I'd like to, but I'll be working with Alice's cousin."

"Then I'll see you in church on Sunday?"

I slowly shook my head no.

"I'll still be working with Lance. I'll be there next Sunday though, for sure."

"Okay, great."

There was a moment of awkward silence between us.

"Well," Jeanette began, "I guess I'd better get going now."

"Leaving so soon?"

I tried not to let the disappointment I felt show on my face.

"Yes, I am. I have to be at Bible study by eight. You're more than welcome to come along if you want to?"

I was fine with going to church on Sunday mornings, but I hadn't quite graduated to attending any Bible studies yet.

"I'll have to take a rain check on that one," I told Jeanette as I got off the bleachers to follow her outside.

"Is it possible to see you again before next Sunday?" I asked, throwing caution to the wind.

"You can always come out here to practice."

"Besides practice?"

"I'm really very busy."

Under normal circumstances, I would have let a conversation like that end right then and there. Whenever a sister told me that she was busy and didn't have the time to see me, all bets were off. However, something in my gut told me to continue in my pursuit of Jeanette. I watched her climb into her car.

"Is there a phone number where you can be reached at?"

I was going for broke. Jeanette sat still for a few seconds before opening her glove compartment and pulling out a scrap piece of paper. I fought to hold back a smile as she jotted down her phone number on the paper and handed it to me.

"I'm usually in by nine each evening, except for Fridays."

"Thank you, Ma'am. I'll keep that in mind."

I finished up my gig with Lance the next day around seven-thirty. By the time I got home and cleaned myself up, it was after nine. Since I wasn't going out anywhere that night, I decided to call Jeanette. When I called her number, she answered on the second ring.

"Praise His name."

I was taken aback by Jeannette's greeting. This girl was definitely serious about the church. It took me a second or two to regain my composure.

"Hello, Jeanette. This is Javier."

"Hey! How are you doing?" Jeanette sounded truly thrilled to hear from me.

"I'm okay. I'm just calling to see how you were doing."

"That was thoughtful of you."

"How did the game go today?"

"We lost," she said sullenly.

"Sorry to hear that."

"It was a close game though. Alice played really good."

"You sound kind of down about losing, Jeanette, and I don't like that. How about I take you out to eat tomorrow afternoon?"

"Aren't you working tomorrow?"

"I should be finished by three. I could pick you up around five?"

I held my breath as I awaited Jeanette's answer.

"I don't know. I have some school papers to grade this weekend."

I would not be denied, at least not without a fight.

"Let me ask you a question, Jeannette."

"Go ahead."

"Do you eat seafood?"

"I love it."

"So you're not game for a ride out to City Island?"

(For those of you who don't know, City Island is a strip of land located off the very northeastern section of the Bronx that is over-populated with tasty seafood eateries.)

"I didn't say that."

That was my cue.

"So what are you trying to say, then?"

Jeanette was silent for a few seconds. My heart fluttered wildly while I waited for her to respond. I had heard from Lance about how this woman had been asking questions about me and what not, now was the time for her to show if she was really interested.

"Could you make it around six?" she asked.

"I certainly can, Jeanette."

I left for Jeanette's house forty minutes early the next day to allow myself some time for disorientation. This was because I got lost every time I drove to Queens by myself. There are too many damn one-way streets in that borough. Even with the thorough directions that Jeanette had given me, I was lost in no time at all. After riding around aimlessly for twenty minutes or so, I pulled out my cell phone and called her.

"Praise His name..."

"Jeanette?"

"Mr. Collins?"

"Yeah."

"Where are you?" Jeanette asked.

"Lost!"

"Tell me where you are and I'll come get you."

Jeanette's Camry pulled up in front of me about fifteen minutes later. She smiled as she rolled her window down.

"Follow me."

"Do I have any other choice?"

We were in her driveway within ten minutes. Jeanette parked her car and then climbed into Jada with me.

"See, you weren't that far away," she said, trying to console me.

"I hate Queens!"

"Don't say that."

"It's the truth."

Jeanette pointed me in the direction of the Robert F. Kennedy Bridge and we were on our way. The Fish Emporium was Jeanette's favorite restaurant on City Island, so we went there. The restaurant's decor seemed kind of tacky to me with lots of plastic fish hanging on the walls everywhere.

The wait for our order was impressively short. After a rather lengthy grace from Jeanette, we proceeded to eat. Jeanette nibbled on blackened catfish while I dug into some crab legs. The food was quite delicious.

"Good, right?" Jeanette asked.

"Not bad at all."

We dined in silence for a while as we savored our meals.

"Can I ask you a personal question, Mr. Collins?"

Hearing that question coming from a black woman always made me uneasy. This time was no different.

"Only if you call me, Javier."

"Deal."

"What's the question?"

"How come you're not married yet?"

I nearly choked on a piece of my crab leg. A sister bringing up questions concerning marriage on their initial date with you was not a good sign. Not at all.

"I guess...because I haven't run across anyone yet who I consider to be wife material."

"And what exactly do you consider to be 'wife material'?"

I knew that shit was coming! I should have chosen my answer more carefully. I couldn't afford to dig myself in a hole any deeper. I decided to do what anyone did whenever they were trying to avoid trouble...play dumb.

"I'm not certain what it is to be honest with you, Jeanette."

"But don't you have any idea what you're looking for?"

Jeanette had stopped eating completely. She leaned slightly over the table towards me as she awaited my answer. I was determined not to give her one.

"Not really. I guess I'll know it when I see it."

Jeanette seemed disappointed by my evasive response. I felt bad about it too, but I knew way better than to continue that type of discussion on a first date.

"Now, let me ask you a personal question."

Jeanette's eyes brightened up.

"What do you wish to know?"

"How long have you been teaching school?"

My subtle attempt to change the subject worked. Jeanette was more than happy to talk about the misadventures of teaching in New York City.

This was the beginning of a series of frequent dates between Jeanette and me. We went out as much as possible. I was still working regularly with Lance at the time so that I could put some money in the bank. Therefore, I was driving myself at a pretty hectic pace.

I took Jeanette to the movies and we went out often for dinner after church service on Sundays. And whenever feasible, I traveled to watch Jeanette play netball. Sometimes Lance and I rode out together to see a game or two if we didn't have any work lined up for us.

I was really happy about the direction that my life was going. So much so in fact, that I called Daddy up one weekend to inform him that I was following his recommendations.

"That's good to hear, son," Daddy said with a chuckle. "When am I going to get to meet this Jeanette person?"

"I might drive down with her one weekend, when the weather gets a little warmer."

"I look forward to meeting her."

"How the women treating you down there?" I asked Daddy.

"Hold on son, I got another call..."

Daddy clicked over to answer his other phone call. He clicked back to me a few seconds later.

"I gotta run, son. I got some personal business to take care of."

"Some monkey business, I bet," I unwisely said.

"You trying to get smart with me, boy!"

"Sir! No Sir!"

"I didn't think so! You know what I can do! Right?"

"Sir! Yes Sir."

"And that's what?!"

"Take my ass out, Sir!"

"Alright then! And say a prayer in church for me the next time you go, dammit! Bye!"

When will I ever learn? I asked myself as I hung my phone up.

CHAPTER EIGHTEEN

By the time March rolled around, Jeanette and I had been dating for about three months and things were going great. Well, just about. I only had one complaint about Jeannette. It was a small issue, but it was a valid gripe nonetheless.

I was known to a lot of the members of Jeanette's church as her boyfriend. Plenty of older sisters in the congregation would often stop us and tell us what a good-looking couple we made.

Whenever this happened, I would merely smile, thank the person, and try to move on. Jeanette, however, seemed to bask in delight every time this event occurred. She would always take my hand and hold it tight, as if we were posing for a photo-op.

Ever since I was first invited into Jeanette's home and saw the numerous wedding magazines that she kept around her house, I knew what her agenda was. I always told myself that I could eventually see myself marrying her, on down the road. Marriage was certainly nothing to be rushing into.

Jeanette, on the other hand, seemed to be just a little bit *too* eager to get married. She was constantly hounding me with questions. How many kids I would like to have? Where would I like to live at if I were married? What was my idea of the perfect honeymoon? There were dozens of others. Jeannette would ask me these questions so innocently that I could never get upset with her.

This was the issue that was on my mind one Sunday morning as I was dressing for church. While trying to adjust my tie, the phone rang. It was Lance. He had an emergency and needed me to help him finish a paint job. (I found out later that the other helper, who had started the job with him, had gotten stoned the night before and his wife couldn't wake him up.)

I quickly called Jeanette and told her what had happened. She was a little disappointed at first, but she said that she understood. Jeanette also informed me that her mother had cooked a special dinner in my honor, and that I should try to be at their house by four o'clock. I told her that would not be a problem.

After finishing my paint job with Lance, I hurried back home and washed up. Looking at the alarm clock on my nightstand, I saw that it was a little after three. I hurriedly put on a gray dress shirt, a nice pair of gray slacks to match, and my pair of brand-new black loafers. I then threw on a light jacket and rushed from my room.

I passed by Tucker in the kitchen. He was drinking some type of health shake concoction that he'd been making lately to help him lose some of the flab from around his stomach. (It didn't appear to be working that much.)

"My, don't we look cute. Where you off to?"

"Not that it's any of your business, but Jeanette's mother made dinner for me."

Tucker looked at me strangely as I headed towards the front door.

"Dinner? At her mom's?"

"That's right," I replied proudly.

"Anybody else coming?"

Tucker seemed highly curious about something. What it was though, I didn't have a clue.

"Not that I know of."

"What's she serving you guys for dinner?"

"I don't know. What's with all the questions?"

Once again, an odd look appeared on Tucker's face.

"Brother, don't you know?"

"Know about what, Tucker?"

A look of amusement came over Tucker's face.

"You really don't know, do you?"

"Know what, Tucker?" I was not in the mood for one of his capers at the moment.

"I thought you said your Daddy talked to you about the facts of life?"

"You know what, dude? I'll see you later," I hissed as I continued towards the front door.

"J.C., wait! This is serious!"

Tucker followed me into the living room with his health shake in his hand. I turned around.

"What's serious?"

"No one has ever explained to you the clandestine significance of, *The Negro Sunday Dinner?* "

I looked at Tucker as if he were speaking Russian.

"Come sit down and I'll explain it to you quickly."

"Can't this wait until I get back?"

"It just might be too late by then."

"*What* might be too late?"

Tucker sat down in our easy chair and motioned for me to do the same. I sighed softly as I walked over and sat on the couch.

"Listen," Tucker began, "in the black community, there is the age-old tradition of sisters inviting their boyfriends over to eat Sunday dinner..."

"So?" I interjected.

"Will you let me finish, dammit?!"

"Sorry."

"Anyway, what a lot of brothers out there don't know is, this is a trap to get you into girlfriend's family...as in marriage."

"Say what?" I asked. (Tucker never ceased to amaze me with some of the stupid things that he could come up with.)

"It's a trap to get you married. If you ever go to your girl's mama house to eat dinner with her and her family on a Sunday, and they're serving you fried chicken, don't eat it! Get out of there quick!"

I sat there for a whole minute observing Tucker, waiting for him to crack a smile. He didn't. He was actually serious.

"What kind of racist bullshit is that?"

I hadn't meant to curse. I had promised myself that I would stop swearing, especially on Sundays, but Tucker had a way of finding the right buttons to push.

"It's not bullshit; it's the truth! If Jeanette's mom is over there with other family members, and they're serving fried chicken, don't eat it! If you do, then you've just unknowingly consented to join the family."

"Who told you this shit, Tucker?" (Dammit! I had cursed again.)

"My Pops," Tucker stated proudly. "The men in the Tucker family have passed this information down to their sons for generations."

I knew better than to pay Tucker any attention, but I just had to ask him a couple of questions to see how sick he really was.

"Is it only fried chicken?"

"Yup."

"Why is that?"

"None of the men in my family really know, but personally, I think it has something to do with the grease it's cooked in."

"What if it's baked chicken?"

"Then you're cool."

"What about eating a fried chicken meal with them on any other day of the week, except Sunday?"

"You still straight."

"What if it's fried chicken on a Sunday, but no extra family is there?"

"That's kind of iffy. I wouldn't chance it myself."

"Let's say that I do eat this particular meal along with Jeanette's family on a Sunday, but I refuse to marry her?"

Tucker looked at me seriously.

"That doesn't happen. You join the family, or else."

"Or else? Or else what?"

"They kill you," Tucker whispered.

"Get the fuck out of here!"

(I was on a roll with the profanity.)

"It's true, J.C.! Remember my cousin Sammy Garrick back in Columbia? He used to live off of Farrow Road, in Greenview?"

"Didn't he mysteriously disappear or something the week before he was supposed to join the Army?"

Tucker sighed deeply as he bowed his head. There was a look of remorse on his face.

"Guess where he ate dinner the Sunday before he finally told his girl that he had enlisted in the service and had to ship out to Texas?"

"Quit bullshitting me!"

"We tried to warn Cuz what he was up against, but he wouldn't listen to us. Sammy thought he had made a clean break from that sister. He was dead wrong." A lone teardrop fell from Tucker's left eye.

It was time for me to leave. However, I had one more question.

"What about you and Paris?"

"Yeah, her family did it to me...only after I was ready for them to."

"Thanks for the information," I said sarcastically to my roommate as I opened the front door.

"If you don't believe me J.C., go ask any brother who's married. He'll tell you that it happened to him too!" Tucker yelled after me.

Jeanette's mom lived above Jeanette in her own apartment, so I didn't have to worry about getting lost in Queens again. I laughed all the way over to the Charles' residence at Tucker's silly forewarning. When I pulled up in front of Jeanette's house, her driveway was already filled with several cars. I found a park in the street. As I walked towards the house, I could hear some of the commotion that was going on inside. It sounded like a serious party.

After I rang the doorbell, I silently cursed myself because I was supposed to stop by the grocery store and pick up some ice cream.

Preoccupied with Tucker's damn foolishness, I had totally forgotten. Jeanette's mother answered her door.

"Hi, Javier!"

"Hello, Ma'am."

"Come on upstairs. Everybody's been waiting to meet you," Lucille Charles said with a wide grin.

When I walked inside Mrs. Charles' apartment, I saw there were twelve other people in the room that I had never seen before. (I knew that none of the men in the room was Jeanette's father. She had told me when we first began dating that he lived somewhere in Florida and was not on good terms with her mother.) Everyone in the room stopped talking and stared at me.

"Everybody, this is Javier Collins."

"Hello, folks," I said weakly.

"Javier, this is my family. Now, I want you to go on around the room and meet everybody. And don't be shy because like I said, we're all family up in here. Dinner will be ready shortly."

I scanned the room and noticed that Jeanette was nowhere in sight.

"Uh, where's Jeanette?" I asked Mrs. Charles before she could take a single step away from me.

"She ran out to get some batteries for her camera. She'll be back soon. Now, go on and mingle."

"I, uh, forgot to buy the ice cream, Mrs. Charles. Maybe I should go back out and get some?"

"Nonsense, son. The important thing is that you're here. Now, go on and mingle!"

Mrs. Charles grabbed my hand and pulled me towards her nearest relative before she hurried off to her kitchen. I felt like the neighborhood thief when he was in his local bodega. Under close surveillance. I was in the middle of meeting the last of Jeanette's family, an older female cousin from Staten Island, when Jeanette finally arrived. I was ecstatic to see her. I excused myself from cousin Thelma, or whatever her name was, and walked over to greet Jeanette.

"Well, look who's finally here."

"Hi, Javier."

We hugged each other lightly.

"What's all of this?" I discreetly whispered into Jeanette's ear as we embraced.

"Just a little family get together," she answered nonchalantly.

"You call this little?"

"It's nothing. Relax."

No matter how hard I tried, I couldn't make myself feel comfortable. Something about this whole scenario had me feeling just a little bit edgy. As much as I hated to admit it, Tucker's little caution kept haunting me.

"Are you okay, Javier? You seem to be jittery," Jeanette asked me with concern in her voice.

"I'm fine, just a little tired."

At that exact moment, Mrs. Charles walked back into the room. She grinned happily when she saw Jeannette and me standing together.

"Dinner's ready, everyone. Let's wash our hands so we can eat."

I waited my turn to go into the bathroom and wash my hands. When it came, I quickly closed the bathroom door and glanced at myself in the mirror. I looked like a nervous wreck.

"Get a grip here, Javier! You know better than to believe anything that Tucker tells you!" There was a loud knock on the door.

"Is everything alright in there, Harvey?"

It was Jeanette's Uncle Pete from Mount Vernon. He had obviously heard me talking to myself.

"Yes Sir! Be right out!"

Uncle Pete eyed me cautiously as I exited the bathroom. When I walked into Mrs. Charles' huge kitchen, I saw that she had the table laid out with an extensive array of food. There was cabbage, macaroni, cornbread, greens, peas, rice, buttered rolls, cranberry sauce, and two huge pans of lasagna!

"You, you made lasagna?" I asked Mrs. Charles happily.

"Yes, I did," she said proudly.

I felt as if a heavy burden had been suddenly snatched from my shoulders.

"You like lasagna, Javier?"

"More than you'll ever know, Ma'am!"

"Great. I'll have to make you some one-day. These here are for Jeanette's class tomorrow. They're having a big party. I've got something else cooked up for you."

My heart sank as Mrs. Charles put the pans of lasagna in her refrigerator. She then reached over to her oven door and yanked it open. Sitting up in there was a large tray of chicken, all of it fried.

"Now, I made all of this especially for you, so I want you to eat up. Okay, son?"

Mrs. Charles smiled at me. I was still in stunned silence.

"Okay, Javier?" Mrs. Charles repeated.

I looked around the room and noticed that everybody was watching me again.

"Yes," I answered submissively.

My brain was churning furiously. There was no way I was going to eat Mrs. Charles' cooking. I still didn't believe what Tucker had told me earlier, but I couldn't afford to take any chances either. The coincidences were too scary to ignore completely. We all sat down at a large table that actually consisted of two tables joined together. I was seated between Jeanette and her mother.

"Would you care to say the grace, Javier?" Mrs. Charles asked me.

I didn't see any problem with praying at the moment.

"Dear God," I began, "please help me…I mean bless me, and all of the other people who are gathered around this table, as we prepare to enjoy this meal that was so thoughtfully prepared by your servants."

Some of Jeanette's relatives called out "Amens" and began to raise their heads, but I wasn't quite finished yet.

"And Heavenly Father," I continued, "please look out for me…I mean us, as we go about our life's journeys. We know that there is *nothing* in this world that you cannot do! And finally Father, please deliver me…I mean us, from evil, as you know it lurks all around me! I mean us! These and other blessings we ask in your precious name, *please!?* Amen."

When I finally raised my head from my prayer, I found all eyes on me yet again.

"Well, that was some grace there, Harvey. Can't say I ever heard one put like that before," Jeanette's Uncle Pete stated, breaking the silence.

"Dig in, folks," Mrs. Charles said.

While the members of the Charles' family attacked the food that was set before them, I waited to see if by chance all of the chicken would be gone before I had to eat any of it. It didn't happen. There was still plenty left. I piled my tray up with everything except bird, hoping no one would notice that I didn't have any. Just as I was about to raise a fork full of rice to my mouth, Mrs. Charles called me out.

"Don't move, Javier!"

I froze as instructed. I slowly glanced over and saw a large two-pronged pitchfork-like utensil in her hand, like the red one the devil carries. Mrs. Charles stabbed three huge pieces of chicken with her cutlery and placed them onto my plate.

"You forgot to get yourself some of my chicken," Mrs. Charles informed me with a smile. I grinned at her sheepishly.

"Sorry about that."

I closed my eyes and thought real hard. As mentioned previously, I had always depended on my evasive instincts to get me out of jams during my quarterbacking days at S.C. State. As I sat there at the Charles' dinner table, I was desperately summoning them up again. After a moment or two, I picked my fork back up and ate my rice. I then started to cough badly.

"Are you okay?" Jeanette asked me with concern.

My coughing continued.

"Here, drink something," Mrs. Charles suggested as she held out a glass of iced tea to me.

I took the glass and drank from it. I then began to cough even harder.

"Excuse me for a minute, folks..."

I stood up from my chair and walked out of the kitchen. I then walked to the bathroom, where I pulled out my cell phone and began dialing. Tucker answered on the third ring.

"What's up, roomie?"

"Call me back in five minutes."

"What?"

"Don't ask questions. Call me back in five minutes."

"Why?"

"Just do it!" I snapped before ending my call.

After flushing the toilet a few times for good measure, I returned to the kitchen.

"Are you alright?" Jeanette asked me when I sat back down.

"I'm okay. Something went down the wrong pipe."

I was taking a bite from my cornbread when my cell phone rang. I pulled it out of my shirt pocket and looked to see who it was calling.

"Excuse me, again," I announced to everyone as I stood from the table and stepped into the nearby hallway. I flipped my cell phone open and then closed it back shut while en route.

"Hello? Are you serious? I'll be right there!" I yelled. I then turned my cell phone off before I walked back into the kitchen with a look of alarm on my face.

"What's wrong?" Jeanette asked with genuine concern.

"My roommate said that there's been a flooding accident at the house. I need to leave now."

Jeanette was crestfallen. Mrs. Charles was clearly upset by the news as well.

"Aw, can't you wait until you at least finish eating first, son?"

"He told me that I should really get over there right away, Ma'am. Our commode just exploded. Sorry."

"You wanna take your plate with you?" Mrs. Charles asked.

"No! I mean, that's okay."

"I insist," Mrs. Charles said as she stood up. "It won't take me but a minute to wrap it up for you. Now you wait right here."

I did as instructed. I said goodbye to all of Jeanette's family as her mother wrapped my plate up. Jeanette walked me to the front door.

"I'm really sorry about this, Jeanette. I'll call you later on."

"Okay. I hope everything's alright."

"It is now…I mean…I'm sure it will be. Bye."

On my drive home, my conscience got the better of me and I began to feel guilty about what I had just done. The further away from Jeanette's house I drove, the guiltier I felt.

There was no use for me to put it off any longer; I had to make amends. When I drove up to the stoplight at the intersection of Hillside Avenue and Queens Boulevard, I spied a homeless woman rummaging through a pile of discarded boxes on the corner. I blew my horn at her to get her attention. When she looked up at me, I motioned for her to come over. The woman smiled with her stained teeth as she approached me. When she reached my driver's side window and held out her hand for some money, I placed the wrapped-up plate of food that Mrs. Charles had given me in her palm instead.

The woman looked at me with surprise as she opened the package and saw what was in it.

"Gee, thanks!"

"You're welcome. Enjoy."

When I walked into my front door, I found Tucker cuddled up on the couch with some young lady. They were passionately kissing away on each other. The television set was tuned to the Knicks and Pacers game, but the two of them seemed more interested in playing one-on-one with each other. They took a timeout, however, when they heard me shut the door hard behind me. I smiled at the young lady and she smiled back. She must have been one of Tucker's new clients, as I had never seen her before.

"Sorry to interrupt, folks."

As I walked across the room, Tucker glanced at his watch.

"Yo, ain't we back kinda early? And what was that weird phone call you made to me all about?"

"I don't wanna talk about it!" I growled before continuing down the hall to my room.

I called Jeanette later on that evening and apologized once again for having to leave so abruptly. When she asked me what I thought about her mother's fried chicken, I honestly told her that I had never tasted anything like it. Jeanette then began discussing her family with me. She made it a point to tell me that from the short period of time that I was around them, I had left a favorable impression with most of the clan; the lone dissenter being Uncle Pete.

We talked a little while longer and then Jeanette told me that she had to finish wrapping presents for her classroom's upcoming party. She also reminded me once again not to miss her big netball game that was coming up that next weekend. I told her that I'd be there for certain.

CHAPTER NINETEEN

I arrived at East Flatbush High around four o'clock. The streets were lined with cars for blocks around. Jeanette's team had made it to the final round of the championship tournament and was now playing last year's champions, a squad from the Wakefield section of the Bronx. By some strange coincidence, every game of Jeanette's that I had attended they had won. So quite naturally, she wanted me to be in the crowd for the finals. The league officials had moved the championship game to the high school gym because it was bigger, and could hold more people.

Unfortunately, it wasn't big enough. I had to stand among the crowd on the floor because all of the bleachers were already filled to capacity. Hundreds of spectators had turned out to witness the final game.

Jeanette's opponents opened the contest with seven unanswered baskets before anybody knew what had happened. That's when Lance's cousin went to work. Playing the goal shooter position for her team, Alice operated like she was possessed. Every time she touched the ball down under the opposing team's basket, she scored. Girlfriend was so dominating that people in the crowd starting chanting "Alice!!! Alice!!!" whenever she got the ball. The whole team rallied behind Alice's performance and by half time, Jeanette's team was down by only four baskets. I spied Lance walking through the door during half time.

"You just getting here?" I asked him.

"Yeah. How's Alice doing?"

"She's getting off out there."

"Good. How about Jeanette?"

"She's been struggling a little."

That was putting it mildly. Jeanette played the other shooting position for her team, goal attack, and had started the game off by shooting four or five bricks at the basket.

During the second half of the contest, however, she redeemed herself by making a couple of shots. Jeanette's defensive game picked up as well and she intercepted two passes late in the game. With less than half a minute left to play, Jeanette's team was still down by a basket. Her coach called a timeout.

I was impressed by the intensity displayed on each of the player's faces as they huddled around their coach on the sideline. When Jeanette's team put the ball back in play, they went straight to their bread and butter, Alice. As soon as Alice caught the pass, she turned and shot it straight into the basket. The game was tied.

On the ensuing play, Alice's opponent accidentally knocked the ball out of bounds when she took her eyes off a pass. Jeanette's team received the ball once more and Alice was called on once again. This time, however, she was guarded tightly and was outside of the shooting perimeter when she received the ball and could not shoot at the basket. That's when Jeanette ran streaking towards the basket and called for the ball. Alice hit her with a perfect pass, and Jeanette stopped and threw the ball up in the air. It went in and they won.

Lance and I exchanged high fives as we went crazy along with the rest of the crowd. I'd never seen a person look as happy as Jeanette was when her teammates mobbed her in the middle of the court. I thought that she would be crushed as teammate after teammate piled on top of her.

"You played great, girl," I told Jeanette as we waited for our food to be served.

"I did, didn't I?"

The team had decided to celebrate their victory by going out to dinner. I didn't want to inhibit Jeanette's celebration with her teammates and told her that I would see her later. She insisted that I tag along, so Lance and I met the team later that night at Chez Sherry's, the popular soul food restaurant on Myrtle Avenue.

"You are way too modest," I teased.

"I am, aren't I?"

We both laughed. Jeanette was sipping on a glass of wine from one of the bottles that a teammate's husband had bought to help liven up the celebration. I was somewhat surprised when she accepted the drink. I got myself a glass of brew so that Jeanette wouldn't feel too conscious about drinking by herself. (As if I needed a good reason to drink beer?)

The wine definitely helped to perk things up. Everyone was having a good time. When our party's food arrived, however, our table was suddenly silent as everyone went to work on their plates. I devoured a generous helping of meat loaf, new potatoes, cornbread stuffing, and green beans that tasted excellent. I was quite full by the time it came to leave for home. I paid for Jeanette's meal along with mine and then kissed her on the cheek.

"Goodnight, Jeanette. I'll call you tomorrow."

"Where are you going?" she asked, looking puzzled.

"Home. You know we've got church in the morning."

Jeanette looked a little dismayed.

"I thought that maybe you could come over and hang out for a little while."

She gave a demure, yet still alluring grin as she spoke.

"It is getting kind of late, Jeanette."

(Actually, the truth of the matter was that I was stuffed and wanted to crawl into my bed and go to sleep.)

"Come on, Javier, I won't keep you up too late. I promise."

While I stood there looking at Jeanette and wondering how to politely decline her offer, Lance tapped me from behind. He was standing next to me and had overheard my conversation. I turned around and faced him.

"You 'bout to blow it, mon," he hissed to me. "The woman wants some *company!* Give it to her."

It was a little after ten when we arrived at Jeanette's house. I figured that I'd sit with her and watch television for about an hour or so, and then take myself home. My plans were changed when Jeanette grabbed me by the arm and pulled me onto the couch with her as soon as we walked into her living room.

"I've been waiting to do this all night," Jeanette said to me as she began to smother my face with tiny, hot kisses.

In the past, Jeanette and I had done some heavy kissing and what have you, but I had always managed to cool it down with her before I became too excited. I knew Jeanette was deeply involved in the church, and committing fornication with her was out of the picture. Plus, I was on my way to embracing religion as well, and could do without any extra temptations.

All of my morals went out the door when Jeanette grabbed my manhood and roughed it up playfully. This behavior from her was totally unexpected. I pulled away from her loving embrace and eyed her suspiciously.

"You're tipsy, aren't you?"

"Of course not!" she giggled.

"Yes, you are," I said as I stood up from the couch.

"What's wrong, Javier?"

"I'm going home because you don't know what you're doing."

I tried to appear noble as hell while I spoke to Jeanette. I would have loved nothing better than to see her butt naked instead, but once again, she was a Christian and I was trying to become one. I also was aware of the fact that I didn't have any condoms on me. I was almost certain that Jeanette didn't keep any around her house.

"For the last time, I'm not drunk, Javier. Can't a woman do what she wants to in her own home?"

Jeanette grabbed me by my arm and pulled me back down onto the couch with her. We began kissing intensely once more. After about ten minutes or so, Jeanette stood up. She pulled me up to my feet as well. We both were silent as she then guided me back into her bedroom.

"I think we've waited long enough," Jeanette said as she took off the silk blouse she was wearing.

"Uh, not so fast Jeanette. If we're going to do this, then it has to be done right. I need to run out and pick up some protection."

Jeanette remained silent as she walked over to her nightstand and retrieved a brand new pack of Trojans from out of the drawer.

"Well I'll be..."

"Now don't get the wrong impression about me, Javier," Jeanette interrupted. "I don't normally buy these things, but I did go out and buy this one pack after you came over here and met my family last weekend."

Needless to say, I was shocked.

"Well, I guess I should say that I'm flattered, Jeanette."

Jeanette continued undressing as she slid her beige linen pants down her long legs and stepped out of them. She then looked at me with an enticing expression on her face.

In the back of my mind, I was hesitant about Jeanette and myself committing the ultimate act of love. But then I reasoned to myself that church folks came into the world just like everybody else did. Right?

I quickly detached myself from the sweater and jeans I was wearing and sat down with Jeanette on her bed. I then reached around under her arms to unfasten her bra. We kissed each other passionately. I made a mental note to myself that if she offered even the slightest bit of resistance that I would stop. Jeanette only kissed me harder as I fumbled with her brassier.

I finally got the annoying thing off her and began to softly massage her perky breasts in my palms. They felt so firm and tempting in my hands that I lowered my head and began sucking ever so gently on the both of them. Jeanette moaned in pure delight as I alternately grabbed each nipple delicately between my teeth.

"Yesss..." she sighed softly.

Jeanette clenched my head and pulled me back up to her lips, where she had a sultry kiss waiting for me. I sucked on her bottom lip for a few delectable moments before venturing off to explore the rest of her body. I slowly kissed my way down her abdomen, licking every inch of it along the way. I took extra time to explore Jeanette's navel with my tongue. She moaned once again in ecstasy as I lapped playfully in it. I licked my way down until I reached the beginnings of her crotch.

On my journey back up to Jeanette's lips however, she grabbed me by the head with both of her hands and shoved my head back down between her legs. Once again, I began to lift my head back up towards Jeanette's face. Once again, she stopped my forward progress and forced me back down between her legs.

"Please, Javier!" Jeanette whispered hotly to me.

That was definitely a no-go. Daddy had always cautioned me that I wasn't supposed to eat anything that did not have a 'sell by' date on it, or wasn't served in a nice restaurant. In my past escapades with females, whenever this situation would present itself, I firmly stated my beliefs on the matter, and usually that was the end of the discussion. I merely made it up to them with a few extra minutes of good, hard loving instead.

"What's the matter?" Jeanette asked inquisitively.

I could tell from her tone of voice that she was trying hard to control her emotions.

"I...I don't do that."

"And why not?"

There was a slight sneer on Jeanette's face.

"I just don't. Never did."

Evidently, that was not a good enough explanation for her.

"What kind of bullshit is that?" Jeanette exclaimed.

I was in total shock! Girlfriend was cussing at me! How she was able to make the sudden transition from a God-fearing good girl to an infuriated female in the bedroom was beyond me. (Or was it?)

"Why are you cursing, Jeanette?"

"Because I'm upset, dammit!"

I tried to think of the proper words to express my views on 'eating out in the bush' as I slid over and sat up beside her on the bed.

"When you come into my bedroom, you supposed to be ready to take that ride downtown on the 'J' train!"

The woman was furious at that point. I really couldn't believe the scenario that was going down.

"Look, Jeanette, don't get so upset. There's nothing wrong with you in particular. I just don't plan to eat down at the 'Y' until I'm married."

"That's going to happen to us one day; so what's the difference?"

I didn't quite understand Jeanette's statement.

"Could you run that by me again?"

Jeanette rolled her eyes as she raised herself up on her elbows and turned to me.

"I said, we're going to get married one day. What's the big deal?"

Evidently, there was a big misunderstanding between Jeanette and me that needed to be cleared up quick, fast, and in a hurry because the last time that I checked I was not anybody's fiancé.

"Married?" I asked in amazement. I was finding it harder to keep my voice calm. Jeanette looked at me as if I were crazy.

"Of course! Why else do you think you'd be in my bedroom now?"

"Who said anything about us getting married?" (As I had stated earlier, I did strongly consider the possibility of marrying Jeanette, but I didn't like for it to be dictated to me. The last time that I recollected, the man was still supposed to ask the woman for her hand first.)

"So what are you trying to say, Javier? You don't want to marry me?"

"I didn't say that, Jeanette."

"Then what's your problem?"

I was way too overwhelmed with the nature of the argument that Jeanette and I had to participate in it.

"You know what? I think you'd better leave," Jeanette stated after I had remained silent for too long.

"I'd better leave? You've got to be kidding!"

She wasn't. Jeanette kicked me out of her bedroom first, and then out of her house as well. I was never so humiliated in all my life. The ride back home was pure torture since I wasn't even able to take a cold shower at Jeannette's place before I had to vacate the premises.

CHAPTER TWENTY

I canceled my plans for going to church in Bushwick the next morning for obvious reasons. Once again, love had thrown a sucker-punch and left me on my butt. The sad part of it all was that I never saw it coming. Jeanette had flipped the script on me.

I wasn't sure if the glass of wine that she drank was fully to blame for her actions or not. If that were the case, I certainly wasn't in any position to condemn Jeanette for her conduct. I had done lots of regrettable things myself after some hard drinking.

The fact that Jeanette automatically assumed that the two of us would be getting married didn't sit too well with me either. I had read often of women who were determined to become a bride and take that stroll down the aisle; Jeanette was living proof.

There was no way in the world that I was going to enter into a permanent relationship with someone who could turn on you like a pit bull. If Jeanette could flip out on me once, she could certainly do it again. Sadly, I concluded that it was best to leave things be.

Instead of going to church service, I went out to the store and re-supplied myself with some cold Guinness. (There was none at the house since I had stopped drinking altogether in my effort to come correct with Jeanette.)

With brew in hand, I sat in my bedroom and hunted through my CD collection until I found my *The Best of Sad Love Songs* disc. I picked Jimmy Ruffin's classic lamentation, '*What Becomes of The Broken Hearted*'. (Daddy liked the oldies so I had to like them, too.) I then sat back on my bed and waited for the music to do its job.

"If you two ever hear me talking about hooking up with another sister again, shoot me!"

Lance, Tucker, and I were at Larry's Lounge sipping on some brew and munching down on a huge plate of hot wings. It was a Friday night. The harsh winter cold had finally disappeared, and we had experienced some pretty pleasant weather the previous few weeks.

I was hanging out with my boys and having a good time. We were raking sisters over the coals at the moment, and I had stated how I felt about them. All of them! As I took a sip from my Guinness, I had a second thought about what I had just said. I gazed over at Tucker, who was eyeing me menacingly.

"You do know that 'shoot me' is just a figure of speech, Tucker?"

He remained eerily silent.

"What the heck happened with Jeanette anyway? You two seemed to be getting along so well."

"She went off on me, Lance."

I was on my fourth brew and my tongue was a tad bit loose. I should have kept my big mouth shut.

"How'd she do that?"

"She cussed me and then kicked me out of her house."

"Why?" Tucker asked.

I had said too much already. It was time to clam up.

"I don't know."

"J.C., you gonna sit here and tell me and Lance that a nice church-going girl like Jeanette just upped and threw you the fuck out of her house? For no reason?"

"Yeah..." I said slowly.

"Come on," Lance coaxed. "You had to have done something?"

Even though I certainly knew better than to tell Lance what actually happened in front of Tucker, I decided to do so anyway. I didn't want to lie to him.

"Actually, she put me out for something that I wouldn't do."

"What?" Tucker butted in.

I was silent as I thought of how best to explain the scenario that had gone down between Jeanette and me. I took another swig from my pint.

"What?" Tucker echoed.

"She got really mad because I wouldn't...she wanted me to...when I refused to..."

"You wouldn't munch her bunch?"

"That's it, Lance."

Lance and Tucker stared at each other with wide grins on their faces. I finished the rest of my pint.

"I told her that I wasn't into all that," I explained defensively.

Tucker looked at me in astonishment.

"And I'm not going to until I get married," I added.

"Boy, you'd better get with the program quick or you ain't never gonna get hitched!" Tucker stated flatly.

Lance nodded his head in agreement. We all sat around the table in awkward silence for a few seconds. I looked over and noticed that Tucker was surveying me again with a sinister look in his eyes. He then cleared his voice and started rapping.

"My girl's Jeanette-and she's my pet-but she won't let-me hit it yet-until I get-my whiskers wet..."

I instantly sprung from my seat and grabbed for him. Lance caught my arm just in the nick of time.

"Let it go, J.C."

"I'm just kidding you, J.C. Damn!" Tucker hissed. "Can't you take a little joke?"

"Not from you!"

I got up and stormed out of Larry's.

Sensing that I was still a little down about my breakup with Jeanette, Lance called me that next Friday and invited me out to watch the big fight. The ex-champ was coming out from prison again, and would be going up against the current heavyweight titleholder. At first, I told Lance no because I didn't feel up to it. When he told me he would be taking care of all of the refreshment expenses as well, I changed my mind quickly. Against my wishes, Tucker chose to tag along with us.

Nobody was showing the fight. We rode around for a whole hour, stopping at nearly every black bar in Brooklyn to try to watch the fight. Evidently, none of the bar owners thought that it was worth it to order the match on pay-per-view.

"This is ridiculous!" I said as we left yet another lounge that wasn't showing the bout.

"Everybody's suggesting we drive to Manhattan," Tucker said.

"Well, if we're going, we'd better head out now because the main event's about to start," Lance stated.

I personally didn't feel like riding into Manhattan. We would be sitting in traffic forever, and the fight would probably be over by the time we located a place that was showing it and found a parking space. I was growing desperate.

"I think I know a spot we can catch the fight here in Brooklyn."

"Where?" Lance and Tucker asked in unison.

"You guys might not feel too comfortable there," I warned.

"Do they serve beer?" Tucker asked.

"Plenty."

"Let's go," Lance said.

We drove to an Irish pub that I had visited once before on Court Street, near my job. When we got there, Lance, Tucker, and I could barely squeeze inside; the bar was packed. I was a little surprised to see the number of other brothers who were there. We all gave each other a tacit 'I-see-you-had-to-come-out-to-this-place-to-catch-the-fight-too!' nod.

There were no tables left that we could sit at. We ordered ourselves some beer and then found a spot over by one of the flat screen televisions. The fight ended up being a real good one. The two combatants went at each other from the opening bell. Everyone in the bar was cheering his fighter on. I was having such a good time that I temporarily forgot about my woes with Jeanette.

As I looked about at all of the drinks that were being served around me, I shook my head in awe. The owner of the place was definitely making some serious money. Lance kept his promise and bought me all the beer I could swallow.

He couldn't drink too much himself, though, because he was our designated driver. Furthermore, as a black man with dreadlocks, the last thing Lance could afford to do was drive around New York City while intoxicated. He was already a suspicious character to some law enforcement personnel.

The champion wound up getting knocked out at the end of the eleventh round. Up until then he had been ahead on points, but had gotten either careless, tired, or both. Whichever the case was, it cost him dearly. The challenger hit him with an uppercut that sent him between the ropes and out of the ring. The crowd went berserk.

"Damn!" Tucker and Lance yelled in unison.

As soon as the fight was over, most of the people of color left the bar. We had to walk six blocks back to where Lance had parked his ride.

"Was that a good fight or what?" Lance asked.

"It sure was!" Tucker said. "I'm glad we were finally able to see it somewhere."

"What did you think, J.C.?"

My thoughts were concentrated elsewhere.

"Did you two see all of those other brothers that were in there?"

"They wanted to see the fight just like we did," Tucker answered.

"That's my point exactly."

"What's your point exactly?" Lance asked.

"There was no place here in Brooklyn where they could hang out and watch the fight."

"No shit, Sherlock," Tucker said.

I stopped and turned to my roommate.

"Don't you get it, Tucker?"

Tucker looked at me in total confusion.

"The next time you're buying your boy drinks, Lance, make sure I'm not around. I hate it when he gets drunk and starts talking in damn riddles."

"What are you getting at, mon?" Lance inquired.

"Brooklyn doesn't have a decent sports bar where the brothers can hang out. You either have to go over to Manhattan, or integrate somebody else's spot around here."

"And you're bringing up all of this to say what?" Tucker asked.

"I'm bringing this up to say that whomever opens a place around here for the brothers would probably make lots and lots of money."

Tucker's expression changed up when he heard his favorite three words: *lots of money.*

"I think you've actually got something valid there, roomie."

"I figured that you would, Tucker."

Lance turned and looked at the two of us.

"Are you two thinking about opening up a sports bar?"

Tucker and I looked at each other and grinned simultaneously.

The die was cast. Tucker and I sat down over the next three weeks and sketched out a business plan for our new enterprise. What we ultimately wanted to create was an establishment where black people could get together and socialize in a warm, friendly, and safe environment. Patrons would be able to enjoy good food and drink, while watching any sporting event they desired.

Tucker had previously put the word out to a couple of real estate brokers that he knew to look out for any possible locations for a second House of Pork. What we decided to do was to open a sports bar that would serve his food.

We also agreed that one of the criteria we would use in selecting a site for our business was that we would be able to buy the building that we were located in. We didn't want to open up a successful operation and then have the landlord jack our lease up on us when it was time to renew. I had seen that done to other businesses several times since I had been in Brooklyn. The proprietors had to either shell out the new exorbitant amount of rent, because they didn't want to relocate their already flourishing business, or move elsewhere and hope that their clientele would follow them to their new location.

To purchase our own building, Tucker and I would have to come up with some serious money for a down payment. We estimated that this would take at least $90,000 dollars. I knew Tucker already had a nice-sized savings account on him, even though he cried broke every chance he got.

I had some money saved up myself from my job at Human Resources, as well as from the numerous gigs that I did with Lance. But the dough I had was nowhere near the size of Tucker's bankroll. I wasn't too stressed about the issue, however, because I knew that I could count on Daddy to have my back financially.

Miraculously, within a month of hunting around, one of Tucker's real estate brokers located an ideal location for us. It was a former Mexican restaurant that was situated on the corner of Dekalb Avenue and St. Felix. The business had gone under and the bank that held the deed to the building was already overwhelmed with foreclosed properties. They were more than willing to bargain with us.

The building we chose was a large elongated brownstone that had been converted for the purpose of cooking and serving meals.

That meant there was plenty of open space inside the structure for what we had in mind.

The kitchen was located at the rear of the first floor and was ideal for Tucker to produce his barbecue creations. The rest of the first floor would be our dining area. The second floor had been the main dining area of the previous enterprise, but for our purposes it would be converted into a lounge.

The fact that Tucker already had a prosperous enterprise in operation made it easier for the two of us to take out a minority business loan for our joint venture. We decided early on that Tucker would be in charge of the administrative aspects of our project. He would be responsible for securing all of the necessary licenses and permits that we would need to build and operate our business. I, on the other hand, would be responsible for handling all of the needed renovations. We would share the task of furnishing the place. Of course, Lance was brought onboard to help me out. The first thing we did, once we were handed the keys to the building, was to repaint it. We picked out a shade of tan for the walls, which would be sure to match the black furniture that we planned to buy. Lance and I then installed track lighting along the perimeter of the walls. This would be used to light the artwork and mirrors that we were going to hang throughout the building.

We installed some wooden bookshelves along a large section of the back wall in the lounge area. These we planned to stock with literature from African-American authors. This would help to give our place a rather homey atmosphere.

Next, Lance and I tore up the food-stained carpeting and brought the ancient hardwood floor underneath back to life by refinishing it.

When it came time to furnish the establishment, Tucker and I went to several restaurant bankruptcy auctions to see what we could possibly save some money on. We didn't want to simply go out and run up bills unless it was absolutely necessary. Our luck paid off. We were able to pick up two mahogany antique bars in fairly good condition. They only needed re-varnishing to bring them back up to snuff.

Tucker and I also found some pretty good deals on dining furniture. Black, just like we wanted. We did have to kick out cash for the seven flat screen TVs that we purchased. We put two of them in the dining area and the rest of them upstairs in the lounge. Lance installed the ceiling and wall mounts that we suspended them from. We also purchased five black couches and placed them upstairs in the lounge area as well.

Tucker then hit upon the idea of decorating the lounge with pictures of famous black athletes. We rounded up photographs of Kareem, Magic, The Doctor, Michael Jordon, Ali, Joe Louis, Jackie Robinson, Arthur Ashe, Walter Payton, Doug Williams, Reggie Jackson, Hank Aaron, Tiger Woods, and those fine ass Williams sisters to start off our collection.

Sports memorabilia from some historically black colleges and universities were also suspended from the ceiling, along with baseball jerseys from the old Negro Baseball League that was in existence until the Major League started integrating blacks into their own organizations.

While the renovation process was taking place, Tucker was busy securing our necessary permits. I disagreed with him when he informed me that we would probably have to grease a few palms in order to get things done quickly, but since he offered to take care of this expense himself, I couldn't object but so much.

Even though Tucker and I had sat down and carefully planned and estimated how much it would cost for us to open our doors, I was amazed at how quickly our money disappeared. We spent money on a new stereo system, which Lance and I rigged up throughout the building so that we could have smooth jazz music playing constantly in the background. We had to pay for the satellite system installation, new security system installation, and the dispensing system for our draft beers.

More money was spent for advertising, cleaning supplies, food stock...the list went on and on. I understood then why so many people were hesitant about starting their own business endeavors. Tucker constantly reassured me that everything we spent money on was necessary and would prove its worth in the long run.

We hired a staff of twenty for starters, including Lance's three-hundred-plus pound cousin, Tank, as our full-time greeter/security person. Tank's main responsibilities were to welcome patrons to our establishment while keeping an eye out for under-aged drinkers and knuckleheads.

Another Level Sports Café officially opened for business during the last Saturday in the month of August. We came up with the name 'Another Level' because you had to take a few steps down in order to enter the building, and also because we were planning to take the Brooklyn sports bar experience to a higher plateau.

We had done an aggressive job of promoting our grand opening around town with flyers and via the internet and it paid off well for us. There was a standing-room-only crowd in the house. A lot of our friends came out to show their support for us. The fact that Tucker was giving away lots of free hot wings didn't hurt our opening day attendance, either.

As previously stated, I was an avowed Yankees-hater personally, but they were definitely good for business. The ball club was having another winning season, and we were packing the place every time they played. I kept my opinion of the Bronx Bombers to myself and went with the program.

I must admit that I was a bit astonished at how prosperous business became. Plenty of brothers kept thanking us constantly; expressing to us how glad they were that we had opened up a spot for them. Tucker made it an unwritten policy of ours to give out free food to members of the N.Y.P.D. This kept police officers constantly swinging by, which added to our overall security. We were lucky to receive a couple of positive write-ups in the area press, which also brought people by to check us out.

After our successful grand-opening, I had gone home that night and got down on my knees and prayed hard that things would continue to go well for us so that I could quit my damn job at Human Resources.

CHAPTER TWENTY-ONE

Financially, I was beginning to blow up—the money was coming in fast—but, physically, I was dead tired. Whupped. Another Level was doing better than we'd predicted, which made me quite thankful; I knew we could just as easily have been hemorrhaging dollars.

Nevertheless, I was burning out. I had my day job, after all. And while it was Tucker's responsibility to open up our sports bar every afternoon—he'd make a beeline to Another Level right after the lunch rush at House of Pork—it was mine to show up there by five-thirty and stick it out until midnight.

From the day Another Level opened, I was there every evening. Working. My Behind. Off. You name it, I did it. I served food, I mixed drinks, I darted out for supplies, I cleaned up. My weekday schedule went like this: I'd wrap things up at Social Services; head straight to Another Level; work nonstop; go home; fall into my bed; sleep for a few hours; get up; repeat cycle.

Right from jumpstreet, Tucker and I both agreed that this hectic schedule would only be temporary. Once we found dependable and honest employees, we'd slow our pace. But that was proving hard to do. The first week of business we fired two folks for hooking up their friends with free beer.

The benefit of never having any time off was that I was saving a lot of money that otherwise would have gone to enjoying leisure activities. I couldn't remember the last time I'd eaten out or gone to a movie or been in pursuit of the fairer sex.

Only at night, when I crawled into bed dog-tired and alone, did I miss female companionship. I'm not just referring to a woman's physical presence, but to her spiritual closeness as well. Not having some sister out there who I could pick up the phone and talk to often depressed me. Jeanette and I had spoken to each other a few times since my expulsion from her bedroom. But there was nothing to our conversations anymore, and we soon stopped calling altogether.

Whenever I wasn't too exhausted from work, I did show up for Sunday worship service somewhere in Brooklyn, though never at Jeanette's church. And when prayer time came, I always asked God to hit me off with a female companion.

One Saturday morning around the end of October, I hopped into Jada and proceeded to the Home Depot for a snake to plumb the toilet in the women's restroom at Another Level. I was driving back down Fourth Avenue, minding my own business, when the cab driver in front of me suddenly swerved over to the right lane to pick up a fare. In the process, he cut off a black BMW that was already in that lane.

It swerved left to avoid hitting the cab. And ran into me instead! The impact knocked me into the median. It took me a few moments to realize that some fool had hit my beloved Jada!

I jumped out of my ride, retrieved my Club anti-theft device from the passenger's seat, and was ready to beat-down whoever had jacked up Jada. "Motherfucker!" I yelled.

(Yep, I was back to cussing full-time.)

I walked around my baby and surveyed the damage. Her rear passenger side door was smashed in, and its window was shattered. I spun around and waited for the BMW's driver to step out. The front driver side of that vehicle was crushed, too, but the dark-tinted windows remained intact.

"Come on out, dammit!"

I quickly memorized the license plate in case the driver decided to speed off. So many people drove around the city without a driver's license or insurance that it wasn't even funny.

The cab was already long gone, and a small group of onlookers had appeared from out of nowhere, probably waiting to see a fight.

When the door of the BMW opened, out stepped a petite, sister dressed in a postal worker's uniform. Right then and there, I figured I wouldn't need my Club. (At least I hoped not.) I would, though, need strength and plenty of it to keep me from snatching homegirl up.

She slowly approached me. Her mouth was opened wide but no words came out. She gazed blankly at her damaged vehicle, paying no attention to my banged-up Jada, which made me even angrier.

"Forget your car! Look at what you did to mine!" I shouted.

She kept staring at the mangled front end of her own ride.

"Look at what you did to my car!" I repeated, louder.

She turned, then, and looked across the street at my smashed up door.

"I'm...I'm so sorry. I didn't even see you."

"Evidently not!" I snapped. "Let me see your papers!"

She stared at me again, saying nothing and looking real stupid.

As if in a trance, girlfriend went back into her car and began rummaging through her glove compartment. I pulled out my cell phone and called the police.

It turned out that the banged-up BMW did not belong to Miss Danielle Davis at all. It was her uncle's. I filled out an accident report with the police, and drove back to Another Level to fix the toilet.

"I bet you wanted to kick her ass?"

Tucker stood behind me in the women's restroom. I was stooped over the toilet bowl forcing the snake down its clogged-up throat.

"I don't wanna talk about it."

"I know I would have. Wouldn't have mattered to me if it was a chick or not. When it comes to my ride..."

"What about all of those car windows that you've replaced after some chick tossed a brick through it?" I cut Tucker off. I was sick of listening to his madness.

He exited the restroom without muttering another word.

I extended the snake as far as it would go into the toilet and it caught onto something. Turning the crank to retract the coil, I fished out a pair of pantyhose. *Now who would do crap like this?* "Women!" I was disgusted.

It took almost three weeks before Jada was repaired. The Nissan dealership had to order another door. When I got her back, though, she looked as good as ever.

About a week after I was back on the road, our prayers for an honest employee to help us run Another Level were answered. Our salvation's name was Luther Simpson. He was a twenty-nine-year-old brother originally from Los Angeles with aspirations of becoming a dancer on Broadway. In the meantime, he needed to pay his rent. We told Mr. Simpson we were looking for somebody who had some managerial experience. He told us he was our guy. Luther gave us some job references who all had nothing but high praise for him.

Luther was an excellent worker; he came to work on time, worked the whole time that he was there, and appeared to be honest. Of course, Tucker tested Luther's integrity several times by leaving the register drawer open, Luther didn't take a dime.

Luther was also an avid black history buff. He sold Tucker and me on the brilliant idea of coming up with trivia questions-of-the-day with free drinks for customers who provided the correct answers without the use of electronic devices.

Luther was a charmer; everybody on the staff loved him. He was also gay. I mention this only to prove that black men of all persuasions are capable of getting along with one another. At first, some of our customers tried to give Luther a hard time. They asked Tucker and me why we hired a gay dude. We made it plain as day that Luther was there to do a job that he was good at, and if anyone had problems with him, they were free to patronize another establishment.

Hiring Luther allowed Tucker and me to get some much-needed rest during the week. We took turns Monday through Thursday working at Another Level. Both of us worked Friday, Saturday and Sunday nights. I spent most of my days off resting up. Tucker, however, went back on the prowl. He was busier than ever chasing women and bringing them by for free food and drinks at Another Level on his days off.

This allowed Tucker to impress the women while making sure the business was running smoothly. Telling his clientele that he owned two successful businesses in Brooklyn usually did the trick for him. So, it was no surprise for me to come home late at night and hear Tucker and some sister making a commotion in his bedroom.

On one such occasion, I knocked on his door.

"What?" Tucker demanded when he finally opened the door.

"I need to talk to you about the business."

"Can't it wait? I'm handling some business of my own at the moment."

"I'd like to discuss it now."

"Give me about another twenty minutes so I can wrap things up in here."

"Okay, Tucker. Twenty minutes, no more."

Fifty minutes later, he knocked on my bedroom door.

"You're late," I announced as he walked in.

Tucker was clothed in only a pair of baggy jeans that sagged around his waist.

"So what's the big issue that you couldn't wait until morning to discuss?"

"Luther came up with another brilliant idea this evening."

Tucker remained silent, gesturing with his hands for me to hurry up and make my point.

"He suggested we hold a Spades party," I said, excitedly.

Tucker was dumbfounded and annoyed.

"You made me stop tapping Debbie so you could tell me this? What is so damn brilliant about throwing a party for a bunch of black folks?"

"I'm talking about the card game, idiot!"

"Oh, now I see," Tucker said.

While the rest of Black America might have been playing Bid Whist, Spades was the premier card game when we were students down at State. And Tucker and I were one hellified team. We were invincible. We'd gotten into trouble with our football coaches on more than one occasion for staying up past our curfew holding late-night Spades tournaments. The idea of replicating that, of hearing all that smack talk across the card table, of pulling in crowds and making all that money at Another Level made Tucker's eyes light up.

The crowd we had that night was standing-room-only, despite the early December chill. We'd set up tables upstairs in the lounge. There was eating, drinking and a whole lot of merriment.

I was downstairs in the restaurant serving food when Tucker called me toward the kitchen.

"Could you take this over to table four, please?"

Tucker handed me a combination platter of chicken wings and ribs and then disappeared back into the kitchen. As I began weaving my way to table number four, I passed Luther, who was delivering a tray of food himself.

"Was I right or what?" Luther asked, patting himself on the back.

"Remind us to talk to you about a raise, Mr. Simpson," I called back to him, grinning.

Table number four's occupants were three females, apparently having themselves a good time. One of the laughing faces, a young lady with short, rust-colored locks and soft, almond-shaped eyes, looked familiar to me. She was in the middle of a chuckle when our eyes met.

It was the same sister who'd smashed into Jada two months earlier, Danielle Davis. I fought back an urge to dump the food I was carrying into her lap.

"Here's your order," I said, sitting down the plate of food. I was trying my best not to sound too impolite.

"Thanks," Danielle snarled back.

The other two women instantly picked up on our mutual antagonism. I spun around and walked off. Being part owner of Another Level, I could ill afford to spar with one of our patrons, especially over something that wasn't business related.

As I walked away from those sisters, I overheard Danielle: "That's the clown that I ran into with my uncle's car."

I bit my tongue and kept it moving back toward the kitchen.

Later that night, Tucker and I were upstairs in the lounge watching and listening. He tapped me on my arm.

"Yo, why don't we get in on a game?"

"Aren't we supposed to be working?"

"Wouldn't you call socializing with our customers working?"

"Maybe, but we can't play in the tournament. We're the ones sponsoring it."

"We'll play some of the losers," Tucker said. "Our work will be already cut out for us, since we know that whoever we're playing against can't be all that good."

I had not planned on playing any cards, but it had been a long time since we kicked some butt. Besides, I needed to sit and rest my aching feet.

"Okay, deal me in," I said.

As fate would have it, Tucker and I were going up against Danielle and one of her girlfriends, Sonya. I started to protest, but didn't. It was only a friendly card game.

"How y'all ladies doing this evening?" Tucker asked after everyone had been introduced.

"Fine," Sonya answered cheerfully as he started shuffling the deck of cards.

Sonya then returned to sipping her drink.

Danielle remained quiet. I did likewise.

Tucker handed the shuffled deck over to Sonya.

"Being that we're such gentlemen, we're going to let you ladies have the first deal."

Tucker's southern accent was heavier than usual.

"We sho' do thanks ya," Sonya threw back, mocking Tucker.

She handed me the deck of cards. I cut them. She began dealing.

"I just want you sisters to know that this is strictly business. So, if we beat you two badly, don't take it personally," Tucker said, chiding our opponents.

"We'll keep that in mind," Sonya said.

I picked up the hand I'd been dealt, and scanned it. I had only one spade in my hand, the four. I gazed across the table at my partner and saw, by his frown, that Tucker wasn't too pleased with his hand either.

"I believe the first bid's on you, gentlemen," Sonya said.

Tucker and I looked at each other and shook our heads in unison.

"I think we'll take a four on this one," he said.

"I'm scared of you two!" Sonya replied, sarcastically, writing down our bid.

"I know we're not trying to talk no noise up in here?" Tucker retorted.

"Never," Sonya stated, then looked over at Danielle.

"How many, partner?"

"One, two, three, four..." Danielle counted. "Five...and a very strong possible." The two sisters eyed each other for a second.

"Wanna try a ten?" Sonya asked. A wicked smile slid across her face.

"Let's do it," Danielle said.

Those girls ran a damn Boston on us! They sho' did! They took all thirteen books. Won every one of them. Tucker and I were stunned.

"Beginner's luck!" Tucker scoffed as he began to shuffle the cards for the next hand.

"I'm dealing this time. Things are going to be different now!"

And things were. The girls only made eleven books the next hand. We lost the game.

"It was really nice beating, I mean, meeting you guys," Sonya jeered as Tucker and I got up from the table.

I looked out of the corner of my eye and saw Danielle sneering.

"Well, ladies, that was a most unusual experience. May I get you two conquerors a drink?" Tucker asked the victors.

"I don't drink," Danielle said.

"I'll take her drink, and mine too," Sonya replied.

Danielle gave her friend a hard stare.

"Here you go," Sonya said, reaching into her pocketbook and handing her car keys over to Danielle.

"Later, folks," I said, before walking downstairs to see what Luther needed help with.

About an hour later, as I was clearing plates away from a table, someone tapped me on my right shoulder.

"Yes?" I asked, apprehensively, looking into the face of Danielle's other friend.

"I don't mean to disturb you, but when you get a chance, could you send somebody into the ladies room? One of my friends was in there sick and she kinda missed the toilet, if you know what I mean."

I understood and gave girlfriend a frown. That was one of the major drawbacks of working in a place that served alcohol and food. Vomit.

"I'll take care of it," I said.

"Thanks," she replied, walking off hurriedly.

I finished wiping off the table and turned around just in time to see Danielle, and the sister who'd just spoken to me helping sickly Sonya out the door. I grabbed a mop and knocked on the door to the ladies' restroom. I received no answer so I went in. Fresh bile was everywhere.

"Crap!"

While mopping up, I noticed a small leather pouch on the floor beside the commode. It contained a driver's license, a United States Post Office worker's identification tag, and forty-nine dollars in cash. Danielle Davis lived on Linden Boulevard, in the East New York section of Brooklyn. I pocketed her pouch and then finished cleaning up her friend's mess.

I finally dragged my behind home at two-thirty in the morning. Taking off my pants, I realized Miss Davis' pouch was still in my back pocket. I had meant to leave it at the bar with Luther, in case the sister came back to retrieve it. She didn't. *Oh well, I'm quite sure she'll show up tomorrow.* I crawled into my bed and fell fast asleep.

CHAPTER TWENTY-TWO

There was no Danielle Davis the following day, Saturday, either. I left her belongings at the bar before we locked up, seeing as I was off the next day. Monday evening the pouch was still where I had left it. I mailed it to Danielle's address the following morning.

That Wednesday evening, as soon as I walked into Another Level, Luther handed me the back of a receipt with a name and a phone number scribbled across it.

"What's this?" I asked him before reading the piece of paper.

"That's the girl's name and number who left her pouch here last Friday night."

I picked up the phone near the cash register and dialed.

"Hello?" a woman answered.

"Yes, may I speak to Danielle Davis, please?"

"This is she."

"This is Mr. Collins from Another Level."

"Yes, I was told that you were the person who found my pouch last Friday," Danielle stated, matter-of-factly.

"That's correct."

"May I ask you where it is now?"

"I mailed it to the address on your driver's license yesterday."

"You put it in the mail, huh?" she asked me, suspiciously.

I didn't like the tone of disbelief in her voice, but I chose to ignore it.

"That's what I said."

"And *when* did you do this?"

"I told you already, yesterday."

"Is that right? I hope that my pouch doesn't get lost somewhere along the way!"

My blood pressure was beginning to rise. That was not good.

"Do you not live over at 528 Linden Boulevard, apartment twenty-four?"

"Yes, I do."

"Well that's the address that I sent your property to. What's the matter, don't you trust your co-workers at the Post Office?"

Danielle Davis was quiet, but I was on a roll.

"As a matter of fact, Ma'am, if you would have come back by here after you realized you lost your pouch in the first place, we wouldn't be holding this conversation now."

"I wasn't around to do that!"

It was time to cut the conversation short.

"The bottom line is that your pouch is in the mail and you should be receiving it shortly."

"Did you send everything back that was in it?"

Girlfriend had gone *too* far.

"Are you questioning my integrity?" I asked, gruffly.

"No. I'm asking about my money."

"Actually, I did take some of your money to pay for the packaging and mailing costs! Now you have a good day!"

I slammed the phone down. A few of the customers turned and looked in my direction, but I didn't care. I was pissed off. It would be quite some time before I did a favor for anyone else I didn't know.

That Friday night we had another crowd in the house because the Knicks were in action. They were battling the Nets, and they were losing. I kept a grin on my face as I periodically gazed up at the television while tending bar. Luther had decided to show me some of the tricks to the trade of bartending. He even let me in on a few specialty drinks that he had created himself, like one greenish concoction that he called 'monster juice.' Luther told me he named it as such because that's exactly what you'd see after drinking the stuff.

"Javier, could you stock the beer cooler while I go get some more orange juice?"

"No problem, Luther."

I squatted down behind the bar and was in the process of pulling some of the warm beer bottles out of their box when I heard a woman's voice above my head.

"Excuse me."

I sprang to my feet to find Danielle Davis standing across the bar in front of me. She was wearing a pair of snug-fitting blue jeans and a beige sweatshirt under her black leather jacket. She also wore a slight look of uncertainty on her face as she eyed me. Her short dreadlocks were pulled back and held in place by a ribbon.

"You need something to drink?" I asked her, coolly. I had forgotten about how upset this sister had made me previously until I saw her standing there in front of me.

"I don't drink."

"Then why are you here?" I asked, nonchalantly squatting back down behind the bar to finish my chore.

"I came by to apologize."

I bounced back up on my feet.

"What was that?"

(Actually, I had heard her the first time, but it didn't sound sincere enough.)

"I came by to say that I'm sorry for the other day."

I turned my head sideways for full dramatic effect.

"I take it then that you've received your pouch?"

"Yes, I did. Thank you."

"Believe me, it was nothing."

"I want you to know that I usually do not behave like that. I've just had a lot of things on my mind lately."

Danielle pulled out a ten-dollar bill from her back pocket and held it out to me.

"You need some change for that?" I asked.

"This is for you."

"Thanks, but that won't be necessary. Keep your money."

I dropped back down behind the bar and finished pulling out the rest of the beer bottles. When I stood back up Danielle was not there. However, she'd left her money on the counter. I looked over at the exit just as she was going through it. I picked up the ten spot and scurried from behind the counter right as Luther was returning with the orange juice.

"Be right back," I informed him as we passed each other.

Danielle was about to turn the corner of the block when I caught up with her. I grabbed her by her arm softly and spun her around.

"Excuse me, but..."

That was all that I was able to get out before Danielle Davis kicked me square in the nuts. I had forgotten that she lived in East New York! Thankfully, my many years of being in almost top physical condition paid off. It took me over five seconds before I collapsed to the ground in agony.

The pain was unbearable. I clutched the money that I was trying to return to Danielle tightly in my left hand, while I clutched myself tightly with my right.

As I lay sprawled on the cold, hard concrete, I thought back to the last time that I had gotten kicked like that. I was about nine years old, harassing General Sherman, one of the goats that Granddaddy kept on his farm down in Yemassee, South Carolina. Now, General Sherman had been old ever since I could remember, and legend even had it that he had been around during the war that his namesake fought in.

Whenever my cousins and I got together down at Granddaddy's, we would always find time to go out and pay General Sherman a visit, much to the goat's dismay. You see, Granddaddy had a lot of plum bushes growing around his farm back then, and whatever plums my cousins and I couldn't eat ourselves, we'd throw at the farm animals. (Wasn't a need to let them go to waste.) General Sherman was one of our preferred targets, being that he was so old that he couldn't move about too fast.

On the day in question, I was down at Granddaddy's by myself, waiting for my cousins from Philly. Their school let out a month later for summer vacation than my southern school did. I was operating a brand new remote-controlled dune buggy that Granddaddy bought me earlier in the day, when it hit the tree stump that the General was tied to and flipped over. I was caught up in playing with my new toy and didn't pay any attention to the General. I casually walked up to the General and bent down behind him to turn my dune buggy back over. After the years of abuse that I had put the poor animal through, General Sherman finally got even.

When I stood up straight again, General Sherman, not forgetting the torment that I had put him through, still had enough fight in him to let me have it with both hind legs. Right in my private area. I immediately passed out.

Granddaddy found me an hour later splayed on the ground and covered with ants. To make matters worse, that damn goat swallowed my remote control.

(General Sherman mysteriously disappeared later on that summer.)

"I'm so sorry!!!" Danielle cried as she bent down beside me. "I thought you were trying to attack me!"

All I could do was grimace in pain.

"Let me help you up?" she offered.

I vigorously shook my head no. I still needed some time to sort a couple of important things out.

Luther was taken aback when he looked up at the front door and saw me limping back through it with Danielle supporting me.

"What's wrong?" he gasped.

"He had a little accident," Danielle answered for me.

I turned and stared at her curiously. Most of the men I knew did not consider getting kicked square in their balls a little accident.

"What happened?" Luther asked her.

"When he grabbed me from behind, I kind of turned and..."

Luther frowned.

"Ouch!" he said.

"It was kind of a reflex," Danielle explained. "I've just recently completed a kickboxing course at my gym."

Luther merely shook his head. Danielle helped me to sit down at a nearby table.

"Would you like some water or something?" she asked.

"That's okay," I squeaked. My voice was now a few octaves higher. What I really wanted was for her to leave. Luther must have read my mind because he grabbed Danielle gently and tried to steer her towards the exit.

"He'll be okay in about a day or so," Luther assured her.

"I just feel so bad about what I did," my assailant moaned.

Danielle Davis would not leave Another Level until I had accepted an offer from her to at least buy me lunch one day soon. I honestly didn't want anything more to do with the young lady because every time I came in contact with her, she wound up causing me some type of grief.

Danielle persisted, however, saying that it would make her feel a lot better. At the time, my main concern was about me feeling better. To hurry up and get her out of my place, I reluctantly agreed. When she asked me where I wanted to go for lunch, I told her that dining where we were presently would suit me just fine. (I was too afraid to go any place else with her.)

CHAPTER TWENTY-THREE

I thought I had seen the last of Danielle after she kicked me in the nuts. But she called me at Another Level three days later to confirm a date to buy me lunch.

"Okay, Miss, what would you like to order?"

"Let me see..."

Danielle was sitting across the table from me in her postal worker's uniform. "I think I'll have another combination platter," she said slowly.

"Okay."

I motioned to Luther, who was standing behind the bar.

"I need one combo platter over here, Luther."

"Coming right up."

"Aren't you going to order anything?" Danielle asked me.

"I was thinking I'd share some of yours. Our combination platter is pretty big...and reasonably priced."

"Okay," Danielle said. She smiled.

For the next minute, we stared at each other in awkward silence. I didn't have anything else to say to girlfriend. My privates were still throbbing from that vicious kick, and I was still nursing an urge to kick her back.

"So, you like working at the Post Office?" I asked, finally.

"It's a job."

"That's true."

"Do you like your job?" she asked.

"Here?"

"How many do you have?"

"I work here and I also work at Human Resources."

"I can't believe I've finally met somebody who gets cursed out at work more than I do."

I had to laugh at that one. *Girlfriend has a good sense of humor.* I thought to myself. Since she was in a good mood, I went ahead and asked her something that was on my mind.

"Can I ask you a question, Miss Davis?"

"You may call me Danielle."

"Okay, Danielle. May I ask you a question?"

"Sure."

"How come you waited so long to come back for your money and identification? Most people I know would have came back the same night looking for their cash—before it was too late."

Danielle took a sip of ice water before answering.

"I would have came straight back myself, but I had to rush out of town when I got home that night."

"What happened?"

"I received an urgent phone call from one of my aunts telling me that my mother had gone into diabetic shock and was in the hospital again. Me and my uncle left for Richmond an hour later. I didn't realize that my pouch was missing until we stopped at a rest area on the turnpike."

"How's your mother doing now?"

Danielle looked at me wearily and sighed.

"She's okay."

"That's good to hear."

"Yes, it is," Danielle agreed.

I didn't mean to, but I caught myself gazing at my lunch host's eyes. Danielle Davis was by no means a bad-looking young lady. Sure, she probably could have used a little more meat on her bones, but other than that she seemed good to go.

A brief jolt of pain in my private area snapped me back to sanity. *What the heck are you thinking about, boy? This girl is nothing but trouble!*

Danielle's order arrived, and we dug in. Girlfriend was petite but she sure could hold her own when it came to eating. She showed no mercy to Tucker's ribs and chicken. I was able to grab two ribs and a leg before she'd scarfed everything else down.

This is what I learned over lunch with Danielle: She's an only child, born in Brooklyn. When she was five, her parents separated, so she moved to Richmond, Virginia with her mother. After graduating from high school, Danielle enrolled at Hampton University but dropped out after two years to take a position at the Post Office, where her mother also worked.

When I asked why she'd quit school, Danielle evaded the question. I could tell from her body language that she was uncomfortable, so I steered the conversation elsewhere.

I also found out that Danielle transferred back to New York when her father fell ill. When he passed away earlier in the year, he left all of his belongings to his only child.

Once back in New York, Danielle concluded that there was more to life than selling postal stamps, so she enrolled at Medgar Evers College to finish her degree in business management. In addition to her Monday-to-Friday regular shift, she worked every other weekend, because the overtime helped pay her tuition. Danielle probably would have kept on divulging her life's story to me had I not looked around and seen that the place was getting kind of busy.

"Well, Miss Davis, I mean, Danielle, I'd really like to sit here longer and chat with you, but I need to get back to work."

If my eyes didn't deceive me, Danielle seemed a little disappointed for a second. She then checked her arm watch.

"Dang! I need to get back myself."

Danielle placed the money for her bill on the table and then we both slowly stood. I extended my hand to her in gratitude.

"It's been a pleasure dining with you, Ma'am. Thanks."

"You're quite welcome. And don't call me 'Ma'am.' I'm not that old, yet."

We both chuckled.

Luther was eyeing me as I returned behind the bar.

"You know, you two make a nice couple."

"We're not a couple of anything."

"Why not? You two obviously like each other."

"Really?" I let out a big fat laugh. "What makes you say that?"

"I saw the way that you two were checking each other out a few minutes ago," he said, after refilling a customer's beer.

"We had lunch together, Luther. That was it. I am done."

"Javier, Luther knows all and sees all. Just now I *know* I saw that sister digging your scene. And you were digging hers too."

I laughed to myself as I refilled a pitcher of stout for another customer.

"I appreciate your expert observations, but I think I'll hold off for right now on dealing with another sister."

"If you say so, boss."

As our conversation turned toward business-related matters, I thought a bit about Danielle and what Luther had mentioned about our making a good couple. Danielle was attractive, and she did seem to have a decent personality, despite my initial impressions. Those almond-shaped eyes of hers were mesmerizing also.

"Which one?" Luther asked, interrupting my thoughts. I gave him a baffled look.

"Huh?"

"I asked which cleaner do you want me to use to mop the floors later on?"

"Oh, use the old stuff. That cheap degreaser Tucker bought is too smelly."

"That's what I was just telling you."

Luther stopped wiping off his area of the bar and stared at me.

"What's on your mind? Danielle?"

"Nothing's on my mind, Luther."

"If you say so, boss."

That following Tuesday evening, when I walked into Another Level, there was a huge bouquet of flowers sitting on the bar. Tucker was behind the bar, serving drinks.

"Who sent you the flowers?" I asked, making my way toward the kitchen area to hang up my coat.

"They're not for me."

"Don't tell me Luther has a new admirer?"

"They're not Luther's, either. The delivery man dropped them off for you about thirty minutes ago."

I stopped and turned around.

"For me?" I asked, trying to suppress my surprise.

"Did I stutter, motherfucker?"

I ignored Tucker's smart remark and walked over to examine the flowers. I pulled off the card, opened it, and started to read:

Mr. Collins,

I hope you enjoy these flowers as much as I enjoyed your company the other afternoon. See you Friday night?

Danielle

There was something else in the envelope. A ticket to a Miles Davis tribute that upcoming weekend at The Coda, one of the premier jazz clubs down in the West Village. I had heard the concert advertised several times over the radio, but by the time I decided to buy myself a ticket, it was already sold out.

How did Danielle know that Miles was my man? I could not recall bringing up Miles' name over lunch, though we had discussed our mutual love for jazz. My thoughts were disrupted when Tucker tapped me on the shoulder.

"Hey, let me know if you want to sell that bouquet, homeboy? I know a chick up in the Bronx who would just love to receive those flowers from me."

"Would you please give it a rest, Tucker?"

Danielle was assertive. I liked that, though I reminded myself that I'm wasn't interested in becoming involved with her. On the other hand, I was kind of blue about missing out on that tribute down at The Coda. And since Danielle Davis already had us tickets to the show...why waste the girl's hard earned money?

The concert was slated to start at eight o'clock. I arrived around seven to give myself ample time to find a place to park Jada. (One of the perks of working for yourself is that you get to take a sick day whenever you need to.)

After circling West Fourth Street and Eighth Avenue for about thirty minutes, I broke down and paid for one of those overpriced parking garages. Not knowing the dress code for the club, I played it safe and went with the old blazer and slacks combination. I gave my ticket to the attendant at the door, went inside and checked my coat.

The Coda's foyer was decorated with old photographs of jazz's aristocracy: Duke, Bird, Coltrane, Ella, Dizzy, Miles, Monk, Prez, and Billie.

I didn't see Danielle anywhere in the main lounge when I peered inside, so I sidled up to the bar for a drink before showtime. I checked my watch after placing my order. It was ten minutes until eight.

I got my beer, and was preparing to find seats for Danielle and me when I spotted her checking her leather coat by the entrance. I did a double take. Danielle looked absolutely stunning.

Her elegant turquoise dress enhanced her small physique nicely. When she turned to me and smiled, I felt as giddy as a teenager on his first date. *Get a grip, J.C., we're still on the solo tip.* I reminded myself.

"Good evening," Danielle said softly when she saw me walking towards her.

"Hello..."

We embraced lightly, and then I quickly pulled away. I didn't want to send the wrong message to girlfriend.

"That dress does you way more justice than your work uniform."

"This old thing?" Danielle teased. "I've had this dress for ages."

"Don't even try it," I laughed. "The price tag is still hanging in the back."

Danielle's almond-shaped eyes lit up in horror as she tried to look at the back of her dress.

"Really?!"

"I was joking."

At that moment, we heard the musicians warming up in the lounge.

"Shall we go in, Ma'am?" I asked as I extended my hand to her.

"Don't call me that!" Danielle hissed under her breath as she took my arm.

I enjoyed the performance thoroughly. Of course none of the musicians were as fly as Miles was with his horn but a few of them came close. For the finale, the whole ensemble of horn players hit the stage with the house band and performed my favorite Miles Davis tune, '*TuTu*'. The audience was on its feet as the band wailed away.

"Pretty good show, huh?" I asked Danielle as we waited in line at coat-check.

"Yes, it was. Thanks."

Is this girl humble or what? I thought to myself.

"You don't have to thank me, Danielle, I should be thanking you."

"For what?" Danielle asked.

"For inviting me here tonight."

Danielle looked at me, puzzled.

"I didn't invite you, Mr. Collins; you invited me. Remember?"

Now it was my turn to be confused.

"When did I do that?"

"When you sent that large bouquet of flowers and that ticket to my house on Tuesday."

I smelled a rat. Ten seconds later, Luther scurried up to the both of us, wearing a million-dollar smile.

"Did you two like the show?"

"It was nice!" Danielle answered.

I simply stared Luther down.

"How about you?" he asked me, still beaming.

"How about telling me what this is all about?"

Luther was un-intimidated.

"That's not the answer I was looking for."

"Then I'm sure you're not going to like the one I'm going to give you tomorrow at work any better."

Confounded, Danielle looked at both Luther and me. She could sense that something was amiss.

"Don't be so negative!" Luther snapped.

Just as I was about to respond to Luther, a tall, suave-looking brother in a dark-gray suit approached the three of us. He was smiling broadly.

"Luther! These must be the good friends that you told me about." The brother had a deep, booming voice.

"That's right," Luther answered. "Cedrick, I want you to meet Danielle and Javier. They really enjoyed the show."

I recognized the gentleman then as one of the musicians who had been playing onstage earlier.

"Nice to meet you. I'm very glad you enjoyed our show," Cedrick said as he shook my hand.

"The pleasure was all mine," I replied.

As I patiently watched Danielle and Cedrick exchange pleasantries, I made a mental note to deal with Luther later. I was still mad about the prank he had pulled, but there was really no need to let Danielle and Cedrick see that.

"Luther told me how much you loved Miles but couldn't get tickets to the show, Javier. So I did him a favor and got some for you. Tell the truth now, you were surprised when you got them, weren't you?"

"You have no idea how surprised I still am, Cedrick."

"Well, I've got to go greet some other people around here. You two take care. Luther, I'll be back shortly."

I deduced that Cedrick and Luther were more than casual friends from the seductive smiles they flashed at each other. Cedrick then continued making his rounds. When Danielle and I stepped outside the building, the temperature had fallen quite a bit.

"Where did you park?" I asked her.

"Over there."

Danielle pointed to the corner across the street, where the entrance to the subway was.

"You came out here on the train?"

Danielle was hesitant.

"I had no choice. My uncle won't let me drive his car anymore."

I suddenly regretted asking her that question. We both had not mentioned how we initially ran into each other.

"I guess it'll be safe if you rode with me back to Brooklyn."

Danielle seemed upset by my comment, until I smiled at her.

"It was only a joke," I told her. "Come on."

We took no more than ten paces down the street from The Coda when Danielle grabbed me by my arm.

"Is there something going on between you and your friend back there that I should know about?"

"You don't miss a thing, do you, Danielle?"

"I try not to."

On the way to the parking garage, I revealed to her what Luther had done.

"How did he get my address?"

"Your guess is as good as mine, Danielle. Anything's possible with internet access and a name these days. I'm sorry that he involved you in this scheme tonight."

"Don't apologize to me," Danielle said. "I had a great time at that concert."

"Yeah, it was pretty good."

When we reached the parking garage, the attendant fetched my ride in five minutes flat, stepped out of my vehicle and looked at me expectantly. Now had I been by myself, I would have left him standing there looking stupid. You see, I don't believe in tipping at establishments that overcharged you in the first place. But with Danielle watching me, I stuck my hand into my pants pocket and fished out seventy-five cents for the attendant.

"Thanks! Now I can retire in style!" the wise guy replied before stomping off.

I ignored that ingrate, climbed inside of Jada and then opened the passenger side door for Danielle. After tuning my radio to the local jazz station, I pulled out into traffic. The digital clock on the dashboard indicated that it was after eleven. My stomach began rumbling, alerting me that I'd skipped dinner.

"Would you care for a bite to eat before I take you back home, Danielle?"

She threw me an odd glance.

"I was referring to your own residence when I said that."

Again, I felt a little light-headed when Danielle smiled at me.

"I'm okay. I ate before I left the house."

We rode in silence for a mile or so, with my stomach rumbling every few hundred yards. I was surprised that Danielle didn't hear it.

"Are you tired?" Danielle suddenly asked me.

Her inflection instantly put me on alert.

"Not really. Why?"

"I'm not ready to go home, yet."

"Oh, you're not?" Danielle's statement had taken me somewhat by surprise.

"Between work and school, I really don't get out much these days. I was just wondering..."

Danielle glanced over at me and hesitated.

"Go on," I coaxed.

I was curious to see what it was that Danielle had in mind.

"I was wondering if we could stop by The Well for a little bit. I've always wanted to check that place out."

This woman must be damn crazy.

"You wanna go and check out The Well?"

I wasn't down for the club scene at all, and especially not The Well.

"I'll pay for you to get inside. That is, if you want to go?" Danielle added. She looked so adorable with her eyes lit up. I found it hard to tell her no, but I did it anyway.

"I don't think so, Danielle. I'm really not up for that. Sorry."

"That's okay. I'll go there some other time," Danielle said with a small sigh. Disappointment was written all over her face.

CHAPTER TWENTY-FOUR

Since it was a Friday night, we had to wait in line for over half an hour before we were able to get inside the nightclub.

"Didn't they have clubs in Richmond?" I asked Danielle, who had pulled out her money to pay for us when we reached the admissions booth, but I told her that her money was no good with me. I paid for myself.

"Of course they have clubs there, but Richmond is not New York City."

"That's a valid point."

I hadn't been out to The Well since I was kicking it with Keisha, but the scenario was still the same. People were milling about everywhere and the dance floor was packed. The deejay was playing the latest rap tune by The Equalizer, which meant the bass in the club's speaker system was thumping extra loud.

I was feeling a bit drained and I was still starving. I knew that a splitting headache wouldn't be too far behind if I didn't procure some food quickly.

"I've got to order me a burger or something," I told Danielle.

"They serve food in here?" she asked, sounding a little surprised

"They do a little something. Nothing too fancy."

Danielle miraculously spied an empty corner and we commandeered it before someone else did. After waiting another twenty minutes, a tired-looking waitress, clad in a skimpy pants suit, took my order for chicken.

In the meantime, I'd ordered a pint of Guinness to sip on while Danielle ordered herself a glass of cranberry juice. She insisted on paying for my food.

"How come you don't drink?" I asked Danielle, trying to kill time until my food arrived.

I could tell from the expression on Danielle's face that she was mulling over something in her mind.

"I used to drink when I first started college. Way too much. In fact, I got kicked out of school partly because of it. Eventually, I had to go and get some help."

That was some real deep info that Danielle had dropped on me and I didn't know how to react. I gazed at her in silence for a few seconds.

"What's the matter?" she asked.

I still didn't know what to say.

"You...don't..."

I decided that it would probably be best to keep my thoughts to myself.

"I don't what? Look like a person with an alcohol problem?"

That was exactly what I wanted to say, but I couldn't let her know that.

"No, not that..."

"What then?"

I tried to think fast.

"It's just that I can't see you as a...you don't..."

(Unfortunately, I wasn't thinking fast enough.)

"Skip it," Danielle said, mercifully.

"Thank you," I sighed, relieved.

I was glad she had let me off the hook. Once my order of chicken fingers arrived, I attacked it with a vengeance. Of course I offered some to Danielle first. She declined, so I polished them off before she could change her mind.

I had just finished eating my last chicken finger when the intro from Frankie Beverly and Maze's hit song '*Before I Let Go*' sounded over the speakers.

Danielle quickly stood up from her chair and grabbed me by the hand.

"Come on, Mr. Collins, let's dance," she said as she pulled on my arm.

I was not in the mood.

"I think I'll pass. You go ahead and dance with somebody else. There's plenty of brothers up in here."

"Come on, Mr. Collins, please?"

"I really don't feel like it, Danielle."

Danielle refused to let go of my hand.

"Just this one song and then I won't ask you anymore. Okay? Pleeeaaaase?"

I was defenseless against those captivating eyes of hers. I gave a sigh of defeat, stood up from my seat and followed. As soon as we were five feet away from our table, another couple helped themselves to it. I looked out at the dance floor and saw that it had gotten even more congested.

Danielle guided me out into the fray and only then did she let go of my hand. Not knowing how good a dancer Danielle was, I politely decided not to demonstrate any of my fancy footwork on her.

"Now I see why you didn't want to dance," Danielle yelled at me over the music.

"And why is that?"

"Cause you can't!" Danielle said before turning her back to me.

Oh no she didn't! I slipped back around in front of her to finish our conversation.

"Can't dance?" I yelled to her. "I'm trying not to embarrass your butt!"

"It's a little too late for that now, isn't it?" she shouted back before twirling around from me once again. That was the last straw.

"Of course you know this means war!" I hollered and slid in front of her once more. Danielle laughed in my face.

"I ain't skurd! Bring it!"

I accepted the dance challenge and hit Danielle Davis with all of my best moves rolled into one. I was well aware that I probably wouldn't be able to walk straight for the next couple of days because of my bad knee, but I had to show Danielle what real dancing was.

She stepped up the pace as well. The deejay began scratching the record and repeating the intro time and time again. I went for broke and squatted all the way down to the floor and began to shimmy back and forth in front of my dance partner. Danielle dropped down in front of me and mimicked my exact moves.

I started to throw a few twirls into my steps then and saw that Danielle was doing likewise. I had some decent competition in front of me on the dance floor, but I wasn't too worried about it. I'd won plenty of dance contests in the past due to my endurance. Sooner or later Danielle would tire out; she'd have to stop and admit defeat.

The deejay then brought '*Outstanding,*' the old Gap Band hit song from the early eighties, into the mix. I began stepping around Danielle in a circle, in perfect time to the beat. When I stopped, she did the same to me.

We danced for the next hour non-stop. The deejay must have played about ten different songs and all of them were the extended versions. I was ready to fall out, but I couldn't bring myself to do it in front of Danielle. She was obviously dragging a bit herself but was not willing to give up either.

"What happened to that one song we were only supposed to be dancing to?" I had tried to yell at Danielle, but it came out more like a whisper.

"You tell me!" she barely yelled back.

"Had enough yet?" I mouthed to her. (I was too tired to try to yell anymore.)

"No. You?" she mouthed back.

The combination of searing heat and exhaustion was too much for me. When my bum left knee started aching, I knew that I was licked.

"You win," I mouthed to her before slowly limping off of the dance floor. Danielle staggered off behind me.

"I'm sure glad you stopped when you did," Danielle whispered to me hoarsely once we got outside, back into the frigid night air.

"Why?" I asked in my own raspy voice.

"I was going to have to, if you didn't."

Danielle noticed that I was walking tenderly on my left leg.

"What's the matter with your leg?"

"Just an old football injury acting up. I'm alright."

I tried to sound as macho as possible, but Danielle wasn't buying it.

"Let me help you."

Danielle threw my left arm over her shoulder and then wrapped her right arm around my waist. If I were not in so much pain at the time, I would have been in heaven. The alluring combination of her perfume mixed with the warm scent of her perspiration was driving me wild.

Crossing the Brooklyn Bridge out of Manhattan on my way home, I reflected upon the night's events. I had gotten tricked into taking a day off from work to go out with a recovering alcoholic, who badgered me into staying out late to go to a nightclub, where I commenced to dancing so hard that my bad knee was killing me. I had enjoyed every second of it.

When I looked over at Danielle sitting across from me, a warm sensation swept over my body from head to toe. I was both pleased and honored that she was there with me. Just as suddenly, I felt bad about how I had treated her the day she ran into me with her uncle's car. I reached over and turned down the volume on my Miles CD as he played his rendition of '*Human Nature*'.

"Danielle?"

She turned and looked at me expectantly.

"Yes?"

"I, uh, I want to apologize for how I acted that day you and I first met."

Danielle smiled and a warm sensation surged through me all over again.

"Oh please, you were mad. Forget about it."

I didn't say anything else to Danielle except to ask her for the directions to her home. When I pulled in front of her apartment complex, a sense of dread crept over me. I didn't want our night together to end. I sighed at the inevitable as I opened the door to get out.

Being the partial gentleman that I am, I had to at least see Danielle to her door, pain or no pain. Two guys were huddled up together not too far from the entrance to her apartment building, smoking a pipe of something that didn't quite smell like tobacco.

"Miss Davis," I began when we got to the entrance door, "I want to tell you that I have enjoyed myself immensely tonight."

"I had a very good time myself," Danielle replied. "And thanks for stopping by that club."

"Believe me, the pleasure was all mine."

I didn't know Danielle enough to try to kiss her, even though I wanted to. Badly.

"Well, good night."

"Goodnight," Danielle said. "Thanks again for everything."

I reluctantly turned around and slowly began hobbling back toward Jada. I was disheartened by the thought that I probably would not be seeing Danielle again.

"Are you going to be alright getting home?" Danielle asked me.

I slowly turned back around and faced her. It was now or never.

"I'd feel a whole lot better if I had your cell number."

(I know that line was corny, but it was the best that I could do on short notice. Okay?)

CHAPTER TWENTY-FIVE

As soon as Luther spied me limping into Another Level the next day around four o'clock, he turned to walk away.

"Luther!"

Apprehension was etched all over his face.

"Yes?"

"You and I need to talk, my man."

"Look, Javier," Luther began as he headed towards me, "I only had good intentions in trying to get you and Miss Davis together. I'm sorry that..."

"Luther!" I snapped again, cutting him off in the process.

Luther stood before me as meek as a lamb.

"Thanks."

A smiled slowly developed over his face.

"I knew it! I knew it! Luther's always right when it comes to these things! You guys had a nice time last night?"

"Yes, we did."

"Tell me how it went!"

I recapped the previous night's events, omitting the part about Danielle out-dancing me at The Well.

"You guys going out again?"

"Yup, this Friday," I told him, smirking.

"You owe me one, boss."

"Yeah, I guess I do."

Luther went back to work. I limped to our business office, which actually was only a storage room big enough to hold a long desk and two chairs. I opened the door to find Tucker on the phone.

"I gotta run now, Linda. I'll call you later on tonight. Okay?"

Tucker didn't wait for her reply, but just hung the receiver up.

"Well, well, well...look at what the cat brought in!" Tucker smiled as he stood up.

"What's up, Tucker?"

I removed my coat and hung it on the back of one of the chairs.

"You're what's up. I tried to wake your ass up before I left out earlier today, but you were dead to the world. What time did you get in last night, Casanova?"

"Let's just say that I barely beat the cows home."

I really wasn't up to discussing my personal business with Tucker.

"So, J.C., did you gut that chick or what?"

"I'm sorry?"

"Did you make Danielle bite the pillow last night?"

"No, I did not. We spent quality time together, if you must know."

"What time is better spent than when you're helping yourself to some fresh poontang?"

"You don't get it, do you?" I walked out of the office in frustration.

"Evidently, you're the one who didn't get it," Tucker chuckled.

That following Friday evening, Danielle met me at Another Level, but would not tell me what she had in store for us. All she disclosed to me was that I had to drive us into the city. I knew we weren't doing anything too elaborate because when I asked her the night before if I needed to be dressed up for our rendezvous, Danielle told me no. She herself was dressed in blue jeans, a wool sweater, and a pair of hiking boots.

When Danielle instructed me to drive up Eighth Avenue after we had crossed over into Manhattan, I objected.

"The traffic's going to be heavy over there because of the Knicks game."

"That's where we're going," Danielle said nonchalantly.

Evidently, I had misunderstood Danielle. Knicks games were always sold out. And the nosebleed tickets that scalpers sold outside the Garden didn't come cheap.

But Danielle stuck a pair of tickets in front of my face.

"How'd you manage that?" My voice was filled with awe and admiration.

"This guy at the job had to go out of town this weekend."

"He gave them to you?"

Danielle looked at me as if I had just sprouted a long horn from my forehead.

"Get real. This is New York."

Yup, homegirl had a valid point there. About the only thing you got free in New York City was a ride to jail if you broke the law.

"You, uh, want me to give you something for them?"

"I wouldn't have bought them if I couldn't afford them, Javier, but I thank you for asking."

I didn't even grumble much about paying for another overpriced parking garage. I was that excited. Even though I had been living in New York for some years, I had never been to a Knicks, or any other professional basketball game. Much to my delight, our seats weren't that bad.

The Knicks were hosting the Atlanta Hawks. The pace of the game was hectic from jumpstreet, or should I say, jump ball. One of the reasons I was able to really enjoy myself that night was because Danielle loathed the Knicks almost as much as I did, if not more. Whenever the Hawks made a basket or made a good defensive play, Danielle and I would applaud...lightly.

When I noticed the annoyance of several of our fellow spectators, I tapped Danielle on her leg.

"We might need to ease up on the clapping a little. Some of these folks around here aren't too happy about it."

Danielle scowled.

"So? My money was just as good as anybody else's to get up in this joint. I'll do as I please."

On the very next play, the shooting guard for the Hawks nailed a three-pointer from way downtown. Danielle jumped out of her seat in delight.

"Yesss!"

The rivalry was on from that point. Many of the Knicks fans around us began cheering extra loudly whenever the Knicks scored a basket or made a good play. By the end of the second period, Danielle and I were getting hoarse from yelling for the visiting team. The game continued to be close in the second half as well.

With less than a minute left in the game, the Hawks scored to take a two-point lead. The Knicks star forward was fouled on the next play and sent to the free-throw line. His first shot hit nothing but net. The entire crowd was hushed in suspense as the ball player focused for the crucial second basket, which would tie the score.

Just as he was about to release the ball from his fingertips, Danielle stood up from her seat, took a deep gasp of breath, and screamed at the top of her lungs: "WATCH HIM MISS IT!!!"

The ball bounced in, and then out of the basket. A Hawks player grabbed the rebound and his team held onto the ball to win the game. The Knicks fans all around us were highly pissed. I nervously tugged on Danielle's sleeve.

"I really think we should go now," I whispered to her.

"Yeah, I think you're right," she replied.

We laughed ourselves silly all the way back into Brooklyn.

"Yo, wasn't that a good game?" Danielle snorted, laughing real hard and gasping for air.

I shook my head in wonderment as I looked at her.

"What?" Danielle asked, still laughing.

"You are one sick sister."

"I'll take that as a compliment. Thanks."

I decided to stop at a quaint little restaurant in Park Slope called the Biscuit Café where they served pretty good country cooking. Fresh baked biscuits were their specialty.

"This food tastes great," Danielle said, digging into crab cakes, candied yams, and macaroni with extra cheese.

"How long has this place been opened?"

"About two years now," I said.

I had ordered the smothered pork chops, brown rice, and cabbage.

"These yams taste just like the ones my Nana used to make me for Sunday dinner," Danielle exclaimed.

"I believe the owners of this place are from Georgia."

Danielle's mentioning of Sunday dinner brought up a question that I had been meaning to ask her.

"Can I ask you a personal question, Danielle?"

Danielle put her fork down and gazed at me with uncertainty.

"What is it?"

"Do you believe in God?"

"Of course I do," she replied. "Don't you?"

"Certainly," I told her. "You go to church?"

Danielle shook her head slowly.

"Not like I need to. To be honest with you, I'm a bona fide member of the CEO Club when it comes to attending church service."

"CEO Club?"

"Christmas and Easter Only."

I nearly fell out of my booth from laughing so hard. A couple of nearby patrons looked over our way to see what the commotion was about.

"You got issues."

"Not me," Danielle replied, smiling and winking mischievously before eating another forkful of yams.

Once again I walked Danielle to her building when I took her home. When we got to the entrance, she turned and faced me.

"Would you care to come up for awhile?"

I wanted to continue my pleasant evening with Danielle more than anything else in the world, but I couldn't.

"Can I take a rain check on that? I plan on hitting the gym early in the morning. This spare tire of mine has been inflating a bit on me lately," I said as I patted my stomach.

"No problem. I understand."

Danielle extended her hand to me.

"Thanks for another entertaining evening."

When I grabbed her hand, I felt a sudden exhilaration flow through my body. *What the hell?* I suddenly pulled Danielle into my arms. I stared into those bewitching eyes of hers for a few moments before giving her a slow, hot, impassioned kiss.

"Damn, dude!" Danielle exclaimed when we came up for air. "If I didn't know any better, I'd swear you really liked me."

"You ain't too bad," I replied nonchalantly.

"What was that?" Danielle asked.

Luckily, I managed to duck the playful swing she took at me.

"Javier, I oughta knock your head off..."

I drove home that night with a warm feeling in my heart. It looked like my prayers for a soul mate had finally been answered.

The next morning, as I prepared to go to the gym, Tucker asked if he could tag along. He had been taking a lot of ribbing from some of his clients about his expanding paunch. I was well aware of my roommate's dilemma. Ever since we opened Another Level, I had not been able to get up early and hit the gym like I used to and it was beginning to show. I needed all the spare time I had on weekday mornings just to get some rest. This meant I was able to workout on the weekends only. That was better than nothing, but it was far from enough.

"You ready to buy a membership?" I asked Tucker while I stood in the kitchen making myself a protein drink.

Tucker had told me that he wanted to purchase a membership to Bronze's ages ago. However, every time I asked him to come with me and join up he had a convenient excuse not to. I had given up asking him.

"My checkbook's right here," Tucker replied as he walked into the kitchen buttoning up his coat.

I grabbed my overcoat and gym bag from the back of the chair next to me and we headed out the front door.

"Why don't I drive?" Tucker offered as we walked down the steps to the sidewalk.

"That'll work."

I didn't have one problem with that at all. Ever since Danielle had sideswiped me in Jada, I'd been using mass transit more frequently.

The parking lot was over halfway full when we arrived. While Tucker filled out paper work to buy a membership, I headed straight for the locker room. I spied my man Tony squatting on a bench lacing up his sneakers.

"Well looka here!" Tony exclaimed as he stood up. "I don't believe it!"

"What's up, Tony?"

We did the brotherman hand-clasp-and-hug thang.

"You are what's up," Tony answered. "Where have you been hiding at?"

"Nowhere. I've just been working hard, my brother."

"You got a new gig?"

"You can say that. I'm over at Another Level."

"Yo, I heard about that place. Been meaning to check it out."

"Come on by and I'll hit you off with the first drink."

"You the bartender?"

"I am, on occasion. Enough questions about me. How's it going with you?"

Tony's smile dimmed.

"I'm getting divorced."

Even as he tried to sound upbeat, his eyes told an entirely different story. Evidently, his wife had had enough of his fooling around. It was a shame that it came to that.

"It's not that bad though," Tony continued. "I'm laying up with this nice little cutie out in Red Hook. She got ass all night long! You gotta come on over and check us out sometime."

"Okay, I can do that."

Tony grabbed his towel from the bench beside him.

"See you out on the floor."

He exited the locker room just as Tucker was walking in.

"You all set now?" I asked him.

"Yeah, after shelling out an ass of money," he muttered.

"Hurry up and change then. I'll be waiting for you over by the treadmills."

After a thirty-minute run on the treadmills, Tucker and I moved over to the stair climbing machines. And after that, we made our way over to the abs machines to get our crunches on.

As we ramped up our workout, music from the exercise room suddenly began to thump and the walls started to vibrate from the pulsing beat.

At least half of the brothers who were in Bronze's at that moment stopped what they were doing and began to congregate in front of the glass-walled exercise area to watch.

In my three years of working out in the place, I had never seen that before. I got up to see what all the commotion was about. And there, in the middle of the pack of sweating sisters, was The Truth, her flawless body jumping, kicking, and bending in perfect time to the music her aerobics class was dancing to.

I could have sworn that a few of the fellas around me were drooling as they watched her body move. When some knucklehead shoved me to the side, I spun around angrily.

"What's going on in there?"

Tucker answered his own question when he peered through the glass. He stood there captivated for a few seconds.

"Yo, who is *that* sister?"

"That, my brother, is The Truth."

"You ain't lying about that!"

"Her real name is Dionne."

Tucker continued to stare at The Truth in awe.

"Man, she can set me free anytime she want to!"

I turned away from the spectacle to resume my workout. I assumed that Tucker had followed me. When I turned around to confirm this, however, I saw that my man was strolling through the glass door that led into the exercise area.

Tucker grabbed two of the plastic steps that were stacked neatly in the corner by the door and plopped them down on the floor, right beside The Truth. All of the brothers looking in from the other side of the glass wall, including yours truly, began shaking our heads in disbelief at bodacious Tucker.

For about five minutes or so, my roommate made a complete idiot of himself trying to perform the routine that the aerobics class was executing. The people around me were falling over each other with laughter. When the women slid over to the right, Tucker slid to the left. While everyone else was kicking up high, Tucker was still squatting down low.

Even some of the sisters in the aerobics class were chuckling to themselves as they viewed Tucker from the corner of their eyes.

And then Tucker began to get the hang of the routine. Eventually, he started to show off. He began putting a little extra bounce in his steps. When he threw a kick, it was done a la Michael Jackson, one hand was placed on his hip and the other one was pointed straight up in the air. By then, everyone in the room was now cheering Tucker on.

"Go 'head! Go 'head! Go 'head!"

The Truth was smiling, chanting and nodding her head with approval as well. Tucker had done it again.

When the song was over, all the women were high-fiving Tucker, who put his steps away and made his way back out into the main area of the gym.

"That wasn't nothing, man," Tucker said to some of the brothers who patted him on the back.

"That wasn't nothing!" he repeated loudly. "I do that at the club every night!"

As Tucker neared me he began to grimace. He was in serious pain.

"Please help me?" he pleaded softly.

I put my arms around Tucker's shoulders as if I was giving him congratulations and then guided him to the locker room. Tucker collapsed from exhaustion on the first bench he reached. He took in big gulps of air in an effort to catch his breath.

"That...that shit almost killed me back there!" he gasped. "Take my keys and drive me to the emergency room right now! I think I broke something on me I still need!"

"Why'd you do it?" I asked curiously as I quickly opened my locker to retrieve my belongings.

"I had to go get her number," he answered between groans.

"What? You got The Truth's phone number?" I asked Tucker in amazement.

"Shiiit, you think I didn't?!"

CHAPTER TWENTY-SIX

"**N**o way, forget it."

"Why not?"

"Because I don't want to, Tucker."

"But it'll be a lot of fun!"

My roommate had begun to worry me. From his first date with The Truth, Tucker was acting bizarre. One day I heard him apologize profusely to a customer after she had complained that her ribs were overcooked. Tucker immediately instructed our cook to prepare another order for the woman.

That was a far cry from his usual. Before, he would have simply scraped away the char back in the kitchen, pour more barbeque sauce onto the meat, and return it to the customer himself with a warm, fake smile.

This new Tucker was an enigma. I cased his room for drugs one night while he was at work. (I was greatly relieved when I didn't find any.)

And instead of hanging out awhile after close of business like he used to do, Tucker always drove straight home and went to sleep if he wasn't out with The Truth.

With the exception of his ex-wife, I had never seen Tucker spend so much time with just one woman.

Still, I felt kind of guilty knowing what I did about my roommate's reputation with women and not sharing it with The Truth. I, therefore, avoided her like the plague.

If it had been another brother that The Truth was dealing with, and I knew that his intentions were no good, I would have probably pulled her coattails about it. But being that she was dealing with Tucker, I had to give allegiance to my man and remain silent. I only hoped that when The Truth did find out what Tucker was really about the emotional damage wouldn't be too great.

Tucker stood in my face as I leaned over the kitchen sink washing dishes. He was begging me to take Danielle and accompany him and The Truth down to Atlantic City for the weekend.

"I said no, Tucker."

My reasons were twofold: one, I didn't believe in giving my hard-earned money to some multi-millionaire casino owners; and two, I wasn't about to ask Danielle to spend a weekend with me out of town because it would look like I was trying to get into her pants.

Unbeknownst to anyone but God, I had made a solemn vow to myself not to become sexually involved with her. If Danielle was the girl for me, and I hoped that she was, then I would ascertain her sexual capacities after we had been joined by God, and before our beloved witnesses, and not a day sooner. A reach for me? Yes. But not impossible, and that was my goal.

"Okay, then, suit yourself."

Tucker began to walk dejectedly out of the kitchen.

"Why do you want me and Danielle to go down there along with you two, anyway?"

My roommate stopped and turned around.

"I think Dionne would be more comfortable if there was another sister there that she could hang out with. Plus, I want her to see the type of positive people that I associate with."

Stunned, I accidentally dropped the plate that I was drying. It shattered into a hundred tiny pieces when it hit the floor. *Tucker was actually concerned about a woman's feelings? This couldn't be.*

Before I could make a move to retrieve the dustpan and broom, Tucker reached into our utility closet and got them out.

"That's alright, bro. I'll get it up."

I accidentally dropped another plate. My roommate never cleaned up after anybody. He barely cleaned up after himself. Tucker eyed me suspiciously as he swept up the debris.

"To be honest with you, Tucker, I'm not too keen on giving my money over to some already rich white men that easily. Besides, I don't think Danielle's schedule would allow her to take a weekend off anyway, so if you want the two of us to tag along with you guys, it'll have to be something on the local tip."

I was sure that I had heard the last of the four of us getting together. Like I said earlier, I didn't want to be around The Truth when she found out the truth about Tucker.

"I know what!" Tucker exclaimed. "How about I cook us all dinner here next weekend?"

There was a look of exhilaration in Tucker's eyes when he asked me that question. I stared at him in wonderment as I slowly stuck one of my soapy hands out and felt his forehead.

"Are you feeling okay?"

Hannibal Tucker *never* cooked for any of his clients before. Even though he made his living based upon his culinary expertise, it was always his female guests that toiled away in our kitchen cooking, or in some cases, trying to cook something.

I personally didn't give a hoot about these folks banging pots in our kitchen, but far too many times than I cared to remember, I had to go and clean up the mess that was left behind. I recall one time in particular when this sister left cornbread batter splattered up on the ceiling! I never did find out how it got up there, or why no one bothered to get it down.

"There's nothing wrong with me," Tucker answered defensively as he slapped my hand away. "Why can't I share my cooking talents with others for free sometimes?"

I briefly considered the notion that perhaps aliens had kidnapped the real Tucker because the man in front of me was definitely not my friend from back home.

That next Saturday afternoon, after we made sure that Luther had everything and everyone in control at Another Level, Tucker set about in the kitchen chopping up this, dicing up that, and mixing up whatever to create some exotic dish that had a funny French name to it. I was expecting Tucker to at least take the easy road and dazzle our company with some variation of his barbecue, but I was wrong. A few days before our scheduled get-together, Tucker videotaped segments of a show on the Cooking Channel and got some creative ideas for his upcoming meal.

What Tucker came up with looked like a fancy meatloaf to me. He made a dressed-up potato and cheese recipe to go along with his special meatloaf, as well as some spinach a la something for the mandatory green vegetable requirement. The Truth arrived at our place a little after seven.

"Look who's here, roomie!"

Tucker reminded me of a peacock as he strolled into the kitchen with The Truth on his arm. She was dressed in a light pink blouse and a pair of black jeans. I was at the counter busy putting the finishing touches on my pitcher of iced tea.

"Evening, Tru, I mean, Dionne."

"How are you doing, Javier?"

"I'm ready to eat."

The Truth laughed politely.

"We're just waiting on his lady friend to arrive, Dionne," Tucker explained to her.

I hoped that Danielle didn't take forever coming over because I was itching to see what that fancy meatloaf of Tucker's tasted like. My prayers were answered when our door buzzer rang ten minutes later.

"Am I too late for dinner?" Danielle asked when I opened the door for her.

After receiving a quick peck on the lips, I closed the door behind her and then helped her out of her leather jacket. Danielle was wearing a beautiful cardigan sweater and some hip-hugging slacks.

"Girl, you look good enough to eat yourself," I replied without thinking. Danielle gave me an uneasy glance.

"Trust me, that was only a figure of speech, darling," I informed her.

"I oughta knock your head off," Danielle mumbled.

After making formal introductions to everyone, we got down to business. Tucker's fancy-looking meatloaf turned out to be a hit with our guests. I soon grew weary of both ladies constantly commenting on his superb culinary artistry. (Nobody commented on my iced tea, even though the pitcher was damn near empty.)

Following dinner, we all sat around the table contemplating what we should do next.

"How about a movie?" Tucker suggested.

"I'd probably go to sleep myself," I informed the group.

There was nothing really playing in the theaters at the moment that I deemed worthy of having to use my credit card to watch. Going to the movies in New York had grown very expensive.

"How about we play a game of Spades?" Danielle suggested. She turned and faced The Truth.

"Do you know how to play, Dionne?"

"Yeah, but I'm not that good."

"That doesn't matter girl; neither are these two."

Danielle pointed to Tucker and me.

"Sounds like a challenge, roomie," I said.

"That it does," Tucker agreed.

We quickly began clearing off the kitchen table. I looked over at Danielle and shook my head in pity.

"Ain't no way you gonna be lucky enough to come up in my house and beat me in a Spades' game."

"Is that what you call what happened to you the last time?" she sneered.

"Yeah, you guys were fortunate when you beat me down at my place of business, Danielle," Tucker answered for me.

Danielle gave Tucker a surprised look.

"You own Another Level?"

Tucker proudly shook his head yes.

"I also used to own the House of Pork over on Livingston. I just sold it a month ago to a group of Rastafarians…for an extremely nice profit."

Danielle then turned to me.

"You work for your roommate? That's nice."

I smiled at her weakly.

"J.C. doesn't work for me, Danielle; he's a part-owner."

My smile grew weaker. Danielle gave me a confused look.

"You never told me that you were a co-owner, Javier?"

Even though Danielle's last statement sounded nonchalant, I knew she was quite upset. I purposely didn't share that bit of information with Danielle because I wanted to know what her values were first.

I wasn't a Bill Gates, or anything close to him, but I had seen a few successful brothers in the past get hooked up with some money-hungry sisters. Those women had all of their bills taken care of and still gave those brothers grief whenever they felt like it.

"I guess I didn't, Danielle. Sorry about that."

"Hey, let's get started people," Tucker ordered.

Danielle continued to eye me funny until we began playing cards. She and Dionne then proceeded to beat us soundly…both games.

"You guys had enough?" Danielle asked with a smug look on her face.

Tucker stared over at me. He was still hungry for at least one victory over our female oppressors. So was I.

"Never!" we replied in unison.

"It's your funeral, people," Danielle remarked casually as she began shuffling the deck of cards. At that moment, we heard a loud thud downstairs. Tucker and I both gazed at each other in dread. Flora and Harry were at it again. Our downstairs neighbors had been relatively silent for the past four or five months, and we'd assumed that they had finally resolved their differences. Evidently, we were wrong. We heard another loud bang below us.

"What's that?" Dionne asked Tucker, who looked over at me for support.

"That's our neighbors downstairs," I answered.

"We kind of get that part," Danielle stated. "What are they doing?" Now it was my turn to look over to Tucker for assistance.

"They're just having another argument," he said casually.

"You mean they fight like this all the time?" Danielle asked in astonishment. I nodded my head in affirmation.

"Why don't you guys do something about it? Somebody could get hurt down there."

For some reason Danielle appeared to be unusually concerned about the fighting going on below us, which had now moved out into the hallway.

"It'll be over in another minute or so," I awkwardly informed our guests.

"This is crazy!" Danielle declared as she jumped out of her chair.

Before I could ask her what she was getting ready to do, Danielle was already on her way to our front door.

"Yo, you'd better go after her, J.C.," Tucker advised.

I shot out of my seat and went into the living room, where I found our front door wide open. *Crap!* I thought to myself as I ran down the stairs after Danielle. I would never be able to sleep peacefully again if she accidentally got clocked by one of Mrs. Jenkins' flying frying pans.

When I reached the bottom of the stairs, I was surprised to find that Danielle had the couple hemmed together in the corner behind the entrance door. She quickly glanced at me momentarily and then refocused on my neighbors.

"You folks ought to be ashamed of yourselves carrying on like this! I can't even enjoy myself at my boyfriend's house because of you two!"

Hearing Danielle call me her boyfriend brought a smile to my face. When Flora and Harry looked over in my direction with a silent plea for help, I quickly converted my smile into a frown in support of my official new girlfriend. Danielle drew herself up into Mrs. Jenkins' buxom chest.

"If you two have to resort to fighting like this, why don't you just go your separate ways?"

Neither of the combatants mumbled a single word. I was just as dumbfounded as they were. It had always been my opinion to keep out of other people's business, unless it involved me personally. Evidently, Danielle didn't think that way.

"Mr. Collins here is a case worker. Why don't you two ask him to try to hook you up with some counseling or something, before it's too late and somebody winds up in jail, or in the morgue?"

Girlfriend was actually making pretty good sense so far, but she was still in danger of getting herself hurt and I couldn't allow that.

"Danielle, come on," I called out to her softly.

My neighbors appeared relieved at my beckoning for her. Danielle ignored me as she turned and faced Mr. Jenkins.

"Do you two go to church, Sir?"

"Yeah...we...we do," Mr. Jenkins stammered.

"And you still carry on like this?"

Mr. Jenkins was at a loss for words, as was his wife. I stepped down from my perch on the bottom step and touched Danielle real gently on her arm. (I wasn't down for getting kicked in the nuts again.)

"Let's go, Danielle."

Homegirl was still pretty worked up, but she reluctantly followed me back to my apartment.

"I don't know what happened to me back there. I've never done anything like that before."

I was driving Danielle back home. Tucker and The Truth appeared to be in the need of some privacy when Danielle and I got back upstairs, and Danielle was so riled up herself after confronting my neighbors, that I figured it was best for everyone to call it a night.

"I guess all of that bitterness from remembering when my own parents used to fight like that in front of me must have come out. What do you think?"

"I think you'd better not do something like that again. Look, if I sound a little harsh, I apologize right here and now, Danielle. It's just that I don't think that I could bear to see you get hurt. I care for you too much."

There, I had said it. An awkward moment of silence followed as we traveled down Bedford Avenue.

"Well, if you cared for me so much Mr. Collins, why did you hide the fact that you own the place where you work at from me?"

"I didn't hide anything from you, Danielle," I responded weakly.

"Then what would you call it? Withholding information?"

"Kinda sorta..."

I was sounding weaker by the moment.

"Why? No, let me guess. You thought that I might be some kind of gold digger?"

Girlfriend had hit the nail dead on the head. I gazed over at her eerily, but said nothing out of guilt.

"For your information, Mr. Collins, I have earned my own money since I was sixteen. I don't need no man to..."

I tried to interrupt.

"Danielle, I didn't mean..."

"No, let me finish! In case you feel that there's anything else you need to hide from me. I've made my own money since I was sixteen, and I'm going to damn sure continue to do so. Okay? I don't have time for anyone with paranoia, Mr. Collins. I've got better things to do!"

I felt five inches tall when I finally pulled in front of Danielle's building. I looked at her sadly as she opened her door to get out. The last thing that I wanted in the world was for the two of us to be at odds again.

"So, you gonna come up or what?" Danielle barked at me.

I knew an opening for forgiveness when I saw one.

"Yes, Ma'am! Let me find a park!"

"What did I tell you about calling me Ma'am?"

"Sorry."

"I oughta knock your head off..."

Danielle's dwelling was classified as a junior one-bedroom. That's New York-ese for an overpriced, studio apartment. She didn't have a lot of furniture in it per se, but she did have enough of the basics to make do. A small stereo system, a television, a bed, a large futon, and a small coffee table. Danielle removed her work uniform off the futon.

"Have a seat," she instructed. She picked up her remote and clicked the television on. I did as ordered.

"I got my cable turned back on, but it's only basic now. That's all I can afford."

"I heard that."

(I wondered if ESPN was included in Danielle's new cable package. I prayed that she still had it.)

"I'll be right back. I'm going to get out of these clothes."

In an effort to keep my thoughts clean, I began surfing the channels on the idiot box. Danielle returned wearing a tank top and sweat pants. She sat down on the opposite end of the futon. I was puzzled by her action. Was she still angry with me about the Another Level issue? I had to find out.

"You still mad at me?"

"Trust me, if I was mad at you, you wouldn't be back up here in my apartment."

Well…that's good to know.

"Uh, Danielle?" I asked with an exaggerated Southern drawl.

"Yes?"

"Where I'm from, when two folks are courtin'? They usually sit a little closer together."

Danielle smiled in spite of herself as she slid down a little further toward me.

"Is that better?" she asked playfully.

I shook my head no.

"Could you come a little closer?"

Danielle scowled as she scooted down closer to me.

"What about now?"

Again, I shook my head no. Danielle slid over some more.

"Okay, what about...?"

That was as far as she got, because as soon as Danielle was within my arm's reach, I embraced her and we began kissing heavily. The good part was that we stayed that way for at least ten minutes. The bad part was that I had an erection after the first two.

I wound up spending the night at Danielle's apartment. On the futon. I had felt so good and relaxed snuggled up in her arms as we watched television that I nodded off to sleep unintentionally. I woke up later on that night with a warm blanket wrapped around me and a pleasantly scented pillow propped under my head.

From around the corner of the L-shaped room where her bed was located, I could hear Danielle sleeping softly. Even though I wasn't lying in bed next to her, I still felt a warm sensation tingling through my body. I softly hummed the tune to my favorite Bob Marley song, '*Is This Love*' as I waited to drift back off to sleep.

The next morning I awoke to the sound of gospel music playing on the stereo.

"About time you got up," Danielle announced as she made up her bed.

"Man, what time is it?" I asked groggily.

"It's a quarter to seven."

"Sorry for dozing off on you last night. Evidently, I was more tired than I thought."

"That's okay. You hungry?"

"Not really."

As I sat up on the futon and stretched, I noticed Danielle eyeing me closely.

"What's up?" I asked.

"I plan on going to church this morning. You wanna come?"

"Huh? It's Easter already?"

The pillow Danielle hurled at me hit me smack in the middle of my face.

We caught the eleven o'clock service at Good Aim Baptist Church, over on Lafayette Avenue. I had zoomed home, bathed, changed clothes, and hurried back to pick Danielle up. She was adamant about making it to the church by nine-thirty. I knew her reasoning for this once I drove by the long line that was outside of the building. Thanks to Reverend Myron Pendergrass' well-publicized involvement in the surrounding community's affairs, his church had a very large membership. The church's congregation was so big, in fact, that they actually had a holding area for members waiting to get into the next service. Dozens of members, mostly females, brought small portable stools along to make the wait more comfortable.

"When was the last time you came here?" I whispered to Danielle.

We had been standing in line for almost an hour and my feet were beginning to go numb.

"Don't start," she threatened.

"No, I'm serious."

"When I first moved back here. The line was much longer then."

"You've got to be kidding me."

Danielle assured me that the service would be worth the wait and it was. The choir and instrumentalists opened devotional service with a rousing song of praise that brought everybody on their feet. The whole congregation was raising the roof in the name of the Lord.

"Yo, this place is funky!" I shouted into Danielle's ear as we raised the roof along with everyone else.

"Didn't I tell you?" she yelled back.

The pastor gave a fervid sermon on moral conduct in the eyes of God. When Reverend Pendergrass got to the part about fornication, I felt as guilty as sin while I sat there in Good Aim because I'd been debating whether or not to try to sleep with Danielle. It was getting harder and harder (pun intended) to resist human nature. Danielle was just that tempting to me. I prayed for strength as I sat next to her in church that Sunday morning.

CHAPTER TWENTY-SEVEN

I tried futilely to convince myself that I wasn't nervous about meeting Danielle's mother. Betty Ann Davis had driven up to New York for a visit with her daughter, and she was adamant about meeting me. She had let it be known to Danielle earlier in the week that she expected to see me at dinner on Sunday.

I had spoken to Danielle's mother only once. She had called while I was at Danielle's apartment one evening working on her leaky showerhead.

From our short conversation, I deduced that Ms. Davis did not pull any punches. She asked me bluntly if there was any other plumbing of her daughter's that I was working on. I caught her double-entendre and politely told Danielle's mother no. I was then advised that, if I knew what was good for me, I'd keep it that way.

That brought my earlier fiasco at Jeanette's family gathering back to my mind. I was thinking about that scary incident as Danielle and I rode the elevator up to her apartment. And, rationally, I knew that Tucker's warning about fried chicken was total nonsense.

It didn't calm my nerves any when Danielle unlocked her front door and the aroma of fried bird slowly wafted into the hallway to greet me.

"Where is he?" I heard Ms. Davis ask her daughter as Danielle stepped into the apartment.

"He's right here, Mama."

"Well, bring him on in."

I felt like a criminal on his way to meet the judge the way the two Davis women were discussing me. I slowly stepped through the door and peered in the direction of Ms. Davis' voice. She was sitting on the futon watching television.

Ms. Davis was a fairly attractive woman who was even smaller than her daughter was. She also appeared to be a bit on the frail side. I knew that this was due to her illness. She looked to be right at home in her over-sized t-shirt, blue jeans, and pair of pink slippers on her tiny feet.

"Come on over here, son," she said.

I shuffled along as commanded towards Ms. Davis.

"Hello, Ms. Davis."

"So, you are Javier Collins?" Ms. Davis remarked after looking me up and down.

"Yes, Ma'am."

"I've heard a lot about you."

"All good I hope," I said with a cheesy smile.

"It was all good. I just hope that it's all true."

My smile disappeared.

"Mama!"

"What? I'm just being honest with him, Danielle. What's wrong with that?"

"Mama, don't start. Please?"

"Alright, alright. How was service this morning?" Ms. Davis asked her daughter. I was glad that she had gotten off my case.

"Good," Danielle answered. "How was the service over at Saint Mark's?"

Danielle's mother had decided earlier that morning to visit the church she attended regularly when she lived in Brooklyn.

"Fine. I see a lot of my old friends are still there," Ms. Davis said as she stood up.

"I don't know about you two," she continued, "but I'm ready to eat. Shall we?"

The entire meal that Ms. Davis prepared was delicious: the beans and rice, collard greens, cornbread, even the fried chicken. I was a little hesitant about eating any of it at first, but then common sense prevailed. Also, I was hungrier than a bear after hibernation; so I wound up eating several pieces.

However, I couldn't help but notice that Ms. Davis seemed to be studying me from across the small dinette table. After dinner, Ms. Davis backed her chair away from the table and stood up.

"You know, Danielle, I've got me a taste for some real lemonade. Would you be kind and run out to the store and pick up a couple of fresh lemons for your mama?"

Danielle didn't look too thrilled about her mother's request. I saw my chance to score a few brownie points with Ms. Davis.

"I'll go get them for you, Ma'am."

I hopped up from the table with enthusiasm.

"You stay right here!" Ms. Davis advised me sternly.

I sat back down. For some reason, a small warning bell went off in the back of my mind. Then it all came to me...I remembered that my parents used to send me to the store to buy lemons, toilet paper, or some other small item whenever they wanted some time alone so that they could go do the nasty. Ms. Davis obviously wanted some privacy for the two of us.

"I mean, I'd like for you to stay here with me, Javier, so we can talk some," Ms. Davis said in a now-sweetened tone.

Danielle looked at her mother uneasily and then looked over at me questioningly.

"Sounds good to me," I said warily.

"Okay then," Danielle said with a sigh. "I'll be right back."

"Oh, take your sweet time, daughter," Ms. Davis said with a smile.

I excused myself and visited the bathroom because I had overdone it with those collard greens. They had my system backfiring like crazy. After about ten minutes, I returned and sat down on the futon next to Danielle's mother.

"So Ms. Davis, do you miss Brooklyn any?" I asked, trying to make small talk.

"Fuck Brooklyn."

My jaw dropped open in disbelief.

"What are your intentions with my daughter?"

"I'm sorry, Ma'am?"

"Don't you 'Ma'am' me! What are you after my daughter for, Mr. Collins?"

I was caught off guard by Ms. Davis' direct line of questioning.

"I'm, I'm not after anything."

"Then why are you spending so much time with her?"

"I like her."

"That's it?"

"Yeah!" I stated loudly. I was trying to keep my cool, but the woman was pushing me! I silently hoped that her interrogation of me would now cease, but unfortunately, her inquisition was far from over.

"You do drugs, Collins?"

"Of course not!"

"You sell drugs?"

"No!"

"Do you know anyone who sells drugs?"

"You looking to buy some?" I was losing my patience with Betty Ann Davis. I was also only seconds away from calling her out of her name as well.

"Don't get smart with me, son! You got any kids?"

I took a long deep sigh before I decided to go ahead and answer the woman.

"No, Ma'am. I don't."

"You sure?"

"I'm positive."

"I damn hope you ain't one of them 'down low' brothers? Cause I know all about y'all."

"Hell no!"

"Who you cussing, boy?!" Ms. Davis barked.

"Sorry, Ma'am."

I had had enough of Ms. Davis.

"I don't have any children, because I'm not married," I remarked slowly before standing up.

"Where are you going?" Ms. Davis asked with concern.

"I'm going to leave now before I say something to you that I might regret. I wish I could state that it was nice meeting you lady, but that would be telling a big fat lie. Tell Danielle I'll call her later."

I turned and started walking to the front door.

"Wait a minute there, Collins!" Ms. Davis called out as she stood up herself.

"Yes?" I said after another long sigh.

"Would you please come and sit back down for a minute? There's something I wish to share with you."

I was still focused on leaving Danielle's apartment until Ms. Davis took me by the arm and walked me back over to the futon. I decided to be polite and lend her my ear. I was still going home after she was finished talking.

"First of all, let me apologize for my behavior just now. I got a little carried away. I am sorry."

Ms. Davis looked at me for some type of response to her apology. I didn't give her one.

"Danielle told you that she used to attend college down in Virginia, didn't she?"

"Yes, Ma'am, she did."

"Did she tell you why she never finished?"

I recalled how when I had asked Danielle about her college experience before, she had avoided answering me and I had left it alone.

"No, Ma'am, she did not."

Ms. Davis sighed softly as she slid over a little closer to me. (I balled my fists up, in case of trouble.)

"Danielle maintained a three point nine grade point average when she was at school, until she ran across a certain young man named Carlos Taylor. He was a smooth talker from Chicago. He told my baby everything that she wanted to hear. He dressed fancy, drove a nice car, and threw plenty of money around wherever he went. Danielle fell head-over-heels in love with him, and her grades suffered."

The seriousness that I saw on Ms. Davis' face convinced me that what she was telling me was true.

"She started drinking, smoking, and I don't know what else, when she moved off of campus the next year without my knowledge, and shacked up with that damn boy."

There was a painful expression on Ms. Davis' face as she continued.

"She never seriously questioned where Carlos got all of his money from, until the police arrested the two of them for selling drugs."

"Really?"

"It cost me and her late father plenty of money to convince a jury that my baby wasn't involved in that damn mess with her so-called boyfriend. During the lengthy court process, Danielle lost the baby that she was carrying from Carlos due to the stress. Soon after her acquittal she started drinking real heavy. We wound up sending her to rehab."

I nodded my head in sympathy for Ms. Davis. Evidently, she had been through a lot with her only child.

"It took a lot of prayer, love, patience, and money to get my baby back on the right track. You can believe that I tried my damned best to talk her out of moving back up here to Brooklyn, but she said that her father needed her. So I had to finally relent. Now she's working hard and going back to school. I'm proud that she's doing quite well for herself."

"I'm sure that you are, Ma'am," I said while un-balling my fists.

I had misjudged Danielle's mother and I felt bad about it.

"So you see then," Ms. Davis continued, "when Danielle kept on mentioning your name to me every time we spoke on the phone, I figured that it was time for me to come up here and check you out for myself. Collins, I do not think that I could stand to go through another ordeal like that again. In fact, I know I couldn't. I'd take someone out before I'd let them mess my baby's life up again."

I re-balled my fists. I truly understood why Ms. Davis was being so protective of her daughter, but I did not condone the idea of the woman making thinly veiled threats.

As soon as I opened my mouth to let her know as such, I heard Danielle's key jingling in the front door lock. She hurried into the room breathing rapidly and leaned up against the door after she had closed it.

"I'm back," she panted. "Did I miss anything?"

"Not really. We were just shooting the breeze. Right, Collins?"

Ms. Davis shot me a hard look, as if daring me to disagree with her.

"Yeah," I answered, meekly. "That's exactly what we did."

"Why are you out of breath? Have you been running?" Ms. Davis asked her daughter.

"I'm not out of breath, Mama," Danielle said as she wiped sweat from her forehead. "Here are your lemons."

Ms. Davis made her lemonade and offered me the first glass. (I sniffed my tumbler cautiously before drinking it.) It turned out to be quite good. She then proceeded to chat with me as if we were the best of friends. Upon the time of my departure, she even hugged me and told me that she looked forward to us getting together again before she went back home. I lied and told her that I did too.

As I lay in my bed later on that night, I thought to myself that maybe it was time for me to seriously consider a future with Danielle. I then began to tally up her merits. Danielle possessed a warm personality, a friendly smile, and a kind heart. She also had a wicked sense of humor. Danielle held a pretty good job with good medical benefits, also.

Danielle did not smoke or drink anymore. I then thought about how pretty Danielle was and the fact that she constantly stayed on my mind. (I won't mention what I thought about every night concerning her.) Furthermore, there were those alluring, almond-shaped eyes of hers. Danielle was a somewhat religious person. The both of us had been going to church steadily for the past few months over at Good Aim Baptist. That fact alone counted double in my book. All in all, out of a total of ten possible points that could have been awarded to Danielle, I gave my girl an eight. (I deducted two points for her mama.)

That rating was still high enough for me, however. I smiled contentedly as I reached over and clicked off the light on my nightstand. *I guess there's only one other thing left for me to do.* I thought to myself before nodding off to sleep.

CHAPTER TWENTY-EIGHT

When I called Daddy and told him I was coming home that following weekend, he immediately asked me what was wrong. I told Daddy that nothing was wrong, and that I had a lady friend that I wanted him to meet. His lone reply was that he'd believe it when he saw it.

I could understand Daddy's attitude because I had made the foolish mistake of telling him a few years back that I was bringing Mandy's cousin, Juanita, home to meet him. I was really excited about finally showing her off to Daddy after I had bragged about her so much. Plus, I wanted Daddy to see that his boy was holding his own when it came to courting big city women.

After arriving at Daddy's house empty-handed, I felt like a jackass when I had to explain to him how his son had gotten kicked to the curb over a damn book. Daddy gave me a stoic look and a firm pat on the back as he told me that that was how the game of love went sometimes. He also stated that Juanita wasn't the girl for me anyway. Daddy then got up and walked out of the room. A few seconds later I heard him dying of laughter in the kitchen.

As I drove Jada across the state line into South Carolina on a Thursday evening, I decided that it was time to forewarn Danielle about Daddy.

"If he seems a little gruff, you have to disregard it. That's just a lot of years of being in the military coming out of him. Okay?" She only smiled at me.

"This is your father we're talking about?"

"That's correct."

"Then how bad can he possibly be?"

"Could you keep that thought in mind for the next three days?"

Danielle laughed at my suggestion, but I was dead serious.

When I arrived at the house, Daddy wasn't there.

"He must have gone out to the store or something," I told Danielle as I opened the front door with my key.

I led Danielle into the guest bedroom, where she would be staying. It was my mother's old sewing room. When I turned around to leave her alone so that she could put her belongings away, I noticed that there was a look of concern on her face.

"You sure it's okay for me to stay here?"

"Positive. In fact, Daddy was the one who suggested it."

At that moment, I heard the front door swing open.

"J.C.?"

"In here, Sir."

I walked out of the room with Danielle timidly trailing behind me. Daddy was in the kitchen setting two bulging bags of groceries down on the table.

"Hello there, son!"

My Spidey senses began to tingle when Daddy turned and hugged me. He never did that! Daddy then freed me and beheld Danielle.

"Miss Davis?"

"Yes, Sir."

"Don't call me Sir! I ain't that old yet!"

Danielle gave me a look of surprise, mixed with alarm from over Daddy's right shoulder when he suddenly picked her up in a bear hug.

"Believe me when I tell you young lady, how glad I am to actually meet you!"

(I pretended that I didn't hear the sarcasm in Daddy's statement.)

"It's nice to meet you too, Mr. Collins."

"Please, call me Daddy."

"Okay...Daddy."

Daddy released Danielle and then refocused his attention back on me.

"How long did it take you to get down?"

"Twelve hours."

"That was pretty good."

Daddy walked back over to the bags that were resting on the kitchen table and began pulling out their contents.

"I'm quite sure you two are hungry from that long trip. What would you guys like to eat?"

"You don't have to cook anything for us, Daddy."

"You didn't hear me say shit about cooking a damn-I mean, I was referring to us eating out, son. It'll be my treat."

We went to a steakhouse that had an all-you-can-eat buffet for
ten bucks a person. Cheaper food was one of the things that I missed
dearly about living in the South.

We gorged ourselves on sliced ham, turkey, roast beef, spaghetti
and meatballs, chicken wings and numerous varieties of fruits and
vegetables. I won't even bring up the desserts. During a trip to the
inclusive salad bar, Daddy nudged me with his elbow.

"That Danielle seems to be a sweet, young lady."

"Thank you, Sir."

We both looked over at Danielle as she sat alone at our table,
dining on roast beef.

"Let me ask you something, son?"

"Yes Sir?"

"What's with the hair?"

Daddy was referring to Danielle's dreads.

"I don't understand what you're asking me, Daddy."

"Is there some kind of religious group or something that she's
involved in up there in New York?"

"No. That's just the way she likes to wear her hair."

Daddy eyed Danielle once again.

"She sure can put a lot of food away for her size, can't she?"

"I guess she can hold her own."

"How come she ain't no bigger?"

"I like her the way she is!" I answered defensively. I
immediately cringed for Daddy's rebuke.

"You plan on marrying this girl?" he asked instead.

I was caught totally off guard by Daddy's inquiry. I had
anticipated him asking me this question when he and I were back at
the house alone somewhere.

"I'm thinking along those lines...yeah."

"Then let me give you a good piece of advice that you'll need to pass on to Danielle." Daddy was loading his plate up with croutons as he spoke.

"In every relationship, no matter how loving, how respectful, or how fulfilling it may be, you can *never* have two bulls in the same pasture. You know what I mean, son?"

I wasn't quite sure where Daddy was going with his statement, but I nodded yes anyway.

"Yeah, I think so, Sir."

"Somebody has got to be the cow!" Daddy instructed.

I understood then what it was that Daddy was trying to relay to me. There had to be a dominating force, a final voice of authority, a last word in every union of love in order to make it run properly. It was some mighty deep stuff to think about.

"I get your point now, Daddy. Thanks for the advice," I said as I piled some sliced mushrooms onto my plate.

"Is uh, that what you told mama when you two got married?"

Suddenly Daddy had a woeful look on his face as he gazed at me. He was thinking forlornly of his deceased wife.

"No. That's what your mama told me."

As soon as the trace of a grin began to appear on my face, Daddy shot me the evil eye.

"Laugh and Danielle's gonna have to drive all the way back to Brooklyn by herself. You feel me?"

"Yes, Sir," I answered meekly. "I feel you."

After dinner, Daddy offered to take us to the movies. I was kind of tired by then, and stuffing myself silly at that buffet hadn't made matters any better. I knew that I would be snoozing away in a nice, cool, air-conditioned theater within the first ten minutes of the film.

Therefore, I declined. Danielle, however, told Daddy that she would be delighted to go with him. With the two of them driving to the new multiplex in St. Andrews, I had a little time on my hands alone. I knew exactly what to do with it.

When my homeboy Cheese got married I had to miss his wedding. I was in the middle of renovations with Another Level, and we were on a tight schedule. I did send him my regards, along with a nice gift, but I still owed my man a congratulatory toast. I also had a few personal questions that I wanted to ask him as well.

"Yo, bartender!" I commanded in a gruff voice as I walked into The Pub and took a stool at the far end of the bar.

Cheese had an odd expression on his face as he slowly turned my way. A look of surprise quickly replaced it.

"Hey, J.C.! What brings you back into town?"

"I brought my girl down for the weekend to meet Daddy."

"You're kidding me."

"Nope. How's everything going with you and your old lady?"

"Fine. I can't complain one bit."

"That's good to hear. Let me buy you a drink."

"What for?"

"You know I gotta give my man a toast since I couldn't do it at the wedding."

Cheese appeared a little hesitant.

"I'm really not supposed to be doing this, but then again, it's not everyday that you come through."

"And it's not everyday that you get married."

"You right about that," Cheese said.

"What's your poison?" I asked.

"You know I'm a Crown man."

"Let's do it."

Cheese promptly began fixing himself a double shot of Crown Royal.

"You doing one with me?"

I looked at my friend oddly.

"I forgot. My bad."

Cheese reached down into the cooler next to him, fished out a beer, and handed it to me.

"To true love," I announced as I held up my bottle.

"To true love," Cheese echoed before we drank to our toast.

"Let me ask you a question?" I said after my swig.

"What's that?"

"How did you know that Stacey was the one?"

Cheese set his empty shot glass back down on the bar.

"That's a tough question."

"I mean, what was it about her that made you want to put the ole hunting gear up?"

At that moment, a rude customer from the opposite end of the bar called for Cheese to come down and serve him another drink.

"Be there in a second," Cheese called out to him. He then turned back to me.

"I...I guess what I did was try to picture myself growing old without her. It didn't look too appealing."

A shiver ran through me as I recalled thinking that same way about Danielle during our drive down the day before. She had fallen asleep in the seat beside me, which allowed me to admire her beauty without her being aware.

"But don't you ever think about hooking up with some of the other women who come through here?"

Cheese laughed.

"Of course, I do. Every straight man thinks about other women."

"What do you do when that happens?"

"Honestly?"

"Honestly."

"I just try to imagine how I would feel if I found out that Stacey was stepping out on me, and those thoughts usually disappear."

"Usually?"

Cheese leaned over the bar closer to me.

"Some of these fine-assed sisters that breeze through here take a little more effort to resist than others."

Cheese's rude customer at the other end of the bar yelled for him once again.

"I said I'm coming over, Black Mack! Hold your damn horses!" Cheese yelled back.

"You better go take care of business, dude."

Cheese waved his hand in dismissal of my suggestion.

"Black Mack can wait. His ass still owes the bar for his tab."

"Well...I gotta be getting back to the house now."

I slipped Cheese the money for the drinks I bought.

"I'll holler back at you before I breakout," I told him as I got up from my stool.

"Yo, I want an invitation when the time come!" Cheese said before I walked out the bar.

When I returned home, I went straight into my old room and fell asleep. I woke up later on that night to find Daddy and Danielle in the living room going through our old family photos.

"This one was when he first started playing football. Javier used to cry before every game because he was scared of getting tackled."

"Really?" Danielle asked my father, giggling.

"The boy was a punk. He was scared of his own shadow."

"Hey! Don't be telling her that!" I said as I stormed into the room.

(I was careful not to raise my voice too loud at Daddy. I wasn't that stupid.) The both of them merely looked at me and laughed at my discomfort.

"You know it's the truth, son. Am I lying?"

I couldn't say anything because I really was scared of being tackled back then. I thoroughly disagreed with that fear of my own shadow part, however.

"I told ya!" Daddy said to Danielle when I didn't respond to his challenge. She began laughing once more. I stormed back out of the room and went back to bed. *At least they're getting along.* I thought to myself as I nodded back off.

I took Danielle to the mall the next morning so she could get her shopping on. She didn't buy that much stuff, which I took as a good omen. On the way back home I stopped by Tucker's family's house to say hello to his moms. I introduced Danielle to Mrs. Tucker and Imani. The four of us chatted for a long time. Mrs. Tucker was extremely pleased that her son and I had gone into business together and were pretty successful so far. I assured Mrs. Tucker that Hannibal was behaving himself up North before I left her home.

During my conversation with Mrs. Tucker, I was surprised to find out that her son had been talking to her a lot about Dionne. Tucker never used to discuss any of his clients with his mom. My man was indeed falling in love.

On the return trip home early Sunday morning, Danielle fell right back to sleep as soon as we hit North Carolina. She had enjoyed her stay and I was really glad. I was also elated that she and Daddy had gotten along so well. The whole trip had been a success.

Well, almost.

There was one low point of my trek down South. As Danielle and I were getting into Jada to drive over to Cheese's house to meet his wife, a tan Chevrolet had pulled up in front of the house blowing the horn. I looked in my rearview mirror and cringed when I recognized the driver of the vehicle. It was Myra. Danielle noticed my unease immediately.

"Who's that?" she asked casually.

"An old friend."

Danielle gave me a funny look.

"I'll be right back," I told her as I unlocked my door.

As I was about to get out of my vehicle, I saw Daddy sprint out from the garage. We glanced at each other with mutual apprehension.

"You go on ahead, son. I'll talk to Myra."

I backed out of the driveway and waved politely to Myra before pulling off. She waved back and smiled slightly while she gawked at Danielle.

CHAPTER TWENTY-NINE

The Cleft Club had been in Harlem for ages. Located on the corner of 125th Street and Lenox Avenue, it was the primary spot for jazz-loving New Yorkers.

It had been a couple of years since I'd visited the club, but the atmosphere was still the same. Dark, smoke-filled, brown curtains covered the walls. And the same don't-take-no-mess-from-nobody waitresses were still employed there. It wasn't unusual to hear an over-amorous patron get jack-slapped for putting his hands where they had no business being.

"What time does your friend play?" Danielle asked.

She was referring to my man Cliff Anderson. Cliff was a brother I had met the first time I patronized The Cleft Club. He was three years older than I and hailed from Camden, South Carolina. Cliff had overheard me ordering a beer and promptly asked me from what part of the South did I come from. Being homeboys, we had kept in touch.

"He should be on any minute now."

I looked at my watch and saw that it was already ten minutes after eight. Cliff told me, when I had spoken to him earlier in the week, that his first set began promptly at eight. I knew automatically to adjust to CP time. Cliff would be starting more like eight-thirtyish.

Danielle had been a bit apprehensive initially when she walked into the club because, from the outside, it looked so raggedy. But, as soon as she smelled the aromas wafting from the kitchen, she loosened up. We dined on some finger-smacking good food and made small talk as we waited for the show to begin. Danielle was still singing Daddy's praises after meeting him the month before. (I kept mum on the subject so she could dream on.)

Cliff finally strolled on stage a little before nine with his sax in hand. He had newly twisted, ultra-short dreadlocks sprouting all over his once-bald head. A keyboardist and drummer, who both went about setting up their equipment, accompanied Cliff.

"Sorry I'm late, people. The subway car I was in ran out of gas!" Cliff said with a chuckle.

No one in the audience laughed. Cliff stopped grinning.

"Boy, I guess I'd better hurry up and give you folks what you came here for."

That pissed-off crowd eased up as soon as Cliff began wailing on his saxophone. He grooved that way, non-stop, for about thirty minutes.

"Boy, he's pretty good," Danielle said, snuggling next to me.

"I told you he wasn't no joke."

"I see that."

After playing for another five minutes, Cliff took a well-deserved break. The audience applauded wildly, Danielle and me included.

"Am I forgiven for being late?" he asked everyone while flashing a big smile.

"No!!!" the audience roared back. (Evidently he forgot that he was up in Harlem.) Cliff took a sorely needed swig from his bottle of water before responding.

"Wait 'til I come back then," he told us. Cliff then hopped off the stage and walked over to my table, where he helped himself to a seat next to me.

"Tough crowd here tonight, huh?" I asked him with a sympathetic smile.

"This ain't bad at all. I can tell you horror stories about playing at a few clubs in Brooklyn." All three of us laughed.

"Cliff Anderson, I want you to meet Danielle Davis."

"How do you do, Ma'am?"

I waited for Danielle to chastise my friend for calling her 'Ma'am'. It didn't happen.

"I'm fine. Nice to meet you."

"You're even more beautiful than Javier told me."

Danielle looked at me first and then looked back to Cliff.

"And how much did he pay you to say that one?"

"Nothing. I'm being sincere," Cliff said.

"Yeah, right," Danielle smirked.

"You guys have any special requests that you'd like to hear?"

"I don't care what it is Cliff, but whatever you play, it's gots to be funky."

Both Cliff and Danielle booed my weak James Brown quotation.

"How about you?" Cliff asked Danielle.

"I don't know? Something by Luther Vandross, maybe?"

Cliff bunched his eyebrows together as he feigned some real deep contemplation.

"I think I can conjure something up," he told us before returning to the stage.

As soon as Cliff reached over and picked his saxophone back up, he stepped over to the microphone.

"At this juncture of the show, I'd like to try something a little different tonight. Me and the boys are now going to take requests from the audience. This first request is for the young lady sitting up here to my left."

Danielle immediately leaned up against me in an effort to make herself less noticeable.

"What's he doing that for?" she hissed.

"Danielle, could you hold your hand up and wave for me one time, dear?" Danielle quickly gave Cliff a pitiful looking wave.

"You call that a wave, girl?" Cliff asked.

The whole audience laughed softly. I could feel Danielle pressing up against me harder. I was trying not to get too hard myself.

"Oh well, anyhow," Cliff said with a sigh of defeat.

Cliff held his horn back up to his mouth and went straight into Luther's hit love song, *'So Amazing'*. The sultry notes that he played seemed to captivate everyone in the audience. I peered over at Danielle and savored the enchantment on her face. Midway through playing the song, Cliff abruptly stopped and looked over at our table.

"Oh, yeah, I almost forgot, Danielle. Your man Javier there wants to know if you'll marry him."

Danielle's jaw dropped open as she turned to face me. When she did, she saw the eighteen-carat gold, single diamond engagement ring that I was holding out to her. It was my mother's. Daddy had given it to me on the last night Danielle and I were down there.

"If you don't give it to her, I might do it my damn self," Daddy had warned me.

"Will you marry me, Danielle?" I asked, staring hard at her.

Speechless, Danielle stared back at me. I could see tears forming in the corners of those almond-shaped eyes as I stood and dropped down on my good knee next to her.

"Please say yes?" I urged under my breath. "Or else I'm going to look like a big dummy up in here."

"We're still waiting for an answer. Aren't we audience?" Cliff asked over the microphone.

"YES!!!" the audience roared back.

Danielle grabbed me by my neck and began kissing me all over my face.

"I can take that as a 'yes' then?" I asked upon coming up for air.

Danielle nodded her head in the affirmative as she began to cry softly. I gently wiped the tears away from her eyes with my thumbs.

"He's good to go, people!" Cliff announced.

"Boo-ya!!!" the audience cheered loudly.

Cliff went back to finishing his song as I hugged Danielle, whose tears began flowing faster.

"Don't let that ring get wet! It might turn green on your finger!"

Danielle looked up at me and giggled.

"Javier, I oughta knock your head off."

It was seven in the morning when I finally got home. I had spent the night at Danielle's house, without sleeping. We had stayed up the whole night discussing the arrangements for our upcoming wedding and, more than that, for our entire future together. Danielle had even awakened her poor mother in Richmond to tell her the good news.

She had suggested that I do the same thing and call Daddy. I knew better than to do something that stupid. Between heavy petting and confessions of our love for each other, I had miraculously abstained from knowing Danielle in the biblical way. Through the course of several erections that night, it had taken all of the inner strength I could muster to stand firm and keep the promise I'd made to myself.

Tucker was in the bathroom shaving when I dragged past him. He was whistling the latest rap tune that was playing over the airways.

"Morning, Javier. Nice to see that you made it in safely," Tucker stated when he saw my reflection move by him in the mirror. (The boy's pleasantness scared me.)

"Morning, Tucker," I replied groggily.

I only had about ten more seconds of strength left to remain standing upright; so I chugged along toward my bedroom. Tucker turned his battery-powered razor off and followed after me.

"You don't sound too hot, roomie. Are you okay?"

"I'm just tired," I told him before dropping across my bed.

"I guess you won't be coming to the gym with me then?"

"I guess not," I mumbled.

Out of the corner of my eye, I spied the Sandman tiptoeing toward me with his bucket.

"If you're too tired to make it to work this evening don't worry about it."

(Tucker's kindness began to nauseate me, so now I had to sit back up.)

"I'll be there. I just need some rest for now."

"Okay, see you later."

Tired as I was, I knew better than not to share my good news with my roommate.

"Oh, yeah, Tucker?"

"What is it Javier? You need something?"

(The queasiness in my stomach grew worse.)

"Do you still have that tux you wore to your wedding?"

"Yeah," Tucker answered. "Why?"

"Cause you're gonna need it to wear to mine."

"You're bullshitting!"

(Now that was the old roommate that I was used to.)

"You guys are really getting married?" Tucker asked with a laugh.

I mentally steeled myself for the marriage jokes from him that were sure to follow. Stuff like being under lock and key, having the old ball and chain on me, or being put out in the doghouse. It didn't happen.

"That's incredible, man."

His last comment incensed me. I bounced up from the bed with renewed vigor. Tucker could see the makings of a knockdown, drag out fistfight in my bloodshot eyes.

"What's so incredible about me getting married?" I asked angrily.

"Nothing. It's just that I'm planning on asking Dionne to marry me, too."

"You're bullshitting!" I blurted. (Hey, old habits die hard.)

"I'm serious," Tucker exclaimed. "I'm going to ask her to marry me next weekend. Hopefully, she'll say yes."

I was dumbstruck. I knew my roommate had changed drastically over the past couple of months, but I had no idea how extreme his transformation actually was. I reached over to Tucker and felt his forehead. He wasn't feverish. Tucker quickly slapped my hand off.

"What's wrong with you?" he demanded.

"I should be asking you that question," I countered. "Are you sure you know what you're doing?"

"I'm the one who was married before. Remember?"

"Yeah, and you're also the one who's been trying to nail every pair of panties that's crossed your path since your divorce. Remember?"

Tucker knew he couldn't deny my allegation. He remained silent as he sat down on my bed.

"Yeah, but this is different."

"How so?" I asked, sitting down beside him.

As soon as my rear end landed on my soft mattress, I nodded off. But only for a second.

"Javier!"

"Huh? What?" I asked groggily.

"I was telling you what was so special about Dionne."

"Go ahead. I'm sorry."

Tucker had a glazed look in his eyes as he reflected upon the virtues of his new true love.

"I really don't know where to begin. She is so sweet and tender, beautiful, sexy, kind, considerate..."

"You've had at least ten of those types of sisters in your life in the past two years, Tucker."

Don't get me wrong, folks, I wasn't trying to give my roommate a hard time, I was really happy to see Tucker settle down again with one woman and quit being a ho'-dog. But the mere fact that he had been out there running so hard, and ahead of the rest of the pack for so long, made it hard for me to believe that he could just throw away his flea collar like that. It was my duty to make sure that Tucker knew what it was that he was about to do. Again.

"What you've said is true, roomie, but I'm telling you, it's real this time. Dionne is the one. I can feel it."

Tucker looked really sincere as he spoke, but his past with women was too heinous. I still wasn't convinced.

"So, you're ready to put up the ole hunting gear too? Throw away your little black book? Bury all of your old bones and leave them covered up?"

"Of course. I've already emptied my cell phone of all of my former clients' numbers. Plus I've already…Javier?"

Tucker realized that his calling was in vain. I was knocked out this time.

CHAPTER THIRTY

It is my personal observation that every female over the age of fifteen has already settled on some grandiose idea, some fantasy about her wedding day. A suitable groom, while essential to the event, becomes a second thought, a mere canvas on which to paint her dreams. Danielle turned out to be no different.

For obvious carnal reasons, we decided to get married as soon as possible. My ability to yield not to temptation was waning by the day. The night after Danielle accepted my proposal, we ate dinner at Peter Gatling's, a popular steakhouse in Brooklyn, to further discuss our nuptials. My bride-to-be wanted to have a big ceremony with lots of bridesmaids, guests, and a huge reception.

Because I was springing for a huge portion of the bill myself, I had something a little more economical in mind. I wasn't one for blowing a huge amount of money on a wedding, which would only last one day, when that same money could be used for something more sensible, like a nice-sized, down payment on a house.

In the past, women always used that tired old line: "It's the bride's day and she should have whatever it is she wants!" to justify the lavish spending. But since it took two to make the thing go right, I figured that the groom should have a little financial say-so, too.

"So, what kind of numbers are we looking at?" I asked Danielle as I cut into my baked potato.

"About nineteen so far," my fiancée replied as she carved into her sirloin. I quickly sized that number up against my savings account.

"Nineteen hundred dollars? I think I can handle that."

"That's thousand, not hundred," Danielle stated nonchalantly.

I choked on my potato.

"Here! Drink this!" Danielle nervously shoved her glass of water into my hand.

"Nineteen thousand dollars? What in the heck for?" I cried, finally able to swallow my food.

By rote, Danielle recited her long list of charges for the wedding coordinator, reception hall, flowers, videographer, photographer, caterer, wedding cake, church, pastor, limousines, and organist. This tally didn't even include the wedding gown, tuxedo rentals, or our honeymoon trip.

"Don't you think that's kind of steep?" I asked after calming down.

I didn't want my baby to think that I was cheap, (which was actually the truth) but I couldn't have her marry me under the impression that I was a negro Rockefeller either.

"I think I fared pretty good," Danielle explained. "Those were the lowest prices I was quoted after calling around."

"Since yesterday?"

Yup, she'd just incriminated herself. A guilty smile slowly spread across Danielle's pretty lips.

"Actually, I'd called around a little earlier."

"How much…a little earlier?"

"Three months ago."

Smiling, Danielle appeared so angelic—and a bit nervous—as she sat across from me. I found it hard to deny her anything that she desired. However, nineteen grand plus was still a lot of loot for a dang wedding.

"And that's the best that you could do?"

"I can call around some more if you'd like me to?"

"I'd appreciate that very much."

Later on that night, back at her apartment, I saw a gleam in Danielle's eyes that said she was ready to make love. We had both had a glass of non-alcoholic wine to toast to our future together and were in high spirits. Things heated up once we started kissing as we sat on her futon, allegedly watching the news.

Next thing that I knew, I had run my hands up under the end of Danielle's pink blouse and was unfastening the straps of her bra. I stopped just as fast as I had started.

"What's the matter, Boo?" Danielle asked, confused.

"I…I can't."

"What's wrong?"

I detected a hint of defensiveness in her voice.

"Nothing's wrong, Danielle. I mean something is wrong. I mean, it's not right." Danielle eyed me oddly.

"That was non-alcoholic wine we just drank, wasn't it?"

"Of course it was. I'm not drunk."

"Then what is the problem?"

I took Danielle's hands into mine.

"Look, if we're planning on spending the rest of our lives together, Danielle, then I think we're gonna need all of the help we can get. Wouldn't you agree?"

Judging from the expression on her face, Danielle didn't have a clue as to what I was talking about.

"Yeah, I guess so."

"I want us to start everything off on the right foot, including having sex. I want us to be right in the eyes of God."

I prayed silently to myself that Danielle would understand where I was coming from because if she didn't and still wanted for us to get it on, I was certainly going to comply. My resistance was that weak.

"Oh, now I see," Danielle uttered as she began tucking her blouse back into her skirt.

I was glad Danielle understood, especially since the both of us had joined the flock of Good Aim Baptist only two Sundays earlier.

"You're right," Danielle continued.

"So, uh, hmmm, what should we do now?" I asked.

"We could play Scrabble, or look at this new wedding magazine I picked up."

"Go ahead and get the game out, Danielle."

The days of my six-month engagement flew by and before I knew it, it was show time! I was broke as hell, nervous as heck, and horny as a brass section in a marching band.

"You ain't ready *yet,* boy?"

"Almost, Sir."

"Quit stalling and let me see what you look like."

I stepped away from my full-length mirror and opened my bedroom door for Daddy. He looked splendid in his black tuxedo. As a matter of fact, he looked almost as good as I did in mine. I was still having a problem with buttoning the collar on my shirt. I felt like I was being choked to death, which I took as a bad sign.

"Everything's okay?" Daddy asked as he walked in my room.

I nodded yes to him, but he wasn't buying it. Daddy always had that uncanny ability to see right through me.

"What's the matter, son? You a little scared?"

Again, I nodded my head yes. Daddy then put his right hand on my shoulder and guided me back over to my mirror.

"Take a look at yourself, son."

I looked at my reflection in the mirror.

"What do you see?" Daddy then asked.

"Me."

"Do you know what I see?"

"No, Sir. What?"

"I see a man. One that I did a damn good job raising, and who is now about to get married and will hopefully, soon raise me up some fine grandchildren."

I never felt more proud to be my father's son than at that moment.

"Thanks, Daddy."

"You're quite welcome. Now, do you still have cold feet?"

I couldn't lie to Daddy, especially not after hearing the sincere sentiment he had just shared.

"Yes...Daddy. I'm afraid I still do."

Daddy stood closer to me and we both gazed at each other in the mirror.

"I understand how you feel, Javier. I really do. Just let me say this to you: I drove a mighty long ways up here to see a wedding. It would be a damn shame to make this a funeral instead..."

"Danielle Denise Davis, do you take Javier Thyrone Collins to be your lawfully wedded husband?"

"I do."

Danielle looked so beautiful in her fancy, white wedding gown that I wanted to cry. I would get my wish later on, when I found out how much she actually paid for that sucker.

All of my family was there to see me get hitched, including my favorite cousin, Cornell, who kept snickering at me every chance he got. Cheese and his wife Stacey had made the trek also to see me tie the knot. Danielle's clan had turned out en masse to see her married off as well. Ms. Davis was over in the front row on her family's side of the church sobbing softly. I hoped that she wasn't over there crying about me being her new son-in-law.

And then I thought of my own mother, which made me a bit melancholy. But I knew that, though she was not physically present, she was looking down on me from heaven.

The entire staff from Another Level turned out to see me jump the broom as well. We had actually closed the place down for my special occasion.

Luther's solo brought the house down.

Lance was there with his new girlfriend, Karina, and she looked absolutely stunning in her gold satin dress. (Not that I noticed her all that much.)

Tucker and The Tru...I mean Dionne, were sitting on the second row on my side of the church taking notes. Dionne had accepted his proposal. Tucker was scheduled to take the plunge himself next year. My roommate and I had agreed to the ingenious idea of having a double wedding because it would have been cost effective for us.

The ladies didn't go for it. They each wanted their own special day.

Mandy, and a few of my other co-workers from Human Resources came out to celebrate with us. Flora and Harry Jenkins were there too, peacefully sitting near the back of the church. I sent up a silent prayer that they would remain that way. There were also many members from the congregation of Good Aim Baptist.

"Javier Thyrone Collins, do you take Danielle Denise Davis to be your lawfully wedded wife?"

It was my turn now and I was scared speechless. I couldn't move my lips to say anything. I wanted to say yes, that I would do it, but my mouth just wouldn't let me. It was embarrassing. Danielle gazed over at me with a look of apprehension in those almond-shaped eyes of hers.

I still couldn't find my voice.

Reverend Pendergrass stared over at me, dumbfounded. He frantically gestured with his free hand for me to hurry up and answer. It didn't do any good, though. Suddenly, from behind me, I heard Daddy loudly clear his throat...

"Yes! I surely do!"

"Thank you!" Reverend Pendergrass sighed. "I now pronounce you two man and wife. Ya'll go on and smooch."

Everyone cheered wildly as Danielle and I kissed each other passionately. It was all over. I was now married, and it didn't hurt as bad as I thought it would. At least not yet.

Our reception was held at the Marriott. Danielle and I were scheduled to head to Prospect Park to take pictures and then return to the hotel to greet our families and guests.

It didn't happen quite that way. We did go out to the park, where we took some excellent pictures. We even managed to draw a small crowd of onlookers during the process.

During the limo ride back to the hotel, however, my libido got the best of me. I couldn't stand it any longer. I didn't want to wait until later on that night to finally know my wife. I wanted her now!

Danielle obviously felt the same way as I did. I could tell this from the way she kept rubbing on my leg during our ride back from the park. As soon as our wedding party stepped into the hotel lobby, Danielle and I walked over to one of the clerks stationed at the front desk.

"How may I help you two?" the young woman asked politely.

"We need a room!" Danielle and I answered in unison.

The clerk understood our plight. She smiled mischievously as she began punching some keys on her computer. I hurriedly gave the clerk two credit cards and told her to pick one. When she was done assigning us a room, I snatched the electronic key (and my credit cards) from out of the clerk's hand. I then marched my wife over to the elevator with me.

"Where in the world are you two going?" Ms. Davis cried out to us in wonderment. Daddy was staring at me with surprise as well.

"We'll be back!" we yelled in unison as the elevator doors closed on us.

When we reached the fifth floor, I dragged Danielle down the hall after me in search of room number five-nineteen. She kept getting her heels caught in her wedding gown and slowing us up! I finally reached the appropriate door and jammed my electronic key into the lock. I opened the door and then turned to Mrs. Collins.

"Come here, you..."

I bent down and swept my almost-blushing bride into my arms.

"This is just like in the movies, baby," Danielle observed happily.

I was in such a hurry to lay Danielle on the bed, that I accidentally banged her head against the door as I carried her over the threshold.

"Ouch! Dammit!"

"Sorry about that, Danielle."

We were both out of our clothes in less than three minutes. I stood frozen in awe as I beheld my wife's naked body for the first time. Danielle looked absolutely gorgeous. She was small, but well proportioned. My wife misinterpreted my hesitation.

"What? What's wrong?" she asked, self-consciously.

"Not a thing," I answered. "Not a damn thing."

We were an hour late for our own reception. The only reason that we showed up at all was because my wife had adamantly refused to indulge me any further.

"We've got people waiting for us downstairs, Javier!"

"Receptions always start late. They'll be fine. Come on, just one more time? Pretty please?"

I pleaded in vain. When we walked into the reception room it got so quiet that you could hear a rat piss on cotton. Either someone from our wedding party had put the word out as to what Danielle and I had been up to, or the grins on our faces gave us away. The entire room suddenly erupted into a thunderous applause.

"AW-RIGHT NOW!!! BOO-YA!!!

"Let's get this here party started!" my cousin Cornell yelled out. As the reasonably priced deejay we hired began to play a record, Danielle and I looked at each other, embarrassed.

"You really think they know?" she whispered.

"You really think I care?" I replied.

"Javier, I oughta knock you're head off…"

EPILOGUE

The last seven months with Danielle have been the happiest of my life. We've only fought one time. It was over what type of car to buy her. I had wanted her to get something not too fancy, so that the thieves would leave it alone, but my wife had wanted something a little spiffier. I let her win.

Someone stole the CD player out of Danielle's red Mustang the second week she had it. I kept my mouth shut though and only mentioned to her that I had been right about nine or ten times.

Even though we've decided to hold off on having any children until Danielle finishes college and finds employment in her field, we have been practicing a lot for that inevitable event. There is nothing, and I do mean *nothing,* that I won't do for my baby. I even take an occasional trip 'downtown' on the 'D' train for her…and when I do, I make all local stops.

We decided not to purchase a house anytime soon. Eventually we plan to move back down South to raise our children. We want them to have a real yard to play in like we did growing up. (Exactly where we move down South will probably be another fight with

Danielle, now that I think about it, because it will *not* be near her mama.)

In the meantime, my wife and I have moved into a spacious two-bedroom apartment in Fort Greene that's not too far from Another Level. I still think the rent is way too high there, but we do live in a nice, secure building.

I plan to leave Human Resources within the next year. Another Level is doing better than ever and my partner already has a real estate agent looking for a location for Another Level Too. If I have anything to do with it, which I do, it will be up in Harlem.

Tucker and The Tru…I mean Dionne, are doing quite fine. I'm happy to report that they are still on schedule to be married. I just hope they do it before the baby arrives.

Luther finally landed a part in an off-Broadway production as an understudy and did an excellent job when he got his chance to go on stage. He has a very good agent now who gets frequent auditions for him. Something tells me that he will not be with us much longer.

The Jenkins' did finally agree to seek some professional help for their domestic disputes and have calmed down tremendously. They still hide from my wife whenever we go and visit Tucker, however. Unfortunately, Daddy is still Daddy.

So there you have it folks. You have now read my personal account of the trials and tribulations I endured en route to finding total happiness. To all of you people out there, who have already found true love, hold on to it. For those of you out there who are still searching for that special someone to share your life with, don't give up the fight.

That person is out there. You just don't know when or where you are going to run into them. Remember not to be quick to pass judgment on anyone. You never know: that person could very well be your soul mate. But do take the time to get to know, really know, that person. In other words, like my Granddaddy once told me, "You can't look up a horse's ass and tell what he ate for breakfast!" Good Luck, Folks!

Mr. Danielle Davis-Collins

About the Author

J.T. Smith resides in Westchester County, New York. This is his first novel. Visit his website at www.jayteesmith.com for more info.